Alfred Draper was born in London in 1924. During the war he served in the Royal Navy and suffered the sinking of two ships beneath him.

After the war he became a journalist and also wrote scripts for the BBC. He became a full time writer in 1972. He is also a contributor to numerous magazines and newspapers.

By the same author

Fiction

SWANSONG FOR A RARE BIRD

THE DEATH PENALTY

Non-fiction

SMOKE WITHOUT FIRE

THE PRINCE OF WALES

THE STORY OF THE GOONS

OPERATION FISH

AMRITSAR – THE MASSACRE THAT ENDED THE RAJ

Alfred Draper

Grey Seal

Futura
Macdonald & Co
London & Sydney

A Futura Book

First published in 1981 in Great Britain by
Macdonald & Co (Publishers) Ltd,
London & Sydney

First Futura edition 1982

ISBN 0 7088 2192 8

Reproduced, printed and bound in Great Britain by
Hazell Watson & Viney Ltd, Aylesbury, Bucks

Futura Publications
A Division of
Macdonald & Co (Publishers) Ltd
Maxwell House
74 Worship Street
London EC2A 2EN

Apart from some famous figures, the characters in this book are all fictitious. *Grey Seal* did not exist, neither did the trawlers who sailed with her. Men who served in Scapa Flow will note that I have taken some liberties and created a non-existent trawler base near Lyness. And those who served in Scapa will rack their memories in vain to recall a Captain Monsey or an Admiral Beynon.

I am deeply indebted to the many people who helped me with background material. I would like to express my special thanks to the Imperial War Museum for making available private papers deposited by trawlermen. I would also like to record my thanks to Stephen Sparrow, Stewart McMorran, and Richard Herd, who all served with distinction in trawlers and willingly placed their experiences at my disposal. To Eddie Horne, who introduced me to Grimsby and many local men who served in Harry Tate's Navy. Lastly, my thanks to Orcadian Peter Baikie for his wartime recollections of the Islands.

1 Lieutenant Commander Crispin Paton buried his head into the upturned collar of his greatcoat like a tortoise seeking shelter in its carapace, but the heavy drizzle still managed to seep down onto his stiff white collar, making it soggy and uncomfortable. The wind whipping across the white-topped Humber estuary made the rain feel like a thousand pinpricks against his suntanned face. After eighteen months in the Mediterranean he was still not acclimatised to the vagaries of an English summer, capable of encompassing the four seasons in as many weeks. He lifted his head, squinted through the wet veil and focused his eyes on the tall, slim hydraulic tower which dominated Grimsby harbour and controlled the lock-system. Paton wondered whether anyone would order it to be camouflaged; it made a perfect marker for a bomber's run in. As he strode purposefully towards it like a ship battling against a head sea, he wondered what on earth he was doing in the fishing port. If he had any sense at all he would be spending what was left of his leave at his parents' home in Hampshire and not trudging through an alien town to take a look at the ship he was due to command and for which he had already developed a deep loathing. By rights he should have felt elated, for it would be his first command, but it appealed to him as much as an arranged marriage between two people who had only seen photographs of each other, and had already decided before meeting that there was no possibility of any affection developing.

As he walked unchallenged through the dock gates he paused by the entrance to an open, low-roofed shed where men in sea-boots and white coats were busy filleting fish with incredible speed and dexterity, tossing the edible parts into heavy metal boxes and the bones and heads into wicker baskets. He called out, 'Excuse me! Can you direct me to Number Two Fish Dock?'

Without even bothering to look up, one of the men replied, 'Pneumonia corner? Two hundred yards on the left.'

Paton thanked him and walked towards a row of metal-roofed sheds perched on a concrete plinth overlooking the harbour. As he turned the corner the wind speared through him and he realized why the locals had a nickname for it.

He ducked to avoid some wooden kits crammed with slithering fish which were being hoisted out of the hold of a trawler moored alongside. In the centre of the shed, boxes were piled high and an auctioneer in a white coat was chanting what to Paton's ears was total gibberish.

The numbness had spread to his feet and he realized that the extreme cold of the water lapping over the welts of his shoes was the melted ice in which the fish were packed.

Paton tapped one of the buyers on the shoulder. 'Do you know where *Grey Seal* is tied up?'

The man did not remove his eyes from the auctioneer. 'She's been warped astern of the one they're unloading. This is her catch we're buying. If you want to nab the skipper you'll have to get a move on. He's not one to hang around once he's tied up. He'll be off in a waiting taxi to get a bellyful of well earned beer.'

Phelp said, 'I'm taking over command,' immediately regretting the bitterness evident in his tone.

Eyes still fastened on the auctioneer the man said, 'The navy must be hard up finding jobs for its officers if they can afford to put a two and a half straight ringer in command of a junk-heap like that. She been requisitioned?'

Paton nodded and said, 'She's just one of many who will soon be flying the White Ensign. It's going to be a race against time to turn her into a fighting ship before the balloon goes up.'

'Bloody panic stations if you ask me. You want to read your newspaper. There isn't going to be any war. Chamberlain has promised peace in our time. It's buggers like you who can't wait for a set to.' The man shrugged in a gesture of dismissal. 'But that's what your kind have been born and bred for.'

Paton had been subjected to similar taunts so often that he did not bother to reply. It was true that since boyhood he had been trained for war, but that did not mean he relished the prospect. But if it did come, he would personally do his damndest to be prepared and see that Britain did not come off second best. If the politicians hadn't been so obsessed with peace at any price the navy would never have been allowed to reach its present run down state. Despite the warnings of some senior officers, the Frocks had adopted the view that any increase in the navy estimates would be construed as belligerency by Adolph Hitler. So there had been relentless cuts, and as a result he had been sent to take over the command of a lousy trawler when he should have been commanding something like a Tribal class destroyer.

He crammed his cap tighter over his head and glanced out towards the slate-grey Humber, where thin plumes of dark black smoke crayoned the horizon beyond Bull Fort and Spurn Head as home-bound trawlers buffeted through the North Sea, their holds filled with fish. How many of them, Paton reflected, were aware that it might be their last fishing trip for a long, long time? It was 12th August 1939. A sense of urgency had at last penetrated the corridors of Westminster and the Admiralty had been instructed to requisition large numbers of fishing boats as soon as they reached harbour.

Paton reached the end of the quay and looked down at the deck of the moored trawler. His spirits plummeted to a new low. The decks were strewn with hawsers, nets, dan buoys and fishing tackle. It was a wonder anyone could work in such a shambles. Everything had a shabby, neglected air about it. Ropes dangled from tackles and the boats were a positive disgrace. The entire ship seemed to be coated with an orange rust and the paint was peeling off the wheelhouse. The hull was daubed with large patches of red lead paint to halt the advancing decay. He walked towards the stern, hoping

9

against hope that he had found the wrong ship, but a glance reaffirmed his worst fears – painted in fading white was the name *Grey Seal*.

Paton shook his head in silent dismay: he was used to serving in ships where everything gleamed and glistened and nothing was ever out of place. I'd be ashamed to hoist the White Ensign on that, he thought. When he had looked her up in the shipping register he had felt dubious: 180 feet long with a twenty-eight foot beam and a coal burning triple expansion engine that was hard pressed to push her 600 tons through the water at more than twelve knots. The actual sight of her was even more depressing.

A rotund man wearing a mould-stained bowler hat and a blue overcoat that almost reached his ankles emerged on the veranda by the bridge and looked up at Paton. 'Don't tell me. I know. She's a bloody sight worse than you expected. Right?'

Paton nodded and said, 'Would you be the skipper?'

'No, he buggered off in high dudgeon when he discovered his ship had been pressganged into the navy. I'm the owner's representative. Better step aboard.'

Paton grasped the ends of the wooden ladder which was the only means of reaching the ship and descended slowly backwards until his feet touched the gunwale and he was able to jump down onto the deck. The bowler-hatted man came out of the wheelhouse, his hand outstretched in greeting. 'Bradshaw. Pleased to meet you Lieutenant Commander. Let's hop into the skipper's quarters.'

The cabin was extremely cramped and contained a small single bunk covered by a crumpled pile of brown blankets. The departing skipper had not even bothered to make it up. In the centre of the cabin was a small table littered with the remains of a half-finished meal which Bradshaw piled untidily onto a tray and dumped outside the door, before gesturing to Paton to take a seat while he rummaged around in a tiny cupboard for two clean glasses. He then produced a bottle of whisky from a capacious pocket, uncorked it, poured out two massive measures, and sat down opposite the naval officer.

'I'm the ship's husband,' he said by way of explanation. 'I was asked to come aboard to make sure everything was all right before the ship was converted. Cheers.' He paused while he knocked back half of the neat drink, then wiped his mouth with the back of his hand before resuming. 'I take it you are the navy officer they said might be dropping in?'

Paton found it difficult to reply as the fiery liquid burned the back of his throat; he would have preferred a little water with it. 'I'm still on leave actually, but as I was passing this way I thought it might be useful to pop aboard and have a look at my new ship.' He hoped the lie was not too transparent. Despair, not enthusiasm, had prompted him to interrupt his leave.

Paton wondered if it showed in his face or his tone of voice for Bradshaw said, 'I suspect you'll be feeling a bit down in the mouth. Not much of a command for a navy man like you.'

Paton glanced around the squalid cabin and tried to hide his distaste. The skipper, whoever he was, had made no attempt to turn it into anything resembling a home. It was as characterless as a hotel room deserted by a bed and breakfast resident.

'I was hoping for something a little better for my first command,' Paton confessed, as he unbuttoned his coat and put his cap on the deck beside him.

Bradshaw replenished his own empty glass and topped up Paton's, at the same time taking the opportunity of having a good look at the young man opposite. A typical navy officer. Twenty-sixish. Good-looking with clean-cut features. Dark hair a bit on the long side, and with that inbuilt confidence brought about by being trained since boyhood to assume responsibilities far beyond his years. Steady blue eyes that were incapable of not betraying his disappointment. Well, if there was going to be a war and if it was anything like the last one, he would have plenty of opportunities to measure up to the good impression he had created.

'I would have thought the skipper would have stayed behind long enough to meet me. I did telephone the owners saying I would be passing.'

Bradshaw said, 'He meant no offence. It wasn't his own vessel. He was merely a hired skipper so there was no sense of loss on his part. *Grey Seal* meant nothing to him. Just a meal ticket. Mind you, a bloody good one. But you have to recognize that fishermen are a breed apart. No doubt you'll end up with some in your ship's company. . . .'

Paton heard the same words repeated by a different voice, as memory transported him back to his recent interview with Captain Foster in the windowless room in the Admiralty. 'Trawler men are awkward sods, Paton. Stubborn to the point of insolence and totally opposed to any kind of routined discipline. Can't stand what they consider to be unnecessary navy bull. But they are the finest seamen afloat with the hearts of lions. They can work fifty hours on a freezing deck in gale force winds and handle lines as if they were on a millpond. They have no respect or affection for the ships they work in. Something you'll have to constantly bear in mind. When they reach port they turn their backs on them, much as a factory worker does when he leaves his place of work at the end of a shift. When they're stony broke they go back aboard. Not how you and I have been brought up to believe a sailor should behave. But if we're going to win this war – make no mistake, it's just around the corner – we're going to need them to keep the shipping lanes clear of mines and a host of other jobs for which we just haven't got sufficient manpower'

It was a long speech for the captain, and Paton listened attentively until he had finished before venturing his own opinion. 'I agree with everything you say, sir. Especially about the manpower shortage. It seems odd, therefore, that their Lordships should consider someone like myself for this appointment. It's hardly using me to best advantage. You've only got to look at my service record to agree that I could be better employed.'

The rancour was lost on Captain Foster who had tapped the long buff-coloured envelope on his desk and said, 'I've got your record here'. It contained Paton's 'flimsies' – the naval term for the character references given by a captain whenever an officer leaves his ship for a new appointment. After Dartmouth, Paton had served as a midshipman in the gunroom of a battleship where his remaining rough edges had been worn down by a routine that was as punishing as possible, without actually being brutal. On promotion to sub–lieutenant, he had joined a County class cruiser in which he had shown the flag in numerous parts of the world and been trained in the serious art of naval warfare. At twenty-four, on getting his second ring, he had been appointed first lieutenant of a Tribal class destroyer which had spent a long period in the Mediterranean. When the ship returned to Portsmouth on the completion of her commission, Paton had been promoted to lieutenant commander; one of the youngest in the Royal Navy. The promotion was well earned for, as the pile of 'flimsies' attested, he was 'an officer of outstanding ability who should go far'.

The grey-haired captain had looked Paton straight in the eye. 'An impressive service record, Paton.' A faint smile flickered across his weather-beaten face. 'On the strength of it, I suppose you feel rather hard done by, eh? Fancy you deserve something a bit better'.

Paton had smiled ruefully. 'I would be less than honest if I didn't admit to being a trifle disappointed.'

'Fancied yourself in command of a fighting ship? Instead of playing Hamlet, you find yourself put in the role of a spear-bearer!'

Paton had sat stiff-backed in the armless chair, carefully working out a reply that would express his own feelings without creating the impression that he was in any way questioning the wisdom of his superior officers. 'They' always knew best.

'I couldn't help reflecting, sir, that all the money that has been spent on my training could have been put to better use. All that gunnery, navigation, torpedo work and what have you, won't be much in demand on a trawler.'

Foster's face had broken into a wide grin. 'You've forgotten one thing in that modest list of your own qualifications, Paton. The gift of leadership. That's why you've been selected for this job. You'll be in charge of a group.'

And with that Captain Foster had enlarged on the difficult task which confronted Paton. Most of the skippers and crews were members of the Royal Navy Reserve and, in the event of war, would immediately be mobilized to man the trawlers which would form the second line of defence against the enemy. The battered, unlovely and unloved ships would be engaged in mine-sweeping, anti-submarine work, and owing to the desperate shortage of destroyers, escort work. There were no finer seamen afloat, but they had no liking for discipline and what they saw as the totally unnecessary spit and polish of the Royal Navy. Therefore, a handful of men like Paton had been selected to weld them into an effective fighting force and to slowly break them into accepting the need for those things which they detested. 'Think of them, Paton, as a football eleven made up of brilliant individualists. They've got to be taught that you never win a game until you start playing as a team.'

Foster had put an avuncular arm around Paton's shoulders and escorted him along the echoing corridors down to the main hall. There, he paused beside a statue of Nelson, an exact replica of the one that stood gazing down on Trafalgar Square. 'I can't help thinking what a tremendous debt of gratitude we owe to him. He inspired men who had been press-ganged into service, and had no great reason to love their ships or country for that matter, to fight and defeat overwhelming odds. You've got a similar job.

'So bear him in mind when the going gets tough. Life aboard a trawler in wartime is about as near to purgatory as you'll ever get.' Foster shook his hand and wished him luck. 'Now go off and enjoy your leave.'

Paton was roused from his reverie by the voice of Bradshaw, the 'ship's husband'. 'You were miles away then.'

Patton suddenly realized he had only been half-listening. 'I'm sorry, I was just recalling a little homily I was given at the Admiralty. It was very much on the same lines as the one you've just delivered.'

Bradshaw filled the glasses. 'In the last lot we always referred to trawlers as being part of the Cinderella navy. Well, the pumpkin in the fairystory turned into a golden coach. When the dockyard has finished with this old tub you won't feel quite so downhearted.'

The tour of inspection that followed did nothing to dispel Paton's mounting sense of gloom. The person who had named her must have had a perverse sense of humour, for she possessed none of the streamlined beauty of the fish-hunting mammal.

He glanced at his wristwatch. 'I'd better be pushing along, Mr Bradshaw. Thanks for showing me round.'

When the two men emerged on deck, the wind had dropped to a gentle breeze, the rain had stopped, and a beautiful rainbow was arching over the docks.

'A good omen,' said Bradshaw. 'Perhaps none of this will be necessary. Old Adolf might have seen the light of day and pulled back from the precipice.'

'If he finds out that this is what we're going to fight him with I should think he'll rub his hands with glee at the prospect of a set-to,' replied the lieutenant commander laconically.

Paton walked back to his hotel and went into the bar where he began to drink steadily without any enjoyment. The bar was crowded and abuzz with conversation centred around one topic: would there be a war or not? Some people were convinced that since Hitler had achieved all his aims without firing a shot he wouldn't push his luck by marching into Poland. Others seemed to relish the idea of having a crack at Jerry and getting the whole thing over and done with as quickly as possible.

One man with a florid complexion bellowed, 'We gave them a bloody nose last time, and we'll do the same again.'

Another countered, 'I'll tell you this for nothing; if Neville Chamberlain's got any sense he'll let Hitler have what he wants. Because if there is a war, it'll all be over in a couple of days. Before you can say knife, the bombers will be over in their thousands, and there won't be anything left of this island.'

A woman paused in the act of raising her glass of stout. 'Poland! What's that to us? Half the country couldn't even tell you where it is.'

Paton listened to them with a mounting sense of depression; their conversation was probably a microcosm of what was being said throughout the length and breadth of the country. To him, the small group personified a nation lacking in leadership.

He did not bother to eat that evening, but went straight to bed with the intention of rising early and going home to plead with his father to pull a few strings and get his appointment altered. He had never asked him a favour; for that would have been totally alien to his upbringing and training. But there always had to be a first time. It wasn't, he told himself, just because his vanity had been offended, it was his genuine belief that he could serve his country better by being posted to a real warship.

Isaac Morris sat in the saloon bar of The Mermaid feeling the comfortable bulge of his wallet against his buttocks as he leaned back in his seat and swapped yarns with other trawlermen about their latest trip. Each was trying to outdo the others with stories of the amount of fish they had landed and how much they had been paid off with. It was a ritual that never varied. The thought of stepping ashore and going straight home with their hard-earned cash never occurred to them. They would spend with all the rashness of a rake going through his inheritance, then when the cash ran out they would book another berth and go off to fish in the most inhospitable waters in the world, where every second was lived on a knife edge of disaster, but where the fish were plentiful and the rewards rich.

It was the only life that Isaac had known since he first booked a berth as a galley-boy when he was fourteen. Born and bred within the sound and sight of the sea, it had never occurred to him to follow any other calling. Now he was nineteen and had already sailed off Iceland, Bear Island,

Spitzbergen and the Barents Sea. The longest period he had ever spent ashore was one week, since his money had never lasted for a more extended spell on dry land. Three of these trips had been aboard *Grey Seal* and it was the latest of these he was bragging about. 'The skipper said he had never seen seas like it, and he should know. There was so much ice on the rigging that we were in danger of capsizing. We had to hack it off with axes, but we never stopped fishing. Our holds were overflowing before the others had got their nets out. We came back so fast we almost blew the boiler up.'

'That's only because you were scared stiff of being caught at sea when war broke out,' said one of his companions jocularly.

'Oh, no it wasn't. The old man wanted to be first in to get the best price. And he did. Who's ready for another?'

Without waiting for a reply, Isaac stood up and clumped his way to the bar. He was still dressed in the sea-boots and clothing he had worn, unchanged, throughout the voyage. His grimy white polo-neck jersey smelt strongly of cod and his face looked as if it had not seen a bar of soap for days.

As he ordered four pints the barmaid sniffed in an exaggerated manner and said, 'Let me get upwind of you before I pass out, Isaac. You should know better than to come into the saloon bar dressed like that. You've seen the notice.'

Isaac had. It was a politely worded, handwritten notice requesting fishermen not to enter the saloon bar in their working clothes. But the fishermen invariably ignored it. They wore their seafaring rig as proudly as any uniform and would only change when they had gone home and had a hot bath in preparation for the evening's binge.

As he carried the glasses back to the table he said, 'You don't really think there's anything in all this war talk, do you?'

'If you'd stayed aboard a little longer and not rushed ashore so quickly, you'd have realized it's more than wild rumour. *Grey Seal* has been taken over by the navy.'

'What the hell for!' The astonishment was genuine. 'She'll be as much use to them as a nun in the knocking shop.' The laughter that his remark aroused delighted him. But it was true. What possible use could *Grey Seal* be to a navy that did nothing but polish brass, holy-stone decks and salute anything that moved. Not that it mattered a damn to him. If he couldn't sail in her, well, there were plenty of other trawlers he could get a berth aboard.

When last orders were shouted Isaac felt a trifle unsteady on his legs, but he put it down to having been at sea so long and not to the beer. As he headed towards his parents' home he noticed that sandbag barricades had appeared outside many of the larger and more important buildings. Air-raid shelters had already been erected in several streets, and many shop windows were crisscrossed with strips of sticky brown paper – they had not been there when *Grey Seal* had sailed.

His parents' home was in a narrow street lined with small terraced houses, the front doors of which opened directly onto the pavement. Nearly everyone who lived there was connected in some way or another with the sea and fishing. He banged the brass knocker shaped like a four-masted sailing vessel and waited for the sound of his mother's footsteps in the passage. When she opened the door he said, 'I'm home, Mum.' Then he kicked off his sea-boots and stepped over the white-stoned doorstep which glistened like polished ivory. It was more than he dare do to put a mark on it.

In the kitchen his father sat in his favourite chair warming his feet before the black-leaded grate that was as spotless as the front doorstep. 'Good trip?' asked his father.

'There haven't been many better catches landed at Grimsby, Dad.' He glanced at the empty sleeve in his father's jacket – the result of an accident with a trawl wire – and did not elaborate. Isaac knew how much his father missed the sea and how much he loathed his job as a postman.

'I suppose you'll be having a few with the lads tonight, Isaac. If you can put up with an old cripple I'd like to muck along and chat over old times.' It was a stereotyped exchange. Isaac could not recall a homecoming when his father hadn't made the same request. The drinking sessions were an umbilical cord. If severed, he would lose all contact with the sea.

Isaac went out to the washhouse at the rear of the house and took down the large zinc bath that was hanging on the wall, carried it into the kitchen and placed it on the hearth in front of the stove, then filled it with boiling water from the two kettles which were on the hob. It never ceased to amaze him how accurately his mother was able to anticipate his return.

As soon as he had squatted in the bath and was decently covered by water, she came in, picked up his discarded clothing and disappeared to put them in the copper before preparing the fish and chips.

As he shaved and washed, Isaac said to his father, 'The navy's taken over *Grey Seal*. They're more than welcome to her. I'm only too pleased to see the back of the old tub. There's plenty of better berths. But do you think things are really that bad, Dad?'

His father wrapped a towel around the handle of the iron kettle with his remaining good hand and added more hot water to the bath. 'If it's God's will there'll be war. If it isn't, there won't.'

Isaac splashed water over the tight curls of black hair that covered his chest and watched the soap trickle down between his exposed knees. 'I've no great desire to fight in a war that's none of my making or wanting. I'll go if I have to, but there'll be no heroics on my part. I've no wish to end up like you.'

Isaac saw the hurt that his remark had caused and mumbled an apology, but he was saved from any further comment by the voice of his mother calling from outside the closed door. 'Table's ready to be laid when you are.'

Isaac stood up, letting the water on his body drain down into the bath, and as his father handed him a warm, dry towel he suddenly laughed and said, 'Imagine *Grey Seal* in the navy, Dad! It's a bit like putting your maiden aunt in the front row of the chorus.'

2 A dawn glow, pale and translucent as a pink rose petal, was suffusing the sky when Lieutenant Commander Paton drove out of Grimsby. He had folded back the canvas hood of his green two-seater Austin Ruby to clear his head of the muzziness induced by too many drinks and to enjoy the cold, crisp morning. The wind ruffled his hair as he drove at a steady sixty miles an hour across the flat agricultural land. Being alone in a car was much akin to standing on the bridge of a ship in a mild sea; very conducive to putting one's thoughts in order. Paton was a relatively simple man who tended to see things in clearly defined blacks and whites; mainly due to the fact that he knew little or nothing of life outside the navy. He had gone to Dartmouth at an age when most boys were thinking of little else but their favourite football team or who would win the Ashes. There, he had been taught to stand on his own two feet and give orders to men with children older than himself. And it had been instilled into him, until it was second nature, that the first duty of an officer was to look after his men because no ship could be efficient if they were discontented. During his progress from the gunroom to the wardroom, he had learned that no officer worth his salt would ever ask a man to do something he wasn't prepared or willing to do himself.

The self-questioning that occupied his thoughts as he drove homewards was necessary to his peace of mind. Did he really believe he could serve his country better by wriggling out of his new command or was it his personal pride he was concerned with?

He spoke aloud to himself: Crispin Vincent Paton, be honest. Are you acting altruistically or are you merely kidding yourself you are?

As his name implied, his family had strong links with the sea and it was the Patons' proud claim that for the past four hundred years there had always been someone, somewhere, serving under the White Ensign. Now he was going home to ask his father to intercede on his behalf and use his rank to get a posting altered. As the miles clocked away, he convinced himself that he was not being a prima donna. Anyone could command a clapped-out old trawler. And so he carefully rehearsed in his own mind the arguments he would put to his father when he arrived home.

As he breasted the brow of the hill overlooking the village, he caught the first glimpse of the four tall chimneys which marked his home. A few minutes later he was driving up the oak-lined drive leading to the house which had been the Patons' safe harbourage after centuries of sailing the world. The trees were said to have been planted by one of his more eccentric ancestors, who believed that Britain's defence depended on the wooden walls of her man o'wars and therefore that there should never be a shortage in time of need.

Rear-Admiral Francis Paton (Rtd.) was standing at the foot of the front steps to greet the arrival of his son. He was wearing an ancient tweed jacket with leather elbow patches and protective strips around the frayed cuffs, and a baggy pair of unpressed trousers. Sitting obediently at his feet was Bosun, a devoted cocker spaniel. It was a scene that had greeted Crispin so many times in his life that it had the permanence of an old photograph.

As his father took his extended hand between both of his own, Crispin could not help noticing how rejuvenated the old boy looked. He seemed to have lost the stoop he had acquired in retirement and his short, grey hair appeared to have recovered some of its former lustre.

'I've never seen you looking so fit, sir. Retirement obviously agrees with you.'

'I've every reason for feeling on top of the world, but I'll save the good news for later. Musn't keep your mother wait-

21

ing, she's dying to know what you think of your first command.'

'That's one of the reasons I came to see you, Dad.'

Crispin had no chance to elaborate, for at that moment his mother appeared at the top of the steps and stood with arms outstretched to embrace him. She invariably delayed her arrival until father and son had met, as if she feared the presence of a woman might inhibit the warmth of their greeting. Members of the 'Silent Service' must never be seen to show too much emotion.

As they sat drinking tea in a bay-windowed alcove overlooking the lawn, Crispin glanced around the room and reflected that the entire history of the Patons was encompassed within the four walls of the house. The rooms were adorned with photographs and portraits of Patons who had served in the Royal Navy along with pictures of their ships. The very first Paton to answer the call of the sea had recorded the event by having the name of his ship and the date he joined her engraved on the lid of a silver snuff box. Subsequent appointments were similarly engraved. It had started a tradition that had never been broken and every Paton had adopted a similar procedure, so that the family heritage was chronicled on snuff boxes, napkin rings and silver tankards.

Crispin's own career was being recorded on the lid of a cigarette box, and he wondered what the reaction would be when he eventually got around to the delicate task of telling his father that he did not want the name *Grey Seal* to be added.

I wonder, he thought, if anyone else has ever sat in this room with a similar intention in mind. He doubted it. The Paton tradition was to obey all orders with unquestioning obedience. Everywhere one looked, there were reminders of that unbroken link and the firm conviction that it was an honour and privilege to serve under the White Ensign. To an outsider, it might all seem a little too obsessive. Even the dining room furniture had naval overtones. The backs of the chairs and the table had three black stripes inlaid with ebony to commemorate the death of Nelson. But it was more than pure sentimentality; a Paton had fallen on the deck of *Victory*.

Crispin was roused from his reverie by his mother's voice. 'Has your father broken the good news to you? We're all so delighted'.

Crispin looked towards his father and said, 'He's been as confiding as an oyster. Come on, Dad, don't keep me in suspense.'

The admiral smiled broadly and said, 'Well, I really thought I'd swallowed the hook. But I had a call from the Admiralty this morning, asking me if I would be prepared to get my uniform out of mothballs. I didn't need any time to consider it. The beach is no place for me. I said yes without a moment's hesitation.'

Crispin said, 'Quite right too. They'll need men with your experience to advise and guide if the balloon does go up.'

His father said gruffly, but with evident pride, 'I'll not be sitting in an armchair. It'll be a sea-going appointment. They've asked me to return as a Commodore of Convoys.' He grimaced slightly. 'The bridge of a merchantman isn't exactly the *Warspite*, but it's not size that makes a ship, it's the men who serve in them.'

Crispin glanced at his father fully expecting to see a reproachful look on his face; his remarks seemed so pointed. Had he anticipated the reason for his visit home? But there was nothing on his face to indicate that he was sounding any kind of warning. He was merely stating what he saw as the obvious.

Mrs Paton beamed and said, 'Isn't that wonderful? I know it's a bit early, but it really calls for some sort of celebration. I just wish your sister could have been here to share the good news, but she pushed off mysteriously this morning muttering something about getting a new job.'

Mrs Paton poured out the sherry and then raised her glass. 'To you both! Crispin on your first command and you, darling, for being rescued from the greenhouse and mower.'

The admiral said rather testily, 'If they hadn't phoned me I would have called on them and demanded a job.'

'As he sipped his drink Crispin knew that he would never mention the reason for his trip home. It was up to him to make sure that *Grey Seal* became a ship of which he would be proud.

Paton stood on the quay at Portsmouth naval dockyard and watched the towering crane wrench the powerful steam winch, used for working the trawl, out of the welldeck of *Grey Seal*. The screeches and groans reminded him of a dentist extracting a reluctant tooth. The cavity that was exposed would become part of a mess deck.

The sound of hammering and riveting filled the air and he shielded his gaze from the eye-dazzling glare of the oxy-acetylene torches that were busy welding and cutting metal. The quay was a tangled skein of electric cables and compressed air pipes. The mizzen mast had been removed so as not to limit the line of fire when the guns were fitted and an open 'monkey bridge' was being erected on top of the closed-in fishing bridge. On the fo'c'sle, the hull frames and deck beams were being strengthened in preparation for the erection of a 'bandstand' which would carry a twelve-pounder gun. Aft, a group of overalled men were busy installing depth charge rails and throwers.

For every man working there seemed to be three who were doing nothing. The lack of urgency appalled Paton and he fumed inwardly. Didn't they realize they were fighting against time? It was his third visit to the dockyard to see how *Grey Seal*'s conversion was going along, and each time he had had to force himself to keep calm and not storm aboard and read the Riot Act.

From long experience he knew that dockyard mateys were not a breed to be rushed; they did things in their own leisurely manner and strongly objected to outsiders telling them to get a move on. By tradition no love was lost between the men who sailed the navy's ships and the men who repaired and maintained them. It was summed up in the derisory sailors' song:

Dockyard mateys children
Sitting on the dockyard wall
Just like their fathers
Doing sweet f . . . all.

But on this particular morning, Paton could no longer curb his resentment and frustration. He was firmly convinced the country was sitting on a powder keg, the fuse of which was incredibly short and burning quickly. Although, technically speaking, the ship was not yet his, he felt compelled to say something about the slow rate of progress. So he strode across the narrow gangplank to seek out the supervisor. In the fishhold, which would soon become the main seamen's mess, he encountered a group of men playing cards on an upturned crate and others just drinking tea. 'Finished for the day?' he enquired sarcastically, but his taunt was ignored. They were too long in the tooth to be riled by a stroppy young officer.

When he finally found the supervisor, he invited him into the empty wheelhouse and, as tactfully as possible, asked him if it was at all possible for him to prod the men into displaying a greater sense of urgency.

The man looked at Paton with ill-concealed animosity, then calmly began to roll a cigarette. 'There're ships all over the dockyard undergoing refits or conversions, and the captain of every one of them is bitching and moaning about how slow we are. So, let me tell you something, the work won't get done any faster by you coming aboard and breathing down our necks. You'll more than likely get them to down tools. Remember, Rome wasn't built in a day.'

Paton retorted angrily, 'I seem to recall a much more appropriate story about Nero fiddling while the whole ruddy city burned down.' And with that he turned and strode furiously across the gangplank.

He knew that it would be better if he restricted his visits to an absolute minimum; no one would thank him if his zealousness produced a dockyard strike. He might just as well return to the 'stone frigate' and bury his head behind a newspaper in the wardroom, along with the numerous other officers who were kicking their heels and desperately trying to restrain their impatience while their ships were being made ready for sea. In a way, Paton mused, the lethargy was understandable; it was extremely difficult for a people who had been lulled into a sense of security to be suddenly aroused to an awareness of the danger at their door. Even the fact that children in high risk towns and cities had been evacuated to the safety of the country had not brought about a full realization of the imminence of war. Parents had gone to stations and taken fearful farewells of their offspring, labelled like parcels and clutching gas masks in cardboard boxes, only to return home to reassure each other that it wouldn't be long before the false alarm was over and the kids back home. In fact, some had already brought them back.

Such thoughts still occupied Paton's mind as he strode through the main gates of HMS *Imperial*: a ship in name only. It was a sprawling conglomeration of tall red-brick barrack buildings which had been added to in hodgepodge fashion since 'Pompey' became a major naval base. Nevertheless, everything within its gates was referred to in nautical terms: there were no floors, ceilings or windows, only decks, bulkheads, deckheads and portholes. There was no left or right: only port and starboard.

In the centre was a parade–ground the size of a dozen football pitches dominated by a towering mast from which the White Ensign fluttered. The staccato bark of orders echoed across it as squads of sailors carried out routine drills.

Fringing the perimeter were cutters and whalers on davits and men were carrying out lowering and hoisting drills under the watchful eyes of petty officers.

At least they were occupying their time usefully, thought Paton, which was more than he could say of himself. He headed for the wardroom. The bar was already doing a lively trade when he entered, and he ordered a pink gin from one of the white-coated stewards and carried it to a table below the windows. The atmosphere was still very much that of a peacetime navy, with stewards in immaculate jackets bustling to and fro like waiters in a West End restaurant. He wondered how long it would be before the whole scene changed. Not long, his intuition told him.

In Grimsby, Isaac Morris felt as unsettled as Paton and his fellow officers. Every morning since his money had run out he had gone down to the docks, haunting the quays to try and find a berth aboard a trawler, but the reply had always been the same: of the few ships putting out to sea, those that were were giving the berths to married men with families, or older men who would not be required in an emergency.

Grimsby had undergone a remarkable change in the space of a few days. Barrage balloons floated above the town and docks like gargantuan sausages, an anti-submarine boom had been strung across the Humber and anti-aircraft batteries established at strategic points along the coast. Posts for air-raid wardens had been set up throughout the town and men wearing initialled tin helmets and blue battledress stood outside, gazing at the sky as if expecting hordes of bombers to arrive at any moment.

The docks were becoming progressively less busy. As ships arrived so they were requisitioned. Morris was told that the same thing was happening to trawlers in Hull, Fleetwood, Shoreham, Falmouth and the Outer and Inner Hebrides.

Eventually Morris gave up going to the docks. There was no point.

At 11:15 on the morning of 3rd September, Isaac, like millions of other Britons, sat huddled over the wireless set, his heart pounding with anticipation. Hitler had attacked Poland two days previously and an ultimatum from the British Government had been ignored, as had a final ultimatum issued at 9 a.m. on the 3rd. Even the most optimistic individual now accepted that war was inevitable and was waiting to hear confirmation of this from Neville Chamberlain's own lips.

The dry sepulchral tones of the prime minister were heard

with sinking feelings by many, but with a sense of elation by others. In some ways the declaration of war came as a relief, for at least the agonizing period of suspense and uncertainty was finally over.

Chamberlain's speech was followed by an official announcement that all naval reservists should report to their nearest Mercantile Marine Office and, although Morris was not in the RNR, he felt that he had nothing to lose by offering his services.

As he hurried towards the docks, a penetrating wail filled the sky and people began to run towards the nearest air-raid shelter. They had all been led to believe that within the hour hundreds of thousands would perish and countless towns and cities would be razed to the ground.

The terror was short-lived. Within minutes another wail, similar in tone but continuous, filled the air and tin-helmeted wardens dashed through the streets shouting, 'All Clear. All Clear.'

When Morris finally reached the Marine Office he was surprised to find it bolted and deserted. He tagged on to a straggling queue of fishermen who had also hastened there and joined them in angry condemnation of the indifference with which officials had responded to the call to arms. Reluctantly, they returned home. Their King and country obviously did not need them.

Paton heard Chamberlain's announcement in the wardroom of HMS *Imperial* in the company of a group of serious-faced officers. There was an air of anti-climax in the room, for the men who had been trained from childhood for this eventuality felt incredibly impotent. There was nothing they could do until their ships were ready.

Spirits soared that evening when a signal was sent to the Fleet. 'Winston is back.' Churchill, one of the few men to sound the alarm bells about Hitler, held pride of place in the navy's affection. With him back at the helm in his old job as First Lord of the Admiralty, everyone would be spurred into a sense of urgency – even the dockyard workers.

That evening, he strolled slowly through the town which, in such a short period of time, had become a totally alien place. The streets were in darkness; not a single lamp glowed and every house and building was blacked-out. Occasionally he heard the strident voice of a policeman or warden bellow out indignantly, 'Douse that light.' The public houses were doing a roaring trade and there were curses and groans as people emerged into the unaccustomed darkness and bumped into each other; or collided with sandbags and other obstacles which had been hastily erected as part of the town's civil defence precautions.

That night he lay on his bed unable to sleep; his ears straining for the ominous drone of aircraft engines and the boom and crash of the retaliating anti-aircraft guns. Expert predictions had warned the government to prepare for at least 250,000 air-raid casualties in the early stages of hostilities. But the sirens remained silent.

After snatching an early breakfast, Paton headed straight for the dockyard where, to his amazement, a sense of immediacy at last seemed to have been injected into the workmen. As he stepped aboard *Grey Seal*, the supervisor who had previously been so belligerent actually welcomed him and offered to show him round to see for himself what tremendous progress had been made since his last visit. 'None of the men really believed in their heart of hearts that it would ever come to a showdown,' he said.

Paton was amazed at the rapid transaction. An ancient twelve-pounder, last fired in anger in the Kaiser's war, had been installed on the 'bandstand' and the monkey bridge completed, right down to the protective quilting on the outside that would act as a guard against shrapnel. On either side of the bridge-wings were twin Lewis guns and another had been sited on top of the galley flat; while regimented rows of smoke floats had been lashed aft below the depth charge racks.

Although the mess decks still smelt faintly of cod and

haddock, they were almost ready for occupation. Every inch of space had been utilized to provide accommodation for three times as many men as she carried during her fishing days. The bulkheads were lined with bunks that could be raised during the day and let down at night. Below them were leather covered seat lockers in which each man could store his personal belongings and in the centre of the mess decks there were three-tiered bunks and tables at which they could eat or write letters. She was beginning to look like a navy vessel, albeit a cramped and overcrowded one.

The Petty Officers' Mess was just as spartan, although there was one slight concession to their seniority: the bunks were self-contained and had curtains round them to afford some minute degree of privacy.

There was even a small hip-bath aft, heated by a steam jet from the boilers. It wasn't exactly luxury afloat, but it was a lot better than many men had cheerfully endured in the past and would no doubt endure in the future.

As Paton toured the ship, he pondered on what kind of men would be sent to serve under him. That was really the most important thing. Given men with stout hearts you *could* turn a sow's ear into a silk purse. Well, he would not have long to wait before he found out.

After three more abortive visits to the Marine Office, Isaac Morris decided to sit back and await events. He did not spend very long kicking his heels in idleness. One afternoon there was a thunderous knocking on the front door and, on answering it, he was confronted by a gaitered petty officer brandishing the staff of a pickaxe. Behind him stood three brawny-looking seamen, with armbands indicating they were on shore patrol duty. The petty officer snapped, 'Right lad, get your skates on. You're coming with us.'

Morris ineffectually tried to explain he'd been trying to do that for the past few days, but there hadn't been anyone available to take any notice. The petty officer warned him not to be stroppy and to keep anything he wanted to say for the officer he would have to appear before. He was, said the PO, for the high jump. It took some time for him to discover that the patrol had been sent to arrest him for failing to report as a reservist, and just as long again for him to explain that he wasn't one, although he was quite happy to accompany them.

Although the petty officer seemed satisfied with his explanation, he said he couldn't go against his orders, which were that Morris should be arrested and taken before an officer who would deal with him on the spot. The warning was delivered in emotionless tones which conjured up all kinds of punishment, from flogging to death before a firing squad.

However, he was given enough time to pack a small suitcase and write a short note to his parents, informing them that he had joined the navy.

Two days later, after a reprimand and a desultory medical examination which merely established that he was capable of walking and breathing, he was issued with a railway travel warrant and ordered to report to HMS *Robin*, a shore establishment on the East coast. At no stage did anyone concede that he was not a reservist and had in fact been pressganged into service.

He was given a short back and sides, issued with two uniforms, gas mask, kit-bag and 'housewife', an open razor and brush, a small wooden name stamp with which to put his personal seal on his belongings, and a hammock and lashings. Then he was photographed holding up a small board on which he had chalked his name, official number, home port and division.

In addition, he was handed Volume One of the *Admiralty Manual of Seamanship* and told to study it during every minute of his spare time. The blue, stiff-covered book, embossed with the fouled anchor of the Royal Navy, contained line drawings of how to tie various knots: reef, sheepshank, sheet-bend, bowline . . . Morris had tied them all in pitch darkness on the heaving deck of a trawler in a force nine gale. Simple illustrations showed how to 'box the compass' – an instrument he had almost been teethed on – and the

31

navigational 'Rules of the Road' were explained in nursery rhyme doggerel: When both lights you see ahead Starboard wheel and show your red.

The book was contemptuously consigned to the bottom of his kit bag, where it remained unopened and unread. To him it epitomized the pusser navy – all spit, polish and bullshit and the belief that there was only one way to learn how to suck eggs – the navy way.

He spent what seemed endless days in pointless square bashing (who was going to march up and down the deck of a ship?), rifle drill, climbing the towering parade–ground mast and rigging in a gas mask that misted over as the air-pipe was squashed by the topmost spar when one rolled over it to begin the descent. (Who would launch a gas attack at sea?) Further numerous head-nodding hours were passed in a darkened Nissen hut, at the end of which was a moonlit seascope dotted with the black outlines of enemy warships; or being shep- herded into an identical building and taught to identify German aircraft. Then he was posted to a ship. He felt like deserting immediately: he was ordered to report to HMS *Grey Seal*. She was all right for catching fish, but he didn't fancy her chances if she came up against any of the ships whose outlines he had memorized.

He fell in on the parade–ground with about twenty other sailors, their kit-bags and hammocks at their feet, small brown 'ditty box' suitcases firmly clutched in their right hands. A petty officer with a nose that glowed with 'grog blossom' eyed them with silent disdain. 'This war is going to last a ruddy long time if you're any indication of the material we've got to fight with,' he muttered. He glared at them ferociously. 'Now is there anyone of you that has taken it into his head to try and smuggle out more than the half-pound of ticklers he's entitled to?' There was no reply from the sullen seamen, and so he fixed his gaze on Morris and said, 'Right, you. Open your kit-bag and let me have a look see.'

Morris untied the top and produced a tin of cigarette tobacco which he dutifully handed over. The petty officer weighed it as if it was about to explode. 'If you've learned nothing else while you've been here, sonny, you at least discovered how to get a pound into a half-pound tin.'

Morris waited for the PO to order him to be marched off to the cells, for the tin did contain more tobacco than he was entitled to. An old hand had demonstrated the impossible. You simply put the tin under the leg of a bunk and, aided by a couple of mess mates, jumped up and down until it was compressed into an almost solid lump. But the petty officer did not say a word. He was simply letting them know he didn't miss a trick and no one could pull the wool over his eyes. 'Right, up in the stern of that lorry and good luck. Believe me, you're going to need it,' he thundered.

The vehicle bumped and bucked all the way to the railway station, where its occupants joined several hundred other sailors all being drafted to ships. A railway transport officer busily shepherded them into several reserved carriages, where they sat for two hours in absolute discomfort before the platform guard blew his whistle and the train slowly pulled out of the station towards an unknown destination.

The carriage was so cluttered that two enterprising ratings stretched out on the luggage racks above the seats. The floor was littered with kit-bags, hammocks and cases as the luggage vans were also filled with passengers; but worst of all there was no corridor to enable them to answer the call of nature.

The journey seemed interminable, with frequent stops for no apparent reason, but at least the halts enabled them to take advantage of the open window. Occasionally they stopped at a station, but they had no idea where they were, for all the station names had been obliterated and when they asked the only response was a finger over sealed lips.

No one seemed at all interested in what awaited them at the end of the journey: the conversation concentrated on women and football, punctuated by the occasional singsong.

Morris glanced around the carriage. 'Anybody here drafted to *Grey Seal*?'

Heads were shaken and one or two murmured, 'No', so

Morris slumped back in his seat, resigned to the fact that he would have to wait until they reached their journey's end before he met any of his future shipmates. Then he heard a voice with an unmistakable Canadian drawl say, 'I've got a berth aboard.'

Morris looked across the carriage towards a towering giant of a man with carrot-coloured hair and held out his hand. 'Isaac Morris. Pleased to meet you.'

The man grasped the extended hand and gripped it in a vice-like hold that would have cracked walnuts. 'Campbell Rhind.' He stared at the man sitting next to Morris and said, 'Swop seats, so we can natter.' It was more an order than a request.

As the huge man eased himself alongside Morris, he fumbled inside the pouch pockets of his tunic and produced a packet of Sweet Caporal cigarettes. 'Last pack. Then I'll have to get used to the horse manure you call smokes.'

Morris accepted a cigarette, lit them both and enquired, 'How comes it that you're joining the ship? You're not English.'

'Canadian,' replied Rhind. 'You're not objecting to a little outside help, are you?'

Morris laughed. ''Course not. Every little helps, as the old lady said when she peed into the ocean. I'm just surprised you got here so quick.'

The Canadian studied the end of his glowing cigarette and said, 'Been here a while now. Working out of Hull as a deckhand. Then the ship got nabbed by the navy and I found myself at a loose end so I joined up. It was that or starve.'

Morris said, 'The same thing happened to me, only worse. I'm going back to the old tub I last sailed in.'

The burly Canadian rummaged once more inside his tunic and produced a flat, half bottle of whisky. 'This calls for some kind of toast.' He put the bottle to his lips and took a long swig, wiped the neck, then passed it on to Morris. 'Here's to keeping our feet dry.'

As the train trundled on its interminable way, Morris

learned more about his companion, who had led a rolling-stone existence for many years. He had been a lumberjack, trapped furs in Alaska and lived with Indians before going off to fish the Newfoundland cod banks and finally joining a trawler which worked off Iceland.

'In Reykjavik I got as drunk as a skunk and filled in three Icelandic policemen who arrested me for being drunk and disorderly. Well, I had no wish to spend several years road-building in that frozen anus of a place, so I broke out of the jailhouse and stowed away on a British trawler. I stayed with her and even went back to Iceland, although I never dared set foot ashore.'

Morris also learned that Rhind's father was a Scot who had emigrated to Halifax in 1912 and joined the Royal Canadian Navy when the First War started. But Rhind could scarcely recall his father – he had been blown to pieces from the deck of a destroyer when an ammunition ship, the *Mont Blanc*, loaded with 3,000 tons of nitroglycerin had broken from her moorings, hit another ship and exploded in Halifax harbour.

'Although it was an accident I still blame the Jerries. So as far as I'm concerned, this gives me an opportunity to even the score.'

Eventually the train pulled into Portsmouth station and juddered to a halt. There was a mad scramble to lower the windows and heads craned out to see what was happening.

A disembodied voice announced over the loudspeaker system: 'Unload your possessions onto the platform and wait beside them until you receive further orders.'

Hammocks and kit-bags were tossed out and the sailors stood in bewildered groups, wondering how on earth anyone could restore some semblance of order to the chaos. The men muttered angrily that it was a typical navy cock-up and they would probably be ordered back on the train to return to where they had set out from. Surprisingly, it was soon sorted out. Leading seamen and petty officers appeared as if from nowhere and began shouting out the names of ships and holding up their hands to indicate they were rallying points.

35

Morris and Rhind shouldered their kit-bags and hammocks and barged their way through the milling crowd to where a chief petty officer with three long service stripes on his arms stood with one hand aloft and a sheaf of papers in the other, bellowing as if to waken the dead, 'Grey Seal's ship's company. Fall in here.'

He was a roly-poly man with tufts of grey hair jutting out from below his cap. 'Dump your kit until we've rounded up the rest of the shower,' he snapped.

The men who were to join Grey Seal reported in dribs and drabs and had their names ticked off. 'That seems to be the lot,' said the chief petty officer, tucking his pencil behind his ear. 'Now get fell in in two ranks. There's transport outside waiting to take you to barracks. Right, quick march.'

The dog-tired men fell into step and followed the petty officer through the ticket barrier.

Rhind edged alongside him and said in a plaintive voice, 'Chief, we've been cooped up like chickens in that cattle truck for hours and we're all parched. Any chance of stopping for a pint?'

The chief turned his head, 'I hope I haven't been lumbered with a load of piss artists.' Whereupon he winked and said, 'If you're paying, you can stand me one in the pub outside. I don't want anyone to see us trooping into the station bar. Gives a bad impression to be seen drinking on duty.'

When the party emerged into the fresh air outside the station the chief pointed to a waiting lorry and said, 'Right, pile your clobber aboard. We'll need one volunteer to keep an eye on it while you have your ale.' He cast an eye over the assembled seamen and said, 'You'll do, son,' and pointed to one hapless youngster. As the youngster's face dropped and before he could protest he snapped, 'Lesson number one. Never volunteer for nothing,' and with that he turned smartly and led the way into the bar of the nearby public house.

The one pint extended to two in the smoke-filled bar and would have been stretched even further if one tactless sailor hadn't remarked too loudly, 'Just like all Chiefies, short arms and deep pockets.' Whereupon they were all ordered to sup up quick and get into the lorry.

'Can't keep the war waiting.' The chief clearly believed that it was his inalienable right not to have to stand his turn.

The lorry formed the tail vehicle of a straggling convoy that drove slowly down the near-deserted streets, through the main gates of the barracks and on to the perimeter of the paradeground.

Against the silhouetted outline of a land-locked whaler the peppery chief told them to be ready on exactly the same spot at eight o'clock the following morning. 'Now go off and get some grub and shut-eye. Likely as not, it'll be the last kip you'll be having for a good while.' The thought seemed to cheer him.

The assembled sailors watched his dark shape disappearing into the gloom and one man remarked, 'We seem to have got ourselves a ripe bastard there. Hard as a ship's biscuit, and they don't come any harder.'

Someone muttered, 'Tight as a duck's arse too, and that's water-tight,' recalling how he had dodged his round.

In the dining room over a table covered with a crisp white cloth, Paton studied the two officers who had been posted to *Grey Seal*.

Lieutenant Brian Phelp, RNR, who was to be his first lieutenant, had been second officer aboard a small cargo passenger vessel that plied between Liverpool and the West Indies. Although only twenty-five, he had put in a lot of sea time and sailed most of the oceans of the world, and like many of his breed had little time for the pusser navy. He admitted, if only to himself, his enrolment in the Royal Navy Reserve had been a cynical move aimed purely at self-advancement; he knew the company encouraged it, firmly believing that a touch of navy discipline would be transferred to its own ships, resulting in more efficient and economical running. RNR men also had a better chance of promotion. Phelp, however, had hoped for something a little more distinguished than 'Jimmy the One' in a trawler.

Midshipman Terence Carnac, RNVR, pink-cheeked and well scrubbed, looked like a lad straight from school. Paton had already elicited that he was the product of a well-known public school and his entire sea experience consisted of weekend sailing aboard his father's yacht at Cowes and rowing on a reservoir in the school's sea cadets' cutter. Posted as additional watch keeping officer, he was as fresh and new as the maroon tabs on the lapels of his doe-skin Gieves uniform.

Paton thought to himself: Well, here we are! Every branch of the navy represented by three men. All summed up in the derogatory but age-old description that mirrored their dislike and mistrust of each other. Himself the straight ring RN officer, 'a gentleman pretending to be a sailor'. Phelp the 'sailor pretending to be a gentleman', and the poor RNVR 'snottie' 'neither, pretending to be both'. Well, it was up to him to see that it didn't matter a damn in *Grey Seal* whether the braid on the sleeves of your uniform was straight, interlinked or wavy. They had got to learn to pull together and turn it into an efficient fighting ship. Healthy rivalry he would encourage; animosity he would ruthlessly stamp out. There was only one way to run a ship – the way *he* had been taught.

In the huge hangar-like shed standing on the quayside where *Grey Seal* was berthed, the ship's company stood in a long single line before the appraising eye of the chief petty officer who had met them at the station the previous evening. By his side stood Petty Officer Harry Reynolds, the engineer, who would be responsible for keeping the engine going.

The chief pointed at the three glistening buttons on the sleeve of his number one uniform. 'I'm Chief Petty Officer John Read, your coxswain. I don't stand for any familiarity or mateyness aboard. Next to the captain, I am the most important man aboard. Some would say *the* most important, but I don't have any delusions of grandeur. What I do have is a giant sized-chip on my shoulder which I might be tempted to take out on you lot. Till Mr Chamberlain cocked things up, I was happily retired running a little sub-post office. But they couldn't fight and win this war without me so it seems. I am a real hard man.' His teeth bared as he snapped out the words. He tapped the three gold stripes on his arm and said, 'Some of you may think they mean "Three badges gold too bloomin' old". They don't. They represent my nickname, "Tiger", on account that I have a nasty, horrible nature. I've been known to have two of the likes of you for breakfast.'

Someone in the near rank sniggered and John Read shook his head slowly from side to side. 'I really hope my ears let me down because if I thought one of you shower had laughed I would have got quite angry.'

Morris could have sworn that he winked slyly to Petty Officer Reynolds, but before he had a chance to reflect on it Read bellowed, 'Ship's company, shun.'

As the men sprang to attention Lieutenant Commander Paton strode into the shed, followed by Lieutenant Phelp and the midshipman.

'Stand the men at ease, Coxswain.'

Paton surveyed the forty men before him. The sprinkling of regulars stood out like a beacon in the darkness. The rest looked a pretty unprepossessing bunch of rookies. But it was better than he had anticipated. At least he had a small but hard core of experienced men around which he could build.

'I'm Lieutenant Commander Paton, your commanding officer. I have a very simple approach to running a ship. It can't be efficient if it isn't happy. When an order is given I expect you to jump to it. But you are not just names and numbers. You are men. Like a chain, we are all dependent on the weakest link and so the surest way of making certain we get through this with our skins intact is to make ruddy sure there isn't one. If any one of you have any personal troubles don't brood on them; come to me or either of the other officers. Cabin doors are meant to be knocked on.'

He then introduced the first lieutenant and the midshipman. 'The coxswain you already know. I met him earlier, and if he scared you as much as he did me then the battle's as good as won.'

There was a ripple of dutiful laughter along the ranks which was promptly stifled by 'Tiger' Read.

Paton continued, 'I've been told that we have two weeks in which to get the ship ready for sea. I'm pretty certain we can do it in half the time. So stow your gear aboard and let's get cracking.'

When the men had earmarked their lockers and bunks or reserved a hammock space, they changed into working rig of navy blue overalls and commenced the thousand and one tasks essential before *Grey Seal* would be made ready for active service. Within a short time the deck was covered with large wooden crates and the air was filled with the screech of nails being wrenched out. Mess deck crockery was taken out of its protective sawdust, carefully counted, then washed and stowed, and mess utensils which included knives, forks, spoons, pots, pans and large fannies for soup and tea, were scoured and polished before being carried into the galley.

Ernest White – immediately nicknamed 'Chalkie' – the ship's signalman and bunting tosser, a gangling quietly-spoken man from Bristol, busied himself on the bridge sorting out his flags and pennants before stowing them in the pigeon-holes of the signal locker. The spotless new White Ensign he carried down to the captain's cabin. After checking the Aldis lamps, batteries and searchlight he hoisted his first signal from the halyards: the red bird-tailed B for Bravo, warning nearby ships that *Grey Seal* would soon be taking on explosives.

The job of ammunitioning was detailed to a party under the hawk-like eye of Leading Seaman James Jenkins, a one-badge martinet from the gunnery school at Whale Island. Straight-backed as the ram-rod from an old muzzle loading cannon, he supervised the loading and stowage of the shells and cartridges for the twelve-pounder and Lewis guns from the tender moored alongside. In normal times, the ammunitioning was carried out in the relative safety of open water, but time was too short for that kind of precaution.

When the ready-use lockers were filled he immediately got the men loading shells into the magazine below the bandstand. The small-arms – six .303 rifles, three 9 mm Lanchester submachine guns and a Lee Enfield with an extra long barrel for throwing a line – were chained and padlocked to a rack in the wheelhouse. Four Webley .45 revolvers were similarly attached to a bulkhead in the wardroom.

In the engine room. Harry Reynolds, the Cockney 'chief', had his four sweat-grimed stokers stripped to the waist polishing the brass work and cleaning the skidproof metal decks with paraffin. 'Don't spare the elbow-grease neither. I don't have to sign a chitty for that. I want to see everything shining like a sixpence on a sweep's backside. I want to be able to eat my grub off the deck.'

After their first meeting, Paton had been more than content to leave Reynolds well alone and let him carry on with getting the engine room shipshape. He had tried to impress on him that he did not consider the engine room the forgotten part of the ship by airing what little he knew about triple expansion engines, but the engineer had been too preoccupied with the filthy state of the machinery. He had muttered with thinly disguised disgust, 'You'll get nothing out of a engine room if you treat it like it was the heads. A engine is like the 'uman heart, sir. It has to be treated with total respect if you don't want it to pack up under you the first time you put an additional strain on it.' He had looked at Patton in a most challenging way and added, 'The bridge might be the brains, but a ship with a dicky ticker is as useless as a runner in a wheelchair, sir.' It was almost as if he was blaming Paton for the condition of the engine room.

Paton had nodded in silent agreement, but this had only encouraged Reynolds to further assert his need for independence. 'So we're agreed on that then, sir. The tiddly topside stuff is your affair, sir. The engine room mine. You ask me for the revs and I'll supply 'em. I 'ave my standards, sir, and if yourn are 'arf as 'igh as mine, we'll get along like a couple of honeymooners, sir.'

Paton had suspected that the liberal sprinkling of 'sirs' was the chief's impregnable bulwark against a charge of insubordination. But he had no quarrel with his approach to the job. If he could instil the same sense of pride into the stokers that was fine with him.

Fresh meat and perishable vegetables were stowed in the larders, the food lockers crammed with tinned food, and emergency rations loaded into the lifeboats and Carley floats. In the galley Charlie Tweddle, a piano tuner in civvy street, sweated over the coal stove preparing a hot lunch. He had joined with visions of becoming a hero only to be sent on a cook's course.

Arthur Hall was one of the few men who had landed on his feet. In peacetime he had been a waiter in a West End restaurant and had rather unwisely mentioned this to 'Tiger' who promptly appointed him officers' steward.

When the failing light made further work on the deck impossible and the order to 'darken ship' was sounded, the activity continued below. It was well past ten o'clock when Paton instructed his number one to tell the coxswain to stand the hands down and inform them that they had done themselves proud.

Paton's own cabin below the wheelhouse was little larger than a boxroom and every inch of space was utilized. There was a single bunk, the mattress of which also served as the back rest of a settee during the day, and below were two long drawers in which Paton stowed his shirts, collars and underwear. Against one bulkhead was a diminutive wardrobe where he hung his number one uniform, greatcoat and raincoat. In the centre, firmly attached to the deck, was a table with two hardback chairs, and near the door a wooden cabinet concealing a hand basin. Above it was a small shaving mirror.

As his job would entail a certain amount of paperwork, he was also entitled to a pygmy-sized desk and on top of this he placed a photograph of his parents and another of his sister Lesley, cradling a plump cat. It would never be much of a home, but that did not bother him; most of his time would be spent on the open bridge.

Phelp and the Snottie who would share the cramped wardroom were also unpacking their personal belongings. Carnac suspected that the first lieutenant was restraining some pent-up frustrations for, from time to time, he cursed aloud and tossed things willy-nilly into the wardrobe rather than stow them carefully. An odd thing for a man accustomed to a life afloat. One frequently repeated phrase bewildered him: 'After the Lord Mayor's Show'. If Carnac had been able to read his thoughts he would have discovered that 'Jimmy-the-One' was extremely bitter about the accommodation. His old cabin aboard the 'banana boat' had been luxury in comparison. And as for the ship itself . . . well, words failed him! With ever-increasing bitterness, he reflected he would have been contributing more to the war effort if he had remained in the Merchant Navy.

Carnac was tempted to ask him what was eating him (after all, they would be living on top of each other for goodness knows how long), but he restrained his curiosity. The first lieutenant might retaliate by questioning him about his own feelings regarding the ship, and he would prefer not to answer. He had envisaged being sent to a big ship, bristling with guns. Instead, he found himself aboard a museum piece with a whole load of responsibilities which he wasn't at all sure he could cope with.

When they finally turned in, Carnac could still hear Phelp muttering angrily to himself. The midshipman formed the distinct impression that the lieutenant was dying to be asked the reason for his ill-humour.

Immediately after breakfast next morning the hands were turned out to begin where they had left off. When the time for Colours approached, Paton went up onto the bridge with the new Ensign tucked under his arm and handed it to the signalman.

Grey Seal's own bosun's pipe swelled the trilling chorus

from scores of ships. On the decks below, the men paused in their labours and faced the slowly rising Ensign. Paton saluted smartly, then he turned and said, 'Well, we've joined the Fleet now, bunts.'

Throughout the morning Tiger Read prowled the upper and lower decks to make certain that no one was slacking. As he passed one group of men he heard a voice singing tunelessly: 'Oh I wonder, yes, I wonder, if the jaunty made a blunder when he made this draft chit out for me'. But he cocked a deaf 'un. He was too old a hand to get ruffled by some seaman wanting to let him know that he wasn't too happy with his lot. Anyway, there was something wrong with a matelot who didn't bitch.

On the bandstand Jenkins, the gunnery 'killick', had two men cleaning the twelve-pounder. The breech was jammed solid with grease that had been there since it was stowed away in an armoury at the end of the First War, while the muzzle looked like a sooted-up railway tunnel. 'When you've finished, I'm going over it with a new pusser's hankie. If I see so much as a smudge on it I'll have you both on jankers,' he warned.

In his cabin, Paton checked the chronometers, binoculars, sextant, and distance-meter which he had personally signed for as they were such expensive items of equipment. If they were lost he would have to foot the bill. Then he went up on the bridge and surveyed the ant-like activity below: slowly but surely, things were taking shape. He turned his attention aft to see how Carnac was coping. Appreciating just how raw the youngster was, he had decided to throw him in at the deep end by putting him in charge of the quarterdeck party. He realized the lad was taking a fair amount of stick from Morris and Rhind, the two experienced trawler hands, who had forgotten more about manillas, hawsers, shackles and capstans than the middie would ever know. They kept lifting their eyes to heaven in mock dismay as he barked out orders in what he hoped was an authoritative voice ringing with the power of command. When someone started singing, 'There's a muck

44

up on the quarterdeck and the wavy navy done it', to the tune of a current popular song, Carnac was stung into threatening to put him on defaulters. Paton overheard it with silent approval; he liked to see the youngster making it perfectly clear that despite his youth he wouldn't take any sauce.

Even so, Paton decided that the Snottie had had enough and he summoned him to the bridge and gestured towards a pile of Admiralty Instructions to Mariners and told him to get the charts up to date by marking in any new hazards, booms and buoys. 'It's a boring chore,' he said, 'but a vital one; many a ship has gone down through a failure to keep charts up to date.' And he added, 'By the way, you did a fine job aft. Keep up the good work. We'll make an officer of you yet.'

The flush that suffused Carnac's cheeks reminded him of a puppy wagging its tail at his master's approval.

When he glanced at his watch he saw that it was nearly eleven o'clock. He descended onto the deck and said to Read, 'Time to pipe "Up Spirits", Coxswain. I don't suppose you've forgotten to see the rum was aboard.'

Tiger Read's face split into an ear-to-ear grin. 'I personally saw to it, sir. Until the lads get a drop of Nelson's blood inside them, I don't think they can consider themselves part of the Andrew.'

'As it's a special occasion we'll bend the rules and let everyone have it neat,' said Paton. 'But we won't make a habit of it.'

Normally only petty officers were allowed their rum neat; the ratings were issued one eighth of a pint of the dark, blood-warming spirit diluted with three parts of water. The dilution was necessary for two reasons: neat rum could have a disastrous effect on men not used to it, but more important it stopped ratings bottling it. Watered rum went off.

Paton thought it was an appropriate time for his officers to join him in a celebratory drink and he invited them to his cabin.

When they knocked and entered, Paton was busy putting the lead-weighted confidential books and codes into the small steel safe resting on a shelf against the bulkhead, held firmly in position by a padlocked steel band that could be swiftly unlocked. The bottom was perforated to ensure it would sink quickly if it had to be dumped overboard in an emergency. On the inside of the door a notice in red letters warned that it should not be dropped in less than six fathoms of water.

As Phelp drank his gin he remarked sourly, 'I hope we never have to go out that far, sir.'

During their brief association Paton had noticed that Phelp took every opportunity to make some disparaging remark about *Grey Seal*. Some time, not just yet, they would have to have a heart to heart talk about it.

Later that night Paton and Phelp sat over the table together drawing up a Watch and Quarters Bill, a daily routine for working ship and allocating an action station to every member of the ship's company. When the orders were posted no man would be in any doubt what his post would be in the event of them having to repel boarders, his duties in damage control, and his boat or raft station in the event of 'Abandon Ship' being piped. Paton was so meticulous and attentive to the smallest detail that the first lieutenant was prompted to remark, 'This isn't a battleship, sir.' To run a scruffy old trawler as if it was a capital ship seemed slightly ridiculous to him.

Again Paton sensed the bottled up resentment. How long would it be before he could no longer suppress it and it burst out, like pus from a lanced boil? Then there would have to be a showdown. Paton did not relish the prospect. But he would not shirk it.

Suddenly from one of the mess decks the sound of voices singing to a mouth organ was heard. Phelp cocked his head and said, 'Listen to that, sir. It's not just me. The men feel the same.'

The regulars were teaching the rookies the navy's own unofficial anthem:

This is my story, this is my song,
I've been in the Andrew too ruddy long.
So roll on the Nelson, the Rodney, *the* Hood,
This one-funnelled bucket is no bloody good.

Paton smiled, 'Not very melodious but encouraging.'

He had heard the same song sung in wardrooms and mess decks in every class of ship the world over. The words meant nothing . . . the ship you were in was always worse than the one you had left. Didn't Phelp recognize that? It was the voices raised in unison that mattered. It was the first faltering step towards comradeship.

'Do you know where the name Andrew comes from, Number One?'

Phelp shook his head. 'Can't say that I do, sir.'

'Andrew Miller was an extremely zealous press-gang officer who impressed so many men into service during the Napoleonic wars that he was said to own the navy.'

'Interesting historically,' said Phelp with the vaguest hint of sarcasm, 'but it doesn't affect the point I was making, sir.'

'Actually it does. Most of the men down there are volunteers. So don't pay too much attention to the words of the song.'

Phelp said, 'I volunteered too, sir. But not for this. Now if you'll excuse me I'd like permission to turn in.'

Paton nodded. 'Go ahead, Number One.' As the door closed he experienced a deep feeling of intense fatigue and knew it was not due entirely to the long hours of non-stop work. How could he instil a sense of pride into the ship's company when his right arm had nothing but contempt for *Grey Seal*?

When 'Pipe Down' was sounded an uncanny silence filled the ship; all that could be heard was the faint hum of the extractors working in the overhot messes. Paton went up onto the bridge and gazed out over the harbour. There was a bright moon and the sky was a filigree of stars, silhouetting the outlines of the impressive warships anchored off shore. He wished he was aboard one of them. He could appreciate Phelp's bitterness. Hadn't he himself felt the same when he first saw *Grey Seal*? But that was all water under the bridge now. Somehow or other he had to create an atmosphere where everyone – officer and rating – wouldn't swop berths for all the rum in the spirit locker. It wouldn't be easy. When you were labelled as part of 'Harry Tate's Navy' it was difficult not to suffer from a sense of inferiority. The derisory comparison with the old music hall artist summed up the navy's opinion of small ship men. The necessary change of heart could only be obtained through example. What was it that Drake had said? 'Everyone must pull together on the rope, the Mariners to haul and draw with the Gentlemen and the Gentlemen with the Mariners'. Somewhere among his belongings was the framed sampler his mother had made bearing those words. He would look it out and hang it in a discreet position in his cabin. Phelp might even get the message.

As he stepped down from the bridge he saw the duty quartermaster sitting on a coil of rope near the gangway, his head buried deep in the collar of his greatcoat. 'Morris, isn't it?' he enquired.

'Yes, sir.'

'When you're on gangway watch you remain vertical, and keep an alert look-out.'

As he went towards his cabin he heard him murmur audibly, 'Who the hell is going to steal this floating scrapheap?' Paton paused, then thought better of it. Morris was a peacetime trawlerman who had yet to learn *Grey Seal* was now *his* ship. He had come from a world where it was the owner's responsibility to look after the vessel in harbour.

'Good night, Morris,' he called. 'And don't forget to slacken the lines as the tide drops. Otherwise we'll be suspended in mid-air.' It was his rather unsubtle way of reminding him that the job was not as meaningless as it appeared, and no one was asked to do anything without a good reason behind it.

But in a way his own ship was the least of his worries. With the help of men like Tiger Read he had no doubt that in time he would blend the ship's company into an efficient combat unit. His real headaches would start when he had to try and get the RNR skippers who would command the other trawlers in his group to follow the same line. They were men used to giving orders, not taking them.

3 At first light next morning, Tiger Read stormed through the mess decks bellowing, 'Rise and shine. Show a leg. Hands off cocks on socks. The sun's in the heavens and waiting to scorch your eyeballs.' It was the first and last time he would be the ship's alarm clock, but today was a special occasion. *Grey Seal* had been ordered to slip and proceed to the coaling wharf; not a long or eventful trip, but a maiden voyage nevertheless. At least under the White Ensign.

Men clambered out of their bunks and tumbled from hammocks and rummaged around for their clothing. Before they had had time to dress Read was shouting, 'Lash up and stow.'

When 'Hands Stand By For Leaving Harbour' was piped, everyone was agog with excitement. Where were they going? Despite their pleas of, 'Come on Chief, let us in on it', Tiger maintained a tight-lipped silence. They would find out in their own good time that they were about to engage in the most distasteful job the navy could chuck at them: coaling ship. It was a task devised by the Devil himself.

Paton stood on the bridge, dry-mouthed and nervous. God, he had better not make a hash of things. He would never live it down. He felt as jittery as a learner driver about to take his test. He bellowed through a megaphone to Phelp in charge of the fo'c's'le party. 'I'll take her out on the stern spring, Number One.'

'Aye, aye, sir,' came back the response.

Paton lifted the brass cover on the voicepipe leading down to the wheelhouse. 'Coxswain at the wheel?'

Read's voice came back, 'Coxswain at the wheel, sir.'

Reynolds, in a faded set of overalls and a sweat cloth wrapped round his neck appeared on the bridge. 'Engine room ready when you are, sir.'

Paton went out to the port bridge wing and looked aft to where Carnac was nervously supervising the quarterdeck party. He unconsciously crossed his fingers, put the megaphone to his mouth and shouted, 'Let go forard, let go aft.'

He distinctly heard someone say in response, 'All gone barmy, all gone daft.' God! Couldn't a navy ship ever put to sea without some wag coming up with that hoary old chestnut!

Paton ordered, 'Slow astern,' and watched the bow swing out as the stern spring tautened. 'Let go the spring,' he shouted. When it was safely inboard he called down the voicepipe, 'Slow ahead,' and heard the clang of the engine room telegraph and Read's confirming voice, 'Engine slow ahead, sir.'

Grey Seal nosed herself away from the jetty and Paton heaved a small sigh of relief: at least that had been accomplished with comparative ease, and he had got the feel of the ship.

He called down to the wheelhouse, 'Starboard twenty.'

'Starboard twenty, sir,' came back the reply, followed seconds later by, 'twenty of starboard wheel on, sir.'

As the ship carved a wide arc to clear other ships, Paton called down, 'Ease to ten.' Then 'Midships,' and finally 'Steady as you go.'

On the fo'c's'le where the hands had been fallen in for leaving harbour, Phelp was fuming silently. He knew where they were going and it seemed absolutely pointless to him to have the hands dress in their number threes. They were going to coal ship, not attend a Fleet Review. In no time at all they would be ordered to change into any old gear to coal ship. The CO was so ruddy hidebound. If that's what the book said, then that's how it had to be done. When would he realize there was a war on and accept that you couldn't run a fishing boat as if it was a peacetime cruiser?

Paton was delighted at the way he had taken *Grey Seal* alongside the wharf; he had hardly flattened the fenders which he had ordered to be suspended over the side from stem to stern.

As soon as the ship secured alongside, 'Change Into Coaling Rig' was piped. Those old seamen who had served in coal burners before the navy switched to oil painted horrific scenes of what they were about to endure, and advised them not to wear anything they valued as it would be worthless by the end of the day. And so the hands emerged from the mess decks resembling a hand of brigands: handkerchiefs were knotted tightly over their hair like skull-caps, some wore football shorts and jerseys, others just combs – the navy issue of one piece underwear.

Hour after hour the men toiled at their labours, shovelling coal into canvas sacks which they dumped into the chutes leading to the bunkers below decks. There near-naked stokers coughed and spluttered as they trimmed the bunkers to make room for more coal, and then more coal. Although they wore cloths over their mouths the dust still penetrated deep into their lungs, until they coughed like men in the last stages of tuberculosis.

Above deck the conditions were a little, but not much, better. As the men heaved, hauled and shovelled, their sweat encrusted the dust on the exposed portion of their bodies until they looked like the cast of a minstrel show. Their eyes and teeth glowing white through the brick-hard deposit of coal. And they sang, not with the enthusiasm of a minstrel group, but simply as an expression of their loathing for the task and a spur to keep them going: Coaling, coaling, coaling. Always . . . .ing well coaling.

A passing vicar would have been appalled to hear the tune of the well-known hymn 'Holy, holy, holy' employed in such a sacrilegious way.

Towards late afternoon more than four hundred tons had been stowed into the bunkers. Enough to keep *Grey Seal* at sea for a month. The triple expansion engine was extremely economical. The three cylinders – high, intermediate and low pressure – ensured that none of the precious steam was wasted. It passed from one cylinder to another with gradually decreasing pressure until every ounce of energy was utilized.

Rhind and Morris were the most outspoken in their criticisms. In all their years at sea, it was a task they had never before been called upon to perform. It was demeaning; coaling was a job to be undertaken by landlubbers especially employed for it. It was a view entirely shared by Lieutenant Phelp. To him it.was another example of Paton's lack of judgement.

When the last of the coal had been trimmed the order was given for the ship to be hosed down. It came as a merciful release for the dog-tired men, who took it as an opportunity to indulge in childish horseplay. They drenched each other with the fire hoses and a couple of men were actually knocked overboard by the powerful jets. However even the hoses and the unexpected dip in the Oggin failed to remove the layer of grime. But they quickly forgot the discomforts they had endured when they had wallowed in the luxury of a hot shower.

Paton had ordered Tweddle the cook to prepare an extra special meal as some consolation for the odious task that had been so speedily accomplished, but despite all the battening down the coal dust had still penetrated into the mess decks. So that when they sat down to eat they could still taste it, like sand at a seaside picnic.

When *Grey Seal* returned to her original berth and 'Darken Ship' was piped, not a sound emerged from the mess decks. Apart from the regular pacing of the quartermaster, the decks were deserted. Tired to the point of near-total exhaustion, the ship's company had just found enough energy to crawl into their bunks and hammocks before sleep engulfed them.

Next morning, with almost sadistic glee, Tiger Read announced that they had a much more colourful job ahead of them: painting ship. There were muted groans of dismay, but few of them were genuine expressions of grievance. After coaling anything else was a doddle. Only Morris seemed genuinely resentful. Once again he felt his pride had been dented; he had never been asked to wield a brush before.

The paint lockers were opened and each man was issued

with a pot and brush and given a section of the hull or upper deck to paint. Makeshift cradles were slung over the side and an air of gay abandon quickly developed as the men sploshed paint over the ship and themselves with more enthusiasm than skill. When the task was completed, the eyesore patches of red lead had vanished and everyone reluctantly agreed that *Grey Seal* looked years younger: like an old lady who had been given an extremely skilful face-lift.

There was an additional source of pride among the ship's company; they had got *Grey Seal* ready for sea in seven days – half the allotted time and comfortably within the deadline set by Paton. And by a fortunate coincidence the task was completed on the first pay day. They filed into the wheelhouse where Midshipman Carnac had set up a table, handed over their pay books and watched their upturned caps receive a small but well earned sum of money.

It was also the first time that shore leave was granted and Paton announced that as many men as possible should be allowed to go. All he needed to remain on board were enough men to tend to the mooring lines and generators.

Through some indefinable almost telepathic process that had existed throughout the navy since its infancy, the men in *Grey Seal* had already selected their 'oppos' and friendships had been established that would only be severed when one of them was posted to another ship or the unmentionable occurred. Men chose the most unlikely people for their 'opposite number'. Tall men invariably paired up with squat ones. Fat ones with thin ones. Hell-raisers with quiet, studious types. Without a handshake or a word being exchanged, Rhind and Morris teamed up together.

When 'Liberty, Men Fall In' was sounded, they stood together in the waist of the ship while Carnac walked along the row of seamen to make certain they were properly dressed and a credit to the ship. The hands had taken immense care with their appearances; their collars were freshly dhobeyed and ironed and the creases in their bellbottoms were like knife edges. Their lanyards sparkled like well-polished teeth.

Their minds were filled with three things: a good meal, a few pints and, granted a modicum of luck, a girl. At the main gate they stood and took a deep breath like released prisoners enjoying their first taste of fresh air and freedom for longer than they cared to remember. Then they split up into twos and threes and went their separate ways. They had been living in one another's laps for what seemed like an eternity, and did not want to see hide nor hair of each other until they returned aboard.

After a meal, Rhind and Morris moved from pub to pub, meticulously buying round for round. The pub crawl was not undertaken in a quest for better or more potent beer, but simply in search of female company.

Eventually they found themselves standing outside an anonymous pub; in the dark they could not make out the name on the swinging sign above their heads. They had almost resigned themselves to a girlless night and were thinking of settling down to spend what remained of the evening in a bout of steady drinking. But the sound of music and merriment filtering through the darkened door gave them fresh hope.

As they pushed their way through the heavy blackout curtains they had to screw up their eyes to see through the thick haze of trapped tobacco smoke. At least the war had given a new lease of life to some people who, not so long ago, had been on the borderline of despair, for the bar was crowded with people who seemed to have plenty of cash to spend. Men who had been unemployed for months had now found lucrative jobs in factories and the docks, and married women who would never have ventured out on their own were now enjoying a new-found freedom behind the backs of their servicemen husbands.

It was one of those pubs which likes to boast character and an affinity with the nearby sea. Seine nets decorated with green glass balls draped from the ceiling and one wall was covered with cap tallies bearing the names of scores of His Majesty's ships which, over a long period of years, had visited the port. The bar itself was adorned with all kinds of curios from stuffed crocodiles to African spears and drums. All exchanged for a drink by hard-up sailors returning from foreign parts.

At the far end of the room a shirt-sleeved man was playing an old upright piano, the top of which was lined with glasses that threatened to spill over from his playing . . . which was more vigorous fhan melodic. A group of people were clustered around the keyboard singing the latest songs which invariably dealt with sorrowful partings, assurances that time and distance would never alter their affections, and the held out promise of happy reunions and all those other sugary sentiments which war seemed to bring to the forefront.

Morris and Rhind found an empty table and promptly staked a claim. Rhind enquired, 'Yours or mine?' Morris retorted, 'Yours. I got the last one, remember.'

The Canadian shouldered his way to the bar and called for two pints and then concentrated on reaching the safety of the table without having them knocked from his hands.

Suddenly an ill-kempt, unshaven man, slightly unsteady on his feet, materialized in front of them. 'Either of you two matelots want to buy a dog?'

Rhind stared icily at the man, then let his eyes stray to the bundle of black fur attached to a length of string. 'Shove off. What would we do with a dog aboard ship?'

The man spoke with the practised whine of the longstanding scrounger. 'I'll have to put him down then. What with rationing and the price of things, I can't afford to feed myself, let alone him.'

Morris fondled the puppy's ears and was rewarded with a good licking and a frenzy of tail wagging. 'How much?' he asked.

The tipsy stranger adopted a weedling tone. 'To you, a quid. Anyone else and I'd ask a fiver. He's a thoroughbred Labrador.'

'I'll give you a packet of duty-frees and five bob. Take it or leave it.'

The man's face registered mock horror. 'What! You must

be bonkers. It's like giving my own child away. Ten bob and the fags.'

The dog flopped down and began to scratch the back of its head with a hind paw.

Rhind protested angrily, 'Come off it, Isaac. Look at its feet. It'll grow to be as big as a bull moose. Anyway, it's alive with fleas. You'd have the whole mess cooty if you took that aboard.'

'All right, all right, Campbell. So we'll have to give him a bath. I just can't stand the thought of the poor little beggar being tied up in a sack and dumped in the harbour.'

The Canadian said scathingly, 'Don't be so soft. He's just having you on. All he wants is the price of a drink. Tomorrow he'll be asking for the dog back.'

Further discussion was brought to an abrupt halt by the man saying, 'I'll take it. You've got yourself a real bargain there,' as he transferred the length of string to Morris's hand.

'What's his name?' Morris asked.

The man said, 'He don't have one.'

As Morris handed over the packet of cigarettes and two half crowns, the man turned on his heels and made straight for the bar.

'What did I tell you?' said Rhind.

But his friend was not even listening. He lifted the dog onto his lap and began stroking it gently. 'His ribs are sticking out like a scrubbing board. Be a pal and do us a favour. Go and get him a pork pie.'

The Canadian could scarcely conceal his annoyance. 'Pork pie! You want to kill him? It's probably still at the milk stage.'

Nevertheless, he got up and elbowed his way to the bar. When he returned with the pie Morris was convulsed with laughter. 'Milk! You must be potty. I just gave him a sip of my beer and he knocked back half the glass. He'll make a proper sea-dog, mark my words.'

The puppy took to its new master without a backward glance at the man who had sold him for a smoke and the price of a few beers. It was certainly ravenous, for it scoffed the meat pie without even tasting it.

As they wended their way back to the ship, the puppy snapping playfully at Morris's bellbottoms, Rhind was still expressing grave doubts about the wisdom of the venture. 'How on earth are you going to smuggle him aboard and get past the duty officer?'

Morris refused to be deterred; it was simple. He would stick the dog down his jumper and while Rhind regaled the duty officer with details of their trip ashore he would slip down into the mess deck.

But there was no need for any subterfuge. Carnac had been told that, as it was the first spot of shore leave for the men, he should make himself conspicuous by his absence and remain in his cabin. Some of the men were certain to be a trifle worse for wear and therefore, technically at least, unfit for duty – which was an offence. Paton had said, 'I don't want a long queue of defaulters in the morning. As long as they can stagger aboard, salute the quarterdeck and get below without injury, that's fine.' So Carnac was already tucked up in his bunk when he was told that all the liberty men were accounted for and safely back aboard.

Morris fed the dog on a bar of 'nutty' before making a comfortable spot for it at the foot of his bunk. Rhind, who slept above, leaned down and whispered, 'What are you going to call him?'

'I've been thinking. What about Jolson?'

The Canadian sounded completely bewildered. 'What on earth for?'

Morris began to chuckle, then started to sing, 'M-a-a-m-i-e, M-a-a-m-i-e. . .' in an excrutiating parody of the well-known singer.

Someone bellowed out, 'Put a sock in it. I'm trying to crash my swede.'

Next morning, by unanimous consent, it was agreed that Jolson should remain. Every ship had to have a mascot. The problem was where to stow him away, unseen and undetected until such time as his presence became acceptable. One wag remarked, 'Stick him in one of the bunkers. With his colour, no one will spot him there.' But Morris was convinced he could secrete him away below his bunk until some more permanent home could be found. His confidence was short-lived. During Captain's Rounds that morning, Paton spotted unmistakable evidence on the deck of the presence of a dog and issued an ultimatum that the animal should be produced topsides in ten minutes, or else.

Morris duly appeared with the tethered Jolson and Paton took one look at the frisky pup and said, 'Well, I don't suppose one more mouth is going to affect the messing arrangements. But he can't stay below deck. Find him a berth in the wheelhouse. And I'll hold you responsible for seeing that he becomes house-trained, or ship-trained.' He patted the dog's head and evoked an immediate and affectionate response. But when the puppy began a frenzied scratching Paton issued another ultimatum. 'Get a bar of pussers' soap and some disinfectant and delouse him.'

And so Jolson became a member of the ship's company.

Soon afterwards, the trawlers *Beaver, Otter* and *Vole* which were to make up the group joined *Grey Seal* and the next two weeks were spent in building up exercises. It was a trying and testing time for Paton, made doubly difficult by the awkwardness of the trawler skippers. So accustomed to acting independently, they found it extremely hard to obey his orders and act in unison. Signals were often unacknowledged or misinterpreted, with the result that group manoeuvres were extremely hazardous and near collisions became commonplace. During one exercise, one particular skipper pulled out of line to do a spot of fishing. Another stubbornly refused to cooperate as, during a routine trip ashore, he had been to one naval establishment where the toilets bore signs 'Officers' and 'Skippers'. It was only when Paton had personally spoken to the senior shore officer and pointed out that such signs were not only offensive to the prickly skippers but prejudicial to the war effort that the word 'Skippers' was discreetly removed.

Paton worked his own ship's company to a standstill. They had, he stressed, to set the standards for the rest of the group. 'Action Stations' were sounded at the most unexpected times and men who had slumped into their bunks hoping for forty winks were suddenly aroused by the alarm bells and forced to summon up hidden reserves of energy in anticipation of the real thing happening one dawn, dusk, or in the middle of the night. There were endless guns drill with dummy ammunition – the real stuff was too precious to squander – until the crews could load, aim and fire in pitch darkness and in all conditions. Phelp was put in charge of the twelve-pounder and he soon discovered that 'Guns' Jenkins had forgotten more about the weapon than he would ever know and happily resigned himself to being little more than a figurehead.

But there were rare occasions when real ammunition was fired and the gun crew, which had been so scathing about the 'museum piece', soon developed a healthy respect for it. Antiquated she may have been, but she was ideal for the job. The separate ammunition – the brass cartridge containing the propellant and the actual projectile – meant that armour-piercing or shrapnel could be fired alternatively if necessary. And, unlike the more powerful four-inch, she could be elevated for anti-aircraft work. Furthermore, the barrel didn't need swabbing or sponging after every round.

Jenkins would only accept one standard: perfection. And when the men on the twelve-pounder or the twin Lewis guns made the slightest mistake he continued the drill. There were simulated depth charge attacks with a British submarine acting as target, during which the Asdic ratings, cooped up in their confined cubicle, were almost driven mad by the incessant ping, ping, ping of their detectors. But they learned to distinguish the real thing from a shoal of fish. They practised boat drill until they could go through the motions blindfolded. In harbour, armed parties were lowered in the whaler to attack buoys representing surfaced U-boats and pelted them with potatoes which they had to imagine were hand grenades. In the middle of a make and mend, they were suddenly called into action to repel boarders with the fire hoses and small-arms.

Sometimes Paton ordered a boat to be lowered in the middle of the night, the oars muffled, and rowed alongside one of the group. Then he would nip aboard and if everyone was asleep he would steal something. Next morning there was all hell to pay when he returned the purloined item to the skipper.

Two of the skippers found the twelve-pounder gun drill ridiculous and frustrating and stubbornly refused to participate. Until more important ships were armed, they had to make do with an imitation main armament made of wood. It added to their resentment and made them more and more convinced that they were poor relations.

Fortunately, it was the period of the phoney war. The British Army in France was threatening Hitler with songs while the civilian population began to wonder if there really was a war on, and a deep sense of apathy prevailed. Paton particularly appreciated the breathing space. True, the war in the Atlantic was very real and a vast amount of tonnage was being sunk by U-boats and surface raiders, but apart from regular sorties by E-boats and U-boats and bomb attacks by aircraft, the coastal shipping lanes had not been subjected to any concentrated assault. When that time did come, he desperately hoped that his group would be ready to deal with it.

When *Grey Seal* and the group returned to harbour after a gruelling spell of exercises in which the men had seldom removed their clothing, Paton summoned Tiger Read and Engineer Reynolds to his cabin and asked them for a progress report over a drink.

The coxswain said, 'They're bored to the back teeth, like firemen fed up with answering false alarms. At the moment there isn't one of them who doesn't tell me that his sole intention is to emerge with his skin intact.'

'A gloomy prediction,' said Paton.

'Not at all, sir. It's what I'd expect. Your average sailor never wants the chance to prove himself a hero. It's only when he's forced to that he does. On the whole I'm satisfied with them. I don't think they'll start ducking when the real stuff is thrown at them.'

Paton turned towards Reynolds. 'And you, Chief?'

The Cockney engineer pursed his lips. 'From the runnin' point of view I got no moans. The stokers know their job and does it well. It's on the 'uman level I've got a 'eadache and one what might only be sorted out by a draft chit.'

Two of them, he went on to explain, had become wordless enemies; they worked alongside each other in silent hostility. In the mess deck when it was necessary for one of them to ask something they did it through a third party. Both were tough Glaswegians who had learned to survive with their fists in the mean, grim jungle of backstreet slum tenements. But that was all the two Jocks had in common. Hamish McIntyre supported the Catholic Celtics while Jamie Ross gave his allegiance to the Protestant Rangers. And the cause of world freedom took second place to the religious and sporting chasm that separated them. The near tribal war which divided Glasgow had been going on far longer than *this* one and would continue unabated long after the victory parades.

'It's too late in the day to think of drafting one. I'd never get a replacement in time, Chief.'

Reynolds said mournfully, 'That's what I thought, sir. It don't affect the efficiency of the engine room, it just makes the two of them thoroughly brassed off and that ain't a good thing for neither of them. Now the other two stokers, they're a completely different kettle of fish. Go together like ham and eggs. Stoker Danvers can't read or write while Cohen fancies hisself as a poet. Christ knows why he wants to shovel coal. He even writes his oppo's love letters. Don't that take the biscuit?'

That's one riddle solved, thought Paton. Due to the needs of censorship every officer had to take the odd turn at reading the ship's company's mail and he had been amazed at how someone as inarticulate as Danvers could wax so lyrical. The arrangement could, however, have damaging repercussions, but that wasn't really his concern. The two men at silent loggerheads were.

'Any point in me having a word with the two Scots?'

'I don't think so, sir. Things like that 'ave a funny way of sorting themselves out at sea, sir.'

Paton decided to end the meeting on a less controversial note. 'That just leaves Jolson, Coxs'n. How's he settling down to shipboard life?'

Tiger grinned. 'If the hands picked up things as easy as that tripe hound, sir, we wouldn't have a thing to worry about. Taken to life aboard like a duck to water. Trots off to the scuppers at sea when he wants to use the heads and nips ashore when we're in harbour. And no stranger can step aboard without him barking his head off. Proper watchdog.' Tiger seemed pleased at the unintentional pun.

Later that day Paton and the other skippers were summoned ashore to attend a briefing, and when he returned he called Lieutenant Phelp to his cabin.

'The dress rehearsals are over, Number One. We've received sailing orders. The group is to escort a coastal convoy up to Scapa. No more dummy runs from now on.'

'Jerry's only got to see us and he'll die of fright,' said Phelp cynically.

Paton sighed inwardly. Despite all his efforts, he had still not managed to enlist the wholehearted support of his first lieutenant. His efficiency was unquestioned and his capacity for hard work limitless, but it was all too robot-like. Entirely professional, but lacking commitment.

Phelp in turn was thinking: He doesn't like me. He just won't accept I'm doing my job as well, if not better, than anybody else. He wants me to love it. And I can't. I'm like a doctor really, I'll do my best for a patient, but I won't fall in love with him. Whatever he says, this tub will always be a fishing boat.

And as he glanced around the cabin he realized how little he knew of Paton. He was very much a loner, stiffly aware of his position as commanding officer and perhaps afraid that familiarity might breed if not contempt, at least an intimacy that might undermine discipline. That was commendable in a ship where there were hundreds of men and officers, but it scarcely applied to *Grey Seal*. Not that he was totally aloof, he had the odd drink with him and Carnac in his quarters, but he ate his meals in solitary isolation and never spoke of anything that revealed a life outside the iron walls of the old trawler. He had not been ashore since they commissioned.

His eyes strayed to the two photographs he had pondered on so many times: the elderly man in baggy tweeds, and the finely-featured women who had Paton's nose and mouth. Clearly his mother and father. Rich and county. Born at the top and rather contemptuous of those who had clawed their way there. And the beautiful but toffee-nosed looking girl, cuddling a cat. Obviously his wife. But Paton was the type who could never unbend enough to talk about something as intimate as love.

'Have a drink, Number One.'

Phelp was almost jerked into an awareness of his surroundings. He accepted politely, but when they sat down together Paton spoke of nothing but the ship and things that needed to be done before morning.

The first lieutenant declined a top-up, only too anxious to get back to his own cabin and Carnac; a bloody good kid who didn't know his arse from his elbow, but a person you could talk to about something other than the ship and the 'Fleet in which we serve'.

Paton lifted the folio of charts he had collected at the briefing, untied the tapes and took out the one that would be of immediate interest in the morning. He busied himself with dividers and a parallel rule and drew a circle with a dot on the chart, to mark the rendezvous point with the merchant ships.

Then he poured himself a drink and sat with the glass clutched between two hands, untouched. The days ahead could prove to be a real testing time for him and all the others aboard *Grey Seal*. He prayed to God that, whatever else happened, he wouldn't fail them. He lifted one hand and held it out. It was trembling slightly.

4 *Grey Seal* and the other trawlers in the group were
steaming in line ahead at minimum revolutions about
three miles off Harwich in that perilous stretch of water
known as 'E-Boat Alley', which began at the Thames estuary
and followed the coastline north up to Flamborough Head. It
was an arbitrary boundary, for the activities of the fast,
powerfully armed torpedo boats which preyed on the coastal
convoys extended far beyond that. They went wherever there
were easy victims. And there were plenty.

Paton rested his powerful binoculars on the rim of the
bridge of the almost motionless ship and scoured the horizon
for any telltale trace of the unwelcome predators who struck
with the swiftness and ferocity of cheetahs on the hunt. Two
lookouts had also been posted on the bridge-wings, and there
was another perched precariously in the crow's nest. He
glanced at his watch and cursed silently; the convoy was
already half an hour late for the rendezvous. He focused his
glasses on the entrance to the harbour and emitted a silent
sigh of relief when he spotted the eight ships being led by two
mine-sweeping drifters sail into view. They were an unexpected but most welcome addition, for as many ships had
been sunk by mines as by enemy aircraft and E-boats. Keeping the shipping lane swept of mines was not a job he would
relish himself, for Jerry seemed to have introduced some
terrifying new mines which the navy had yet to find an answer
to. Apart from the conventional mines which exploded on
contact, there were others which seemed to be triggered off
magnetically or simply by the sound of a ship's engine. There
was even one with a delayed action mechanism. Together,
they were exacting a terrifying toll of valuable and difficult to

replace shipping. The sea was dotted with the masts, funnels and superstructure of ships which had fallen victim to these unseen menaces. Until some of the mines were recovered intact and the boffins were able to examine them and come up with a solution, the east coast would remain a graveyard for countless ships and the men who sailed in them.

Paton studied the approaching ships like a shepherd casting a protective eye over his flock. There were two small tankers and six cargo vessels of various shapes and tonnage. One was an extremely ancient cargo vessel that lay so low in the water her plimsoll line was no longer visible, her holds were packed solid with cement. Her sea going days were numbered, for she had already been consigned to a watery grave as a Scapa Flow block ship. It seemed ironical to Paton that he was charged with doing his utmost to ensure she remained afloat only to be sunk on arrival at their destination. Paton turned to Chalkie White and said, 'Bunts, make a signal telling them to take up their appointed stations.' As the Aldis winked out the message in morse Paton remarked bitterly to Phelp, 'It would have to be a lovely day, darn it.'

The sea was as smooth and placid as a boating pond with a gentle swell that scarcely moved the mast from the vertical. The wind was so light it would not have registered on the Beaufort Scale. The sky was almost cloudless except for a few misty strands which reminded him of the dappled underbelly of a mackerel. Visibility was perfect. These advantages were far outweighed by the disadvantages.

When the ships took up formation Paton ordered the trawlers to sail in line ahead, forming a protective shield to seawards. The speed of the convoy was set at seven knots, the speed of the slowest ship. The forenoon watch passed uneventfully and the gun crews who had been closed up at action stations since dawn began to fret and question the need for it.

Phelp said, 'Shall I stand them down, sir?'

'No. In these conditions they could never get back in time to man the guns. Have the cook rustle up some ki and sandwiches and have them sent round the ship.'

The only man who was relieved was the lookout in the crow's nest. No man could be expected to remain in that position, clinging to a small handrail for longer than two or three hours at a stretch.

Despite the slow speed, the merchant ships seemed to have considerable difficulty in maintaining station. And when he signalled them to close up his messages were ignored more often than not. Furthermore, the amount of smoke they were making was alarming; in the breezeless conditions the plumes of black smoke rose into the sky like Indian signals. The trouble was that some of the trawlers were making just as much smoke, and when Paton sent a signal to *Otter* pointing this out he received a curt reply, 'What do you want me to do – wash the ruddy coal?'

When dusk – a particularly dangerous and vulnerable period – came and passed without any sign of the enemy, Paton told the first lieutenant that the men could stand down and go to their messes for a meal. The duty Asdic rating, however, remained at his post in his cubicle, listening for any contact that might herald the presence of a U-boat. Even under the comforting blanket of darkness, one could never cease to be ever-vigilant against the unseen enemy.

Paton, who had been on the bridge since they sailed to meet the convoy, looked dark-eyed with fatigue and strain.

'I'm going down to snatch forty winks, Number One. You'd better do the same. The Middie can take over. It'll do him the world of good.'

When Carnac presented himself on the bridge, Paton handed over the watch giving him the course to steer. The merchant ships were steering on the stern light of the ship ahead, and as long as the weather remained fine there was not a lot to worry about on that score. 'Call me if you have the slightest problem. And don't worry about bothering me unnecessarily. Better safe than sorry.'

Paton went down to his cabin, took off his duffle coat and shoes and stretched out on his bunk. Within seconds he had dozed off; the dangers lurking outside were instantly dismissed. It was a form of mental discipline which he convinced himself was necessary. One had to delegate at some time or another. If and when the testing time came, a captain who was totally exhausted and not mentally alert was a menace to the ship and the men for whose safety he was responsible.

Midshipman Carnac stood by the binnacle and watched the phosphorescent glow as the bows parted the water. He could just make out the dim, dark shape of the trawler immediately astern and the straggling blur of the ships to port. He occasionally caught a glimpse of a stern light as one of them veered slightly off course.

He had never felt so alone or vulnerable before. He was in sole charge of *Grey Seal* and his mind went through all the things that could possibly happen and what he would do in response before calling the captain. He was positive of one thing: he wouldn't panic unnecessarily and earn Paton's disapproval. He wished more than anything that, given time, he could be as unflappable as the CO. Nothing seemed to worry *him*.

On the bridge-wings he could see the shapeless outlines of the lookouts, their heads buried beneath the hoods of their duffle coats; he hoped they hadn't nodded off.

'Port lookout, anything to report?' he called.

'All quiet, sir,' came the reply, and he rebuked himself for being so untrusting. He repeated the order to the starboard lookout and received the same reply. He didn't want the first man he had spoken to to feel as if he was being singled out.

Towards the end of the watch continuous peering into the darkness began to have a hallucinatory effect. Carnac began to feel as if he was sailing the ship down an endless avenue of trees. He rubbed his eyes but the illusion persisted and he began to experience the first pangs of panic. Then he heard the sound of footsteps on the bridge ladder and fear gave way to immense relief. Four minutes to midnight, just before the end of the First Watch – Phelp clambered up to relieve him.

'Nothing to report, sir,' he said. Carnac made it sound as if he had been to hell and back.

Phelp smiled in the darkness and patted him on the

69

shoulder. 'Well done, Middie. I fully expected the alarm bells to be ringing all night. That's what I did when I kept my first solo watch as a young officer. Now pop off and get your head down.'

As Phelp acknowledged the new helmsman who had taken over the wheel he marvelled at Paton's ability to remain in his cabin. If he had been the captain he would have been worried stiff at the thought of a mere boy being in sole charge. He would have been up and down to the bridge like a jack-in-the-box.

A refreshed Paton lay on his back in his bunk staring into the darkness, seeing nothing but the glowing end of his cigarette and reflecting how strange it was that tobacco was tasteless when you couldn't see the smoke. He wondered why on earth he had lit it. He heard the clump of Carnac's feet descending the ladder from the bridge and was sorely tempted to call him in and ask him how it had gone, but resisted the urge. Carnac was doing a man's job and was therefore entitled to be treated like one.

At three-thirty, with half an hour to go before the commencement of the Morning Watch, Paton clambered up to the bridge. 'Morning, Number One.'

'Morning, sir. Been as quiet as a churchyard.'

'Let's hope it stays that way.' He took a deep breath of sea air and expelled it noisily. 'Pity we can't do the whole trip in darkness.'

At dawn the ship's company was closed up at 'Action Stations' and a signal was hoisted, warning of a change in course and giving the new direction to be steered.

Phelp swept his binoculars along the convoy looking for the acknowledgement to be hoisted. 'Damn it, sir, there can't be a lookout po... on one of them. No one's seen it.'

Paton glanced astern and muttered sourly, 'The same seems to apply to their escorts.' He brought the bridge of the trawler astern into closer focus but could see no sign of activity and suspected that the skipper was conning the ship from the relative comfort of the wheelhouse. 'Bunts, semaphore "Capten, art tha sleepin' there below?"'

White stood, legs apart on top of the signal locker, his red and yellow hand-flags held aloft until he received an acknowledgement that he had been spotted. Then his arms moved stiffly spelling out the message word for word as Paton dictated it. Paton chuckled loudly as there was a sudden flurry of activity on the bridge and the signal flying from *Grey Seal*'s halyards was hastily repeated. Within minutes it was being flown on the other trawlers whose vision had been obscured by the wayward trawler. But the merchant ships still remained in blissful ignorance.

Paton called out impatiently, 'Execute the signal, Bunts.'

As the flags were hauled down, Paton gave the alteration of course to the helmsman and waited breathlessly to see what would happen. The escorting trawlers turned with the precision of guardsmen on the parade ground, but the merchantmen maintained course until they realized almost too late what was happening. Suddenly their masters seemed to become aware of the situation, but were not at all sure what they should do about it, and some swung to port, others to starboard. Within minutes ships were cutting across each other's bows and collisions seemed inevitable. Men rushed to the sides and lowered fenders. Sirens hooted and the water was threshed into a white frenzy as some of the masters ordered 'Full astern' on their engines.

Paton gazed at the ensuing chaos and shook his head in mock dismay; but his anxiety became very real as one of the smaller vessels made a violent alteration to course and came steaming bows on towards *Grey Seal*. Paton bellowed down the voicepipe, 'Hard a port. Emergency, full ahead!'

By steering directly towards the approaching ship he could narrow the angle of approach and minimize the risk of collision.

The orders were repeated with unruffled calm by the helmsman and *Grey Seal* responded like a horse being spurred. The lookout in the crow's nest had to cling onto his handrail like grim death to prevent himself being hurled over-

71

board. Her bow began to swing with ever increasing speed towards the approaching vessel. Then when a head-on crash seemed inevitable, the merchantman also made an emergency turn and the two ships passed abreast of each other at a distance that was little more than thirty or forty yards. They were so close that Paton was able to bellow through a megaphone, '*Quo Vadis*?'

The two-fingered gesture that the trilby-hatted master gave him was a clear enough warning that his attempt at humour was unappreciated. It was followed by an infuriated bellow, 'How am I expected to know what your ruddy silly flags mean?'

There was no time for Paton to reply that it was assumed that every captain and signalman had studied the code books which had been issued at the convoy briefing, for by then the merchantman was well clear and desperately struggling to rejoin the other ships which were trying to resume station after the hectic game of nautical dodgems.

Phelp whistled softly through his clenched teeth. 'Bit too close for comfort, that, sir.'

When some semblance of order had been restored out of the chaos Paton turned to Phelp and said, 'Well, it had to happen sooner or later, Number One. Thank God it was sooner. At least we know it won't happen again. From now on they'll keep their eyes peeled on our halyards and know it's not washing we're hanging out.'

Phelp was not so conciliatory. 'If they carry on like that, we won't have to worry about the enemy. They'll do the job for him.'

Paton smiled broadly, 'Let's not be too hard on them. They're not used to sailing in company. Unlike us, they've yet to learn the importance of team work. Remember how we bitched at all those seemingly pointless exercises?'

He did not elaborate on what he was attempting to imply. In any case there was no need, for Phelp smiled in return. 'Point taken, sir.'

Half an hour later Paton hoisted a signal indicating a

minimal alteration to course. It was totally unnecessary and unplanned; he simply wanted to find out if an important lesson had been learned from the debacle. It had. The signals halyards of every ship were immediately festooned with identical flags and when the executive was given they all obeyed the order, if not with clockwork precision, at least with commendable zeal and promptness.

Paton lifted the top off the voicepipe leading to the engine room and blew hard into it to sound the whistle at the other end. He replaced the top and waited for his own whistle to sound. When it did he said, 'Hope I didn't give you too much of a scare, Chief. We had a bit of a flap on.'

Reynolds, grimed with coal dust, a sweat-cloth wrapped round his bare throat appeared on the bridge and said, 'What was all that about, sir? The lads below nearly jumped out of their skins.'

Paton explained briefly what had happened but did not make too much of it. He was a firm believer in letting the engine room know exactly what was happening topsides for he knew that dangers were tripled when you could not see them. Therefore, when the men in the engine room received a series of emergency orders they invariably feared the worst. The greatest dread of stokers and artificers was to be entombed below decks in a sinking or flooding ship.

Reynolds shrugged it off as if it were of no importance. 'Served a useful purpose though, sir. It made 'em jump to it like scalded cats. At least I know they can pull their fingers out when necessary.'

Paton glanced at the convoy, now steaming in near perfect formation. 'Panic over,' he said with genuine relief.

But it was a short-lived respite.

From the crow's nest an excited voice began bellowing almost hysterically, 'Bridge, bridge.'

Paton looked up and saw the lookout gesticulating frantically and vaguely to starboard, his binoculars dangling round his neck.

'Sir, sir. Ships. Ships.'

73

Paton put the megaphone to his lips and called back, 'Give your report properly, lookout. We'll understand it much better then.'

The solitary figure aloft was seen to visibly compose himself, although he continued to point with an extended arm and finger. 'Green two-oh. Unidentified objects approaching, sir.'

Paton acknowledged and immediately began scanning the horizon to starboard. No sooner had he picked up three distant blobs that were so small that he could not identify them, than the lookout on the bridge wing announced that he too had seen them, adding the vital addition, 'Approaching fast.'

The alarm bells clamoured furiously and the men who only seconds before had unwound were once again taut and tense.

Paton kept his glasses focused on the approaching dots until he could see white plumes of water being ploughed up by their bows. Gradually the shapes took form. Without glancing up he bellowed to Phelp, 'E-boats! At least three of them.'

Phelp went down the ladder, his feet scarcely touching the rungs, and raced towards the bandstand where the crew of the twelve-pounder were already at their stations with tin hats and white anti-flash gloves on.

Chalkie White, the signalman, said, 'Ship astern has spotted them too, sir.'

'Acknowledge and tell them to hold fire until they're within range.'

Paton crouched over the compass binnacle and took a fix on the centre E-boat. The angle remained constant although the shape was growing larger by the second. There was no doubt about it, they were coming in for a bows-on attack. He realized just what they were up against.

The Schnellboote with its vastly superior armament and powered by twenty cylinder V-form Daimler Benz diesel engines, could run rings round the sluggish trawlers. And if they broke through the slender cordon they could annihilate the unarmed merchantmen with their guns and deadly torpedoes.

Paton signalled to the remainder of the group to close up

while he turned *Grey Seal* towards the approaching enemy. Head-on, he could bring most of his armament to bear.

At the twelve-pounder, Guns Jenkins stood as calm and composed as if it was just another dummy run. He occupied the layer's position and as he peered through the range-finder he barked out orders to the trainer and words of encouragement to the crew and loaders.

Phelp stood near the rail gazing at the approaching enemy. He was responsible for estimating the distance and spotting the fall of shot, but he had no sophisticated range-finding instruments at his disposal so it was more a matter of 'by guess and by God'. He estimated the E-boats were about seven or eight miles off.

He heard Jenkins bellow, 'Layer on.' Then a second voice, 'Trainer on.'

'We'll give the buggers a real mixture. H.E., and armour-piercing.'

Paton shouted through his megaphone, 'Shoot when you're ready, Number One.' There was a sudden ear-shattering chatter as Morris on the starboard Lewis opened up. Paton turned in annoyance and shouted, 'For God's sake man, wait until they're in range. You're just wasting ammunition we might well need.'

Through his glasses, Phelp could now clearly see the E-boats with their two torpedo tubes gaping like menacing mouths on either side of the bow. They did not look at all like the tiny harmless models he had studied so carefully in the recognition hut. Then he saw a white puff of smoke which was followed by a reverberating crack. He ducked automatically as something screamed and whined angrily overhead and he turned to see the missile splash noisily but harmlessly in the sea way beyond.

'Fire,' he shouted, and the deck beneath him juddered as the lanyard was jerked and the twelve-pounder recoiled. There was a deafening bang which almost ruptured his eardrums and he could clearly see the 'brick' as it soared towards the target. He cursed loudly when he saw it fall well short. 'Up six hundred,' he ordered. There was a clatter and clang as the breech was opened and the empty casing bounced onto the deck. Immediately a new projectile and cartridge were rammed home and the lanyard yanked. This time it was closer to the target, but still short.

By now they had been joined by the twelve-pounder from *Beaver* the other trawler armed with a real gun, and their shot was much closer.

'Come on, Guns. We can't have them giving us a lesson,' Phelp implored.

Grey Seal's next shot was bang on target for it struck the centre E-boat just for'ard of the bridge. Unfortunately it failed to explode and the damage was minimal.

'Commence independent firing,' yelled Phelp in a voice so excited it resembled a hysterical screech more than a firm command.

Jenkins, as calm and composed as if it were a practice shoot, slightly depressed the muzzle to compensate for the diminishing range. Round after round sped towards the oncoming torpedo boats with such relentless accuracy that the Germans were forced to alter course. But they were as dedicated and courageous as the men facing them and they pressed on with the attack.

With their vastly superior speed and greater manoeuvrability, they seemed to be able to anticipate the fall of shots as they formed into single line, made a wide sweep, then came in from astern between the trawlers and their precious charges. The roar of their engines was deafening.

As they raced through almost obscured by their own spray, the E-boats raked the escorts and the merchantmen with a withering hail of fire from their secondary armament. *Grey Seal's* Lewis guns chattered in retaliation and several men on the leading German ship were seen to throw up their arms in almost melodramatic gestures and topple overboard into the water.

Paton could clearly see the ensign with its black cross fluttering arrogantly from the stern.

He ducked automatically as bullets thudded into the quilted

padding below the bridge, followed seconds later by the sound of shattering glass and splintering woodwork as a burst of bullets hit the wheelhouse.

Paton glanced quickly towards the merchantmen and saw that they had already suffered considerable damage. Small fires had broken out on some of their decks and men were busy trying to extinguish them with hoses and buckets of sand. Boats hung crazily from their davits where the falls had been shot away, and through his glasses he could see the odd dark shape slumped over machinery or lying inert on the blood-stained decks. 'Round one to them,' he murmured silently to himself.

It took no time at all for the E-boats steaming at forty-five knots to clear the convoy, and Paton watched in impotent rage as they made a wide sweep and headed out to sea and disappeared over the horizon.

Phelp cupped his hands over his mouth and shouted, 'It looks as if they might have had enough, sir.'

'Don't let's fool ourselves, Number One. They'll be back. With a vengeance.' He shouted to White, 'Signal the convoy to close up,' then leaned over the voicepipe and said, 'Get someone to tell the sparks to break radio silence and ask for immediate assistance.'

As he spoke the three E-boats reappeared in the distance, their sterns well down and their bows almost clear of the water. They fanned out, bouncing and bobbing as they literally skimmed the waves. This time it will be tin fish, thought Paton. And his fears were confirmed as he saw men gathering by the torpedo tubes.

The twelve-pounder on the fo'c'sle opened fire and the shell landed between two of the enemy craft. A direct hit was going to be a question of pure luck against such a small and fast-moving target. The crack of the gun echoed across the water as Jenkins and his team fired and reloaded as fast as they possibly could. *Beaver* was giving valiant support, but her gunnery was just as erratic. Great spouts of water erupted around the Germans, causing them to swerve off course. But they continued the attack with dogged determination. The deafening bang of the twelve-pounders was joined by the cacophonous rattle of the Lewis guns, which put up a deterrent curtain of tracer and armour-plated bullets.

The Germans, sensing that they could accomplish their mission without resorting to torpedoes, adopted precisely the same tactics as they had for their first attack. They suddenly made a violent alteration to course and steamed up from astern between the trawlers and the merchant ships.

Paton could quite clearly see the captain of the leading boat as it thundered past with guns blazing. He was crouched low on the bridge wearing his cap at a jaunty angle, his jersey as white as his bow wave.

Morris, his teeth gritted into a ferocious smile, emptied an entire pan of ammunition as the three boats roared past at less than a hundred yards. He saw his bullets smacking into the hull of one boat and men toppling doll-like into the sea as his fire created havoc amongst the gun aft.

Unable to restrain his excitement he ceased fire and jumped up and down, his hands held high. 'I got some of the bastards. I got some.'

But the return fire from the E-boats was just as devastating and accurate and Morris's mind was brought back to his gun as bullets tattooed a pattern of holes in the funnel and richocheted off the deck.

Once again the E-boats exacted a deadly toll as they sped along the slow moving line of merchant ships. The orange-red flashes from their guns were clearly visible as they were aimed at point-blank range towards their opponents. Men fighting the fires dropped like axed trees and their shipmates slithered and fell on the thick red welter of blood deposited on the decks. Machine gun bullets thudded into soft flesh leaving a gruesome sewing machine pattern on the dying sailors. One ship had a gaping hole in her bow and the wheelhouse of another had been shattered to matchwood.

One departing shot from *Grey Seal's* twelve-pounder sheered off the mainmast of the tail end E-boat and Phelp cursed aloud. 'A foot lower and we would have sent them to Davey Jones.'

Once more the Germans headed out to sea and the fearful din of the guns gave way to an eerie silence.

Paton snatched up his megaphone and called in turn to each of the guns, 'Report any casualties.'

The reply from the twelve-pounder was encouraging: only one man had been hit; a shrapnel splinter had ploughed a neat furrow across his forehead. Morris reported that he had a slight graze but it was nothing to worry about.

Even so Paton walked across the bridge wing to make sure and was amazed to see Jolson sitting beside Morris, happily wagging his tail and looking as if he was thoroughly enjoying himself. 'Jolly good gun dog, sir.'

The captain felt strangely moved and muttered angrily, 'You just keep him out of harm's way, Morris. Remember, we don't carry a vet.'

Returning to the binnacle he fixed his glasses on the horizon. This time it had to be torpedoes.

He summoned the engine room on the whistle pipe. 'Chief? Stand by to give me all you've got. Even if it means blowing the boilers up. At least we'll be doing it and not Jerry.'

Back came the cheery response, 'In that case, sir, you'd better slacken off the funnel stays otherwise they'll get so 'ot the 'ole thing'll collapse.'

Paton realized that unless he did something dramatic the E-boats *must* get through and totally annihilate the sluggish group of merchantmen. A sudden, desperate idea occurred to him. He let his eyes stray momentarily from the open sea while he shouted to the wheelhouse, 'Send up Mr Carnac. At the double.' It was an incredible gamble, but there wasn't time to weigh up the chances of it failing or succeeding. One thing *was* certain, however; if it went wrong *Grey Seal* would be consigned to a watery grave.

He did not need the lookout's cry of, 'E-boats on the starboard bow', to tell him what his own eyes had already recorded. There they were, steady as a flight of homing geese.

Minute blobs gradually getting larger and larger in the single circle of his glasses.

Carnac pounded breathlessly onto the bridge and saluted. 'Sir?'

'I haven't got time to explain this in detail,' Paton cast an eye seawards, 'as you can see for yourself. But we might save the convoy. I want the depth charges set to maximum depth. When I lower my hand I want you to drop two off the stern and fire four off the throwers. Now jump to it if you want to live long enough to get your first stripe.'

Carnac was completely bewildered: they were being attacked by surface vessels, not U-boats. Nevertheless, he sensed the urgency in his captain's voice and knew better than to question him. He scuttled aft and repeated the orders to the leading torpedo rating with an assurance he did not feel, and with what he hoped sounded like some degree of confidence and a perfect awareness of what they were doing.

The torpedo rating primed the depth charges and set them to a maximum depth. 'You wouldn't like to explain what the captain and you have in mind, would you, sir?'

'I wouldn't,' snapped the midshipman.

'I thought not, sir,' he said miserably.

Paton moved away from the compass – there was no need to take a bearing on the approaching ships, they weren't going to disappear. He strode to the chart-table and took a hurried look: they were in nine fathoms of water. He did a quick sum in his head. The timing mechanism of a depth charge was controlled by the size of a small aperture which let in water. One set at 500 feet took roughly fifty seconds to explode. The depth of the water did not affect the timing, for it would sit on the seabed until that period elapsed. The real danger was whether or not they could get out of the way in time. If they couldn't the stern would be blown off.

'Bunts, signal to the other escorts, "Make Smoke Urgently!"'

Even in the heat of battle *Otter* replied cheekily, 'Haven't I been doing that?'

Paton did not mind. A sense of humour in a crisis was worth its weight in gold. There scarcely seemed time for his order to have been passed to the quarterdecks before the huge smoke-making cannisters were tumbling off the ships and thumping into the sea. Great clouds of dense, black smoke billowed from them and in an incredibly short time an almost impenetrable black shroud had enveloped the three escorts and effectively blotted out the merchantmen from the attacking E-boats. It struck Paton as rather humorous. Not so long ago he had been warning everyone that smoke could endanger the safety of the convoy, yet here he was relying on it to rescue them. He would have dearly loved to drop his own but dared not risk it. It was vital for him to have uninterrupted vision.

He called to Phelp on the bandstand, 'I'm turning to engage them, Number One. Open fire as soon as you like. And hang on to something solid. You'll need it.'

He crouched over the voicepipe, 'Starboard ten. Slow ahead.'

As the ship answered, the helm and the bow swung round towards the enemy and he felt the palms of his hands become clammy with sweat. Mathematics had never been his strong point, yet somehow or other he had to estimate extremely accurately how quickly the gap was narrowing. He did a rapid calculation.

The boom of the twelve-pounder was followed by the first lieutenant's urgent command, 'Rapid fire.' Paton nodded in silent approval. Whether they were thinking of their own skins or fearing the whiplash of Jenkins' tongue he did not know or care. But the old gun banged away with such rapidity it sounded more like a pompom. No one was issuing any orders, they were simply firing as fast as they could reload. As shells cascaded in the path of the E-boats they were joined by others from the supporting trawler.

Paton whistled the engine room. 'Right, Chief. When I give the order you can push the pistons right out of their cylinders.'

Steadying himself on the binnacle he watched the gap

gradually narrow. All the while, he was mentally ticking off time and distance and forcing himself to remain icily cool. Rather incongruously, he thought, he found himself thinking of the old white hunter friend of his father's who had been charged by a rogue elephant and dropped it dead at his feet. He had explained his lack of fear with the words, 'That was no time to get the shakes.'

'Full ahead,' he called to the engine room and to the wheelhouse, 'hard a starboard.' With the single screw rotating clockwise he knew that a turn to starboard would be that much quicker. Smoke belched from the tall funnel coating the deck and those on it with greasy soot and red-hot embers. The unfortunate men who got scorched cursed the engines more than they did the Germans.

The guns of the E-boats were pounding away and Paton could hear the bullets pinging against the hull and thudding into the quilting surrounding the bridge and gun emplacements. The E-boats were now so close he could see the men on the bridge and upper deck quite clearly. Then, as *Grey Seal* completed a full circle and presented her stern to the enemy, he jerked his arm down. He saw the men on the depth charge rails roll their deadly cannisters into the sea and the two throwers hurl dark black objects high into the sky. As they fell, almost lazily towards the sea, he saw the torpedoes leap out of their tubes like greyhounds unleashed from their traps.

The twin Lewis guns on both wings and the galley-flat maintained a continuous chatter of fire. Their loaders were breathless with the exertion of replacing fresh drums of ammunition.

Paton glanced at the second hand of his watch and saw it tick round with agonizing slowness. Every second seemed an eternity. Had he got a duff load of depth charges? Or had he miscalculated or missed out something vital?

Then suddenly the sea astern erupted into mountains of towering white foam and the boom of the explosions echoed across the placid water, drowning the crack and chatter of the guns. Each charge contained three hundred pounds of TNT and the shallow water had almost trebled their effect. Water deluged the bridge and washed over the deck like a tidal wave. The explosion lifted *Grey Seal*'s stern clear of the sea and she shuddered from bow to stern as if she had run aground.

For two or three neverending seconds her enormous single screw rose clear of the water and raced in the air, before the stern came down with a bone-juddering crash that lifted men like dolls and hurled them across the deck, their hands reaching out in desperation for anything solid to cling on to. Paton thought his last moment had come when something black and heavy crashed into him, throwing him flat on his back with a force that jarred from head to heel. For one agonizing moment he feared that he had lost his sight.

Then a reassuring voice enquired, 'You all right, sir?' and he realized that the bunting tosser had cannoned into him and was now covering his head with his body. They rolled apart and Paton struggled to his feet and steadied himself against the bridge parapet, to watch in awe as the centre E-boat was lifted out of the water and tossed, like a terrier from the jaws of a mastiff, across the forecastle of the starboard boat. Through the flurry of spray he heard the sound of rending metal and the crunch of splintering timber as the two craft collided. The E-boat which had been hurled off course was straddled across the other vessel; so that they resembled some grotesque maritime monsters mating. The sea astern was immediately whipped and churned into a whirlpool of creamy foam as the powerful diesels went full astern. Slowly and laboriously the two boats uncoupled. They were too tied up for the moment with their own problems to present any danger and he cast his eyes towards the merchantmen to see if any of the torpedoes had struck home. Paton was immensely relieved to see all his charges still afloat and steaming steadily in line.

The port side lookout yelled, 'Don't worry about the tin fish, sir. They all passed harmlessly astern of the convoy. Bit difficult to aim straight when a depth charge goes off under your backside, sir.'

The lookout had spoken too soon and too optimistically. For no sooner had he got the words out than there was an enormous bang as if some gigantic dry stick had snapped, and the bow and stern of the block ship rose almost vertically above the water like two outstretched arms. The torpedo had struck her amidships and the cement-filled holds had intensified the force of the explosion, causing the ship to break in two and rise V-shaped above the sea. There was surprisingly little smoke and no fire at all as the two halves began to settle. Then they literally disintegrated as the boilers burst and a column of steam rose in the air, making the sea hiss and bubble like a cauldron. A minute later there was nothing to be seen.

Beaver's fo'c'sle gun was still thumping away and Paton eased the engine to 'Half Ahead' and brought *Grey Seal* back on her original course to enable her own twelve-pounder to rejoin the fray.

The E-boats were game and gallant opponents, for they continued to return fire although the two which had collided were clearly in considerable difficulties. Through his binoculars Paton could make out small groups of men busily rigging towing lines and attempting to pass them to the undamaged craft. It was obvious they were in no condition to mount a fresh attack and he was sorely tempted to give chase, but he realized that his first duty lay with the merchant ships entrusted to his care. In any case, the E-boats were now underway and heading homewards. A chase would have been pointless; damaged though they were, they were still capable of showing the trawlers a clean pair of heels. Quite apart from that, they would have already signalled their position to base and announced the presence of a very slow and vulnerable convoy. The response was anybody's guess. It could mean more E-boats, planes or, perish the thought, a force of destroyers.

Paton watched the Germans limp away licking their wounds and vanish over the horizon. A signal was sent to *Otter* ordering her to search for survivors from the block ship.

It was, he realized, no more than a token gesture; no one could have survived.

He summoned Phelp and Carnac to the bridge and told them to stand down the hands and see they got a hot meal and a drink inside them before closing up again. The first lieutenant could not conceal his irritation; the men needed a long stand easy. 'They've been through a pretty rough time, sir. It's their first taste of action and they're pretty tuckered.'

'I know that, Number One, but we can't be sure the E-boats won't carry out on the spot repairs and return. One goal up at half-time doesn't mean the match is over.'

Phelp was just about to remonstrate when the captain cut him short. 'Please, no arguments.' His body was just one dull ache from the collision with White and he realized it was making him short-tempered – he could have sounded a little more appreciative.

The ship was handed over to Carnac whilst the captain and first lieutenant went on a tour of inspection to see what damage had been inflicted and the casualties suffered.

In the engine room they found Reynolds anxiously checking his dials, pipes and pressure gauges with the meticulous thoroughness of a mechanic examining the engine of a Formula One racing car. The two Scots stokers were working alongside each other firing the boiler; with such effortless ease there was something almost poetical in their movements. But they did not exchange a word and Paton could not help but reflect that it might have been better if the engineer had separated them. It was too late now, though, and he just hoped the chief knew what he was up to.

Reynolds, wearing an oil-stained singlet, wiped his brow with a wad of cotton waste and said, 'Everything seems to be in one piece, sir. Although the prop shaft is knocking like my old lady's knees when the rent man calls. We won't know 'ow bad it is till a diver goes down and has a decko. But don't worry, sir, she'll get us to Scapa. They certainly built these old tubs to last.'

He reached for a tin jug with a flat lift-up top that was

85

resting on a hot-plate near the furnace. 'Cuppa?' he asked, producing three not too spotless enamel mugs.

Paton eyed the jug with thinly concealed distaste and nodded. The tea was so thick you could stand a spoon upright in it. Reynolds, it seemed, didn't believe in ever emptying it; he simply added a handful of fresh tea to the grouts. Paton took the proffered mug ånd the chief added a generous dollop of thick, sugary condensed milk, but even this could not hide the taste of pure tannin.

'Come on, Number One, mustn't decline the chief's hospitality.'

Phelp saw the glint of amusement in the captain's eyes as he took the mug and stirred in the milk. He could not suppress a shudder as he sipped it. 'What on earth do you put in it, Chief – old socks?'

'You need lots of somefing 'ot and strong in this bakehouse to replace the sweat. Cold water's no good, sir. Beer's best, but beggars can't be choosers.'

The three of them made a quick but thorough inspection. One or two of the hull plates were seeping water where the impact of the depth charge explosions had loosened rivets, but *Grey Seal* had been built to withstand the might of the most punishing seas and Paton was surprised it wasn't far worse.

'I'll do my best to see I don't tax the engine too much, Chief, but it's not really up to me. It's up to Jerry.'

Reynolds grinned proudly and patted the side of one of the pistons as if he were an owner congratulating his mount in the winners' enclosure. 'I couldn't 'ave asked more of 'er, sir. She was like an old lady lifting her skirts and running for a bus.'

Paton looked towards the two toiling stokers. 'I'm proud of you, lads. It must be very hard to concentrate on your duties when you can't see what's happening topsides.'

He hoped it might encourage some slight rapport between the two men but they simply replied, 'Thanks, sir,' and kept on shovelling.

When they emerged on the upper deck they examined the

appalling damage caused by the enemy guns. Rafts, boats and hatch covers had been splintered to matchwood. The protective quilting round the bridge hung in tatters. The funnel was like a sieve and there were stomach-churning pools of blood on the glass-strewn deck. Paton dreaded the task of checking the casualties. Judging from the devastation there might not be enough fit men to see them safely home.

But as he toured the ship he was relieved to discover that they were far less than he had feared. One rating had a gaping wound across his forehead where he had been struck by a flying piece of metal, but he brushed it aside. 'I've cut myself worse shaving, sir.' Two men in the quarterdeck were nursing broken limbs received when they had been hurled across the deck by the depth charge explosions. But they insisted they could remain on duty once they had been put in splints. Several had been hit by bullets but their wounds were like a badly bleeding nose – they looked far worse than they were. Not that there was much Paton could do to relieve their pain. The ship carried no doctor, only a rather primitive first-aid chest containing wound dressings and other bare essentials. It was far better for the men to be patched up and allowed to remain at their posts. Lying on their bunks was the worst possible thing.

'Keep your chins up, lads,' he said. 'We'll soon be in Scapa. Then you'll realize what a picnic you've been through today.'

Even the wounded managed to summon up a smile.

Paton nodded to the first lieutenant. 'We'd better go for'ard.'

On the bandstand Jenkins and two ratings were cleaning and oiling the gun whilst the remainder of the crew were gathering up the empty shell cases and stowing them away.

Phelp said, 'We'll have to make a careful check of the ammunition we expended and enter it in the gunnery log. I bet someone ashore will bitch that we used too much.'

Jenkins said cheerfully, 'Nothing like a little bit of action for an opportunity to cook the books, sir.'

Paton said, 'I don't anticipate any queries about the amount of ammo we used, Guns. As a matter of fact, if there's a check someone might express surprise we used so little. But I'm sure that next time you'll be able to increase the rate of fire.'

Phelp could barely conceal his annoyance; the gun crew had worked hard and efficiently and a word of encouragement, even praise, would not have gone amiss. It was only when he caught a glimpse of the faintest suggestion of a wink from Jenkins that he realized the gunner took it all with a pinch of salt. The old sweat knew the ways of the navy too well to be upset and was perfectly aware that the captain was more than happy with their performance.

'Maybe a tot of neat rum will speed the lads up a bit, eh Guns?'

'You bet it will, sir.' The old salt said, 'Hear that lads, the captain's pleased with you. Which is more than I am.'

Jenkins knew an issue of 'Harry Neaters' would be far more appreciated than any verbal encouragement. The old man wasn't the hard bastard he liked to pretend he was; he just didn't wear his heart on his sleeve like his two and a half rings. But it was in the right place.

When they returned to the bridge, Paton took over from Carnac and told him to rig the loudhailer.

'I'll steam down the convoy, Number One, and you can ask them to report any damage. Get yourself a signal-pad, Middie, and make a note of their replies. Not that we can do anything about it at this stage.'

As *Grey Seal* steamed abeam of the merchant ships, men could be seen busy on the decks cleaning up and hosing down. Some paused in their labours to wave and shout, 'Well done the Navy.'

When they came abreast of each bridge, Phelp asked the master to report any damage and casualties. Although they had received a fearful pummelling there wasn't a vessel that would be unable to continue the voyage. Fourteen men had been killed, another dozen seriously wounded, and a score or more had minor injuries. Every master firmly declared that he would press on.

Having seen to his wards, Paton turned his attention to the trawlers and there the answer was pretty much the same: heavy casualties but a grim determination to see it through.

Vole's skipper called out, 'That stunt with the depth charges was a stroke of genius, sir.'

Paton took the loudhailer and called back, 'Thanks, but it was very much a team effort. The bloke who runs the last lap in a winning relay mustn't claim all the credit.'

One hour passed, then two, and Paton began to experience a feeling of relief; for some obscure reason the Germans had not reappeared. It wasn't up to him to reason why. He was simply extremely grateful. Perhaps his own signal requesting assistance had been intercepted by the enemy and they feared it had been answered. Now if the convoy could just plug along until darkness provided a protective shield, he would be more than happy. It was pointless to think further ahead than that. He would have to adopt the same attitude as the prisoner in a cell who ticked off each day, comforting himself with the knowledge that his ordeal was gradually coming to an end.

Tiger Read appeared on the bridge clutching a steaming cup of ki, the hot nourishing drink made from slices scraped from a solid block of navy-issue cocoa. 'Thought you might like this, sir. I slipped some of my tot in it.'

Paton accepted gratefully; for a man to share his tot with an officer was a rare and generous sacrifice. 'You'd better not let any of the lads know about this, Coxswain. They'll suspect you of currying favour and looking for a draft chit.'

Read watched his captain sip appreciatively at the drink. He could smell the hot rum from where he stood. 'To be honest, sir, it isn't all my tot. Some of the hands chipped in with a few drops. That Rhind is turning out to be a bit of a card, sir. Know what he said? Not issuing rum to officers is the only way the Admiralty has of keeping men like him on the lower deck.'

Paton made himself sound deliberately casual. 'How do you think they shaped up, Coxswain?'

Read replied, 'I didn't see a lot of what went on, cooped up in the wheelhouse, sir, but I was very happy with them, sir. Naturally, I didn't go round patting their heads. Don't want them to have to rush off to slops and buy new caps. Mind you, sir, they didn't think the officers exactly let them down.'

Paton relished these rare moments of informality for they enabled him to get to know what the men were thinking and at the same time leave it to Read to pass on to them what their captain felt.

'Between the two of us, Coxswain, I think we've got the makings of a really first-rate ship's company. Still quite a few rough edges to smooth off though.'

Suddenly the starboard lookout bellowed, 'Aircraft bearing Green one-five, sir.'

Paton glanced towards the bow, his hand automatically reaching for the alarm bells.

Read quipped, 'It looks as if those rough edges are going to be rubbed off quicker than we wanted, sir,' and was already on the rungs of the ladder and on his way to his action station at the wheel.

The barrel of the twelve-pounder was being raised to its maximum elevation and the Lewis gunners were peering through their ring sights although the aircraft were still well out of range.

The first lieutenant focused his binoculars on the small dots in the sky, but was unable to identify them. Of one thing, however, he was certain: it wasn't the RAF paying a courtesy call.

'Load with shrapnel, Guns, and open fire as soon as you can. Even if we don't hit them we might drive them off.'

On the bridge, the captain glanced anxiously along the line of merchantmen and was happy to observe that he would not need to send a 'Close Up' signal. The convoy was maintaining a constant speed and keeping well nigh perfect station; there wasn't a straggler among them. They had learned one very important lesson fast.

He watched the Germans break formation and begin to lose height. God, I could do with a few pompoms and Oerlikons.

Once again he cursed the short-sighted men who sent ships to war with decoy guns. If *Vole* and *Otter* had real twelve-pounders instead of wooden replicas the odds would be that much shorter.

He picked up his megaphone and bellowed once more to Phelp. 'Issue the small-arms, Number One. It'll keep some of the hands occupied if nothing else.'

Phelp sounded almost cheerful as he shouted back, 'Very good, sir. Remember what David did with his sling.'

Paton glanced quickly round the ship: the men on the port and starboard Lewis guns seemed calm enough and their loaders were standing by with fresh pans of ammunition. Regrettably their field of fire was limited by the protective guard-rails which had been erected to prevent over-enthusiastic gunners blowing away part of their own ship. The third Lewis, above the galley, was the only gun that provided any real defence against an attack from the stern. He would have one or two very strong words to say about the inadequacy of their armament when he came to write his battle report. Assuming, of course, they survived.

The aircraft were still little more than bird-sized dots and Paton had no idea what class of plane they were. He began to count them: one, two, three, four, five, six. They in no way resembled the machines he had studied so carefully on the identification charts and the Germans were not charitable enough to give him a top view, elevation, side view and nose-on picture of themselves.

There was no time for further reflection as the silence was shattered by the crack of the twelve-pounder, followed immediately by *Beaver* opening fire. Cottonwool puffs appeared in the sky as the guns hammered away. But they seemed to have as much of a deterrent effect as a catapult against a flight of eagles.

Above the boom of the guns Paton could now distinguish the incessant throb of the aircrafts' engines and what had seconds ago been mere shapeless dots now began to assume an identifiable form. They looked like dragonflies; bulbous

91

noses with a long, pencil-slim fuselage. Pictures flashed through his mind relating what he had learned to what was now before his eyes.

There was no doubt about it: they were Dornier 215 four-seater reconnaissance bombers. Memory provided him with the statistics that would soon be confirmed in a painfully practical manner. Speed, take or leave a few miles an hour, in the region of 290, and the capacity to carry a 2,200 lb bomb-load. It had originally been introduced as a fast civilian mail plane, but that had been a mere disguise for its real purpose in life. Fast, highly manoeuvrable and heavily armed, it was perfectly suited to attacking shipping.

As the bombers broke formation he reflected bitterly that the pilots of the Luftwaffe, unlike the men they were attacking, had had plenty of practice. The Spanish civil war had been an ideal training ground, and they had obviously learned that you attacked your targets from as many different angles as possible, and were discerning when it came to selecting their prospective victims. As they came in at little less than a thousand feet they ignored the trawlers and concentrated on the much more important cargo ships and tankers.

Paton could clearly make out the black and white cross on the fuselage and the swastika on the twin tail-planes.

On the deck of *Grey Seal* men crouched behind anything that afforded the slightest protection and loosed off with .303 rifles and whatever else they found to hand.

One of the bombers attacked the starboard line of ships from astern, while another attacked the port column from the opposite direction. The others zoomed in from midships and on the quarter. At times it seemed as if a mid-air collision was inevitable. Not that any of the watching sailors would have objected.

Paton waited with bated breath for the bombs to come tumbling out of the bomb-bays, but during the first attack the planes relied entirely on their guns. The illustrated charts had described them as being defensive; two 7.9mm machine guns firing forward and two on movable mountings above and below the crew compartment – but there was nothing defensive about them at the moment. Orange flames flickered from the muzzles as they raked the ships from all angles. The tracers, which could be seen very clearly, seemed to be heading towards their targets with astonishing slowness.

The planes wheeled, turned, and gathered for a second attack as if they were giving an aerial display. As they came in even lower, Paton saw the flaps of the bomb-bays open like trapdoors. They were so low he could see the helmeted figure of a front gunner with startling clarity. Great mushroom gouts of water erupted as the bombs fell into the sea and exploded on impact, submerging the upper decks and superstructure of the merchantmen with tons of water. One fell so close to one of the cargo ships that it tilted over at a perilous angle and for a moment Paton thought it must go down. But it righted itself and emerged shedding water like a retriever from a lake.

Above the clamour of the gunfire he heard Morris cursing wildly and turned to see him pounding his hands on the jammed Lewis gun. On the deck below the wheelhouse the big Canadian, Rhind, was lying flat on his back and blazing away, looking as if he was enjoying every second.

Directly ahead an enormous mountain of water soared skywards to be followed by a devastating bang which echoed across the sea. When it cleared, one of the minesweepers had vanished. The Dorniers were now almost brushing the masttops as if the bomb aimers had been given orders to drop their deadly cargoes straight down the funnels of the ships. They were in and out so quickly the gunners had a mere three or four seconds in which to fire. But time had ceased to have any real meaning; seconds became hours and minutes an eternity.

One ship halted in its tracks as a bomb sliced off the stern as cleanly as a wire cutting through cheese. Another emerged from a curtain of spray minus its bridge.

Then a great roar that could be heard above the terrifying din came from the fo'c'sle as one of the aircraft was seen to be heading out to sea with black smoke pluming from one of the engines. Phelp roared in triumph, 'We've hit one of the bastards at last, sir.'

The bomber gradually lost height until it pancaked into the sea, to be enveloped in a shower of spray.

The bellow of triumph immediately turned to howls of despair as the Dorniers transferred their attention to the impudent trawler which had had the temerity to shoot one of them out of the sky. Three of the aircraft began a concentrated attack from different angles which made it extremely difficult for the gun crews to decide which target should have priority.

Grey Seal heaved, rolled, and plunged bows deep into the water as she shook from stem to stern under a pattern of explosions which came perilously close to overturning her. Bullets shattered equipment to smithereens, tore gaping holes in the deck and turned the funnel into a smoke-belching colander.

It was a terrifying ordeal for the men manning the guns, and Paton felt a glow of pride that such novices could contain their fear and continue to fight back against the overwhelming odds.

But if it was a nerve-shattering ordeal for the men up top it was sheer agony for the sweating men battened down in the engine room. As the ship lurched and rolled from the hammer blows they could only visualize what was happening in the clean fresh air above the water line. They began to fear that each fresh impact would herald their last moment on earth, and they would depart it amongst the hiss of scalding steam and ice-cold water. It was a nightmare that had often tormented their sleep and woke them sweating and shaking with fear. Now it was no hellish dream but stark wide-awake reality.

The four stokers had an almost overpowering urge to toss down their shovels and race up the ladder; but they resisted with a superhuman effort and continued to fire the boilers. Their blackened faces had a devilish appearance when they were caught in the glow of the brightly burning fire.

94

Reynolds screamed abuse at the invisible enemy as his jug of tea was hurled through the air. 'You'll pay for that, you sods,' he shouted and waved a clenched fist in the air.

To Hamish McIntyre, it seemed as if one of the pilots was endowed with the gift of telepathy for a series of extremely violent explosions, far closer than any previous ones, suddenly rocked the ship.

'Knock it off, Chief. I think he heard you.'

As he spoke he felt an agonizing blow on the head which felled him like a pole-axed cow. When he staggered to his feet he saw that the restraining timbers across one of the bunkers had disappeared and the coal had broken free and stopped a few feet short of the boiler. He glanced anxiously around him for Jamie Ross, the man who had been shovelling in silence beside him seconds earlier.

Reynolds was clinging to a pipe, shaking his head dazedly and wiping away a thick trickle of blood that was running down his forehead and seeping into his eyes.

'Jamie's disappeared, Chief.'

Reynolds peered into the semi-darkness and swore aloud. 'The bloody coal's shifted. He must be somewhere underneath.'

He grabbed a shovel. 'Come on, let's get the poor bugger out before he suffocates.'

'Better use our hands,' grunted Hamish, 'otherwise we might chop his head off.'

The men dropped on their hands and knees and began to tear at the slowly moving mass of coal. All the time they kept shouting, 'Where the hell are you?' But there was no response and they pressed their ears against the coal straining to pick up the slightest sound.

Then from somewhere beneath the black mound they heard a muffled voice reply, 'Here! Get me out, for Christ's sake.'

They located the spot and worked like demented squirrels trying to unearth a misplaced store of nuts, as they clawed and tore away at the imprisoning mass with reddening fingers.

Reynolds called out, 'Quick here. I've got a hand.'

Hamish kept shouting words of encouragement as he tried to find the head of the buried man, for the most important thing was to expose his mouth and nose to the air. A grey-black blur appeared and whispered hoarsely, 'Any of that tea of yours left, Chief? I'm choking.' Their hands worked feverishly until they had exposed the stoker's head. Hamish crooked his finger and stuck it in the gasping mouth and hooked out the choking coal dust. Then he took off the sweat-cloth wrapped round his neck and carefully cleaned the man's eyes and nostrils.

Once Jamie's life was no longer endangered Reynolds summoned the bridge and reported the danger and asked for any spare men to be sent down immediately to erect a makeshift barrier and stop the coal from moving any further.

As McIntyre cleared the last remaining lumps of coal from Jamie's face, he said, 'You all right, Jock? Still in one piece?'

Ross said, 'Thanks Hamish. That gave me a nasty turn. Couldn't see or hear a ruddy thing. I could just feel the bumps.'

Seconds later he was hauled clear from his suffocating tomb and, as he felt his limbs gingerly to see if he was still in one piece, he said, 'I'll not forget that.'

Hamish fumbled in his trouser pocket and pulled out a rumpled packet of cigarettes. 'Here, have a smoke. There's nothing like a drag for settling the nerves.'

As the stoker sat on the coal which had so nearly been his grave and took a long draw at the welcome cigarette, he said, 'I thought you would have left me there to rot, Hamish.'

'And end up doing your stint of shovelling? No fear. In any case, what would life be like not having someone not to talk to.'

As the seamen who could be spared clattered down the ladder and got to work replacing the coal to its former position, the four stokers resumed their duty of firing the ship. Ross and McIntyre chattered like two women over a garden wall as they hurled coal into the furnace. Reynolds walked over and patted them both on the shoulder. 'Blimey, it took a lot to get you two nattering. For God's sake don't ever fall out again. I don't think my old ticker could stand it if it takes something like this to get you together. I'd better make some fresh tea.'

The impact had hurled Paton across the bridge like a tennis ball struck from the centre of the racquet. He careered into a sharp corner of the chart-desk and groaned in agony as a pain like a sword thrust shot through his chest. When he picked himself up and staggered to the compass he was astonished to see the ship was still afloat. He coughed and a searing pain brought tears to his eyes and forced him to double up in agony. It felt as if a red-hot poker was imbedded in his ribcage. At best it was a cracked rib, at worst . . . He dared not contemplate. In any case, there was nothing he could do about it. He called down to the wheelhouse, 'Everything all right, Coxswain?'

Read's reassuring voice came back up the pipe, 'I'm having to carry a bit of port wheel, sir, to keep her steady. Rudder could be buckled, but nowt to panic over.'

'Good for you, Cox.'

'What's going on out there, sir? Can't see a ruddy thing from here.'

'Nothing much. Jerry's feeling a trifle playful.' He replaced the cover on the voicepipe, sympathizing with the men in the wheelhouse who could hear and feel everything yet see nothing, however this was no time to provide a running commentary.

He wondered just how long the Germans could continue with their attack. Every time he thought it was over they regrouped and renewed the assault with increased tenacity and ferocity. At least two more ships had been severely damaged. One was listing badly to port and the other was hardly making any headway. But at least the odds had shortened.

One of the trawlers had scored a direct hit on another of the Dorniers which had headed towards home with flames streak-

97

ing from its underbelly. Whether or not it reached base they would never know for it was still airborne when it disappeared out of view.

He scanned the horizon as the remaining aircraft withdrew and prepared for another attack. He heard Morris shout, 'Don't worry, sir. I've cleared the Lewis. I'll bag one of them if it's the last thing I do.'

'That's the spirit,' he called back.

Then they were back. As the remaining planes peeled off, picking out their individual targets, he saw one that was almost skipping over the wave tops, it was flying so low. A momentary panic seized him. The pilot seemed intent on suicide. He's going to crash-land on us, he thought.

The plane was mast-high as it came in and he could see the propellers rotating.

Morris lined the plane in his ring sight. 'Don't panic. If you don't get him he'll get you.' His heart was pounding and his mouth was dry with fear, but he waited although his finger itched to press the trigger. It was seven or eight hundred yards away and plumb in the centre of the sight when he fired.

'Right, Fritz,' he screamed, 'here's where you get your feet wet.'

The plane seemed on the point of taking his head off when he pressed the trigger and emptied a whole pan of ammunition in the few seconds it took for it to come within range, and then fly out of it. He saw tracers hammer into the nose compartment and wing, and perspex and pieces of metal fall away.

His loader turned his head as the plane roared overhead, 'You've hit him, Isaac. You've *hit* him.'

One of the engines spluttered to a halt and the propeller suddenly ceased to rotate. A tracer must have pierced a wing fuel tank for flames suddenly appeared and began to lick their way along the fuselage. The bomber banked, turned away from the convoy and began to climb as fast as it could, its remaining engines screaming in protest.

Morris jumped up and down and the loader embraced him. 'I got him. I said I would, didn't I?'

Paton shared their sense of triumph and a feeling of elation spread through his tired frame; but it was no time for anyone to relax. 'All right Morris,' he bellowed, 'get another pan on. It's not over yet.'

But it was. What appeared to be mushrooms suddenly drifted across the sky as four of the crew baled out and pulled their ripcords. The abandoned Dornier stalled, then disappeared in a bright orange glow that plunged seawards to be extinguished like molten metal plunged into a blacksmith's trough.

Grey Seal's crew began shouting in jubilation as the remaining aircraft disengaged and began to head for home. Roars and cheers from the merchant ship could be heard echoing across the water. From the fo'c'sle Phelp called out, 'We've driven them off, sir. The buggers bit off more than they could chew.'

A new sound filled the air and one of the lookouts reported, 'Aircraft astern, sir. Ours I think. I hope.'

Paton swung his glasses and immediately recognized the squat hump-backed shape of four Hurricane fighters in unmistakable RAF green and brown camouflage. They were heading at high speed towards the departing Dorniers, which were under full throttle in a desperate effort to gain height and escape the lethal fire of the eight Brownings mounted in the fighters' wings. It would be a close-run thing. The Dornier had a maximum speed of 298 mph; which was only 20 mph less than a Hurricane flat-out. If the Germans could hang on, the British fighters with a limited range of 480 miles would be forced to turn back. But the bombers were at a disadvantage; they lacked altitude. For the first time during the battle the odds were with the home team.

Paton picked up his megaphone. 'I think their arrival scared them off more than we did. Never mind, Number One, we didn't disgrace ourselves.'

Once more the urgent voice of a lookout demanded his

attention. 'Ship approaching fine on the starboard bow, sir. Destroyer. One of ours, thank God.'

Steaming at full speed towards the convoy and tossing up a gigantic bow wave was a sleek V and W class destroyer, an Aldis blinking from her bridge. White repeated each word aloud as he acknowledged it. 'Do-you-need-a-nurse-maid?'

Send back, 'No thanks. Baby can look after herself. She's not only learned to walk she's cut her first teeth.'

Chalkie White grinned like a mischievous schoolboy as he sent off the cheeky reply.

'Add: If you want to do something useful pick up some very wet Jerries,' said Paton.

The parachutes could be seen floating lazily towards the sea and as the destroyer altered course to pick up the survivors she flashed a further message: 'Will do. Good luck and well done Harry Tate.'

The long, sleek ship moved over the water like a grey whippet and Paton felt envious. That was the navy he knew. Powerful turrets fore and aft, quick firing anti-aircraft guns as plentiful as a porcupine's quills and torpedoes amidships. If he had been commanding a ship like that the Germans would have shoved off much earlier. But there was no time for contemplating what might have been; the convoy had to be shepherded and tended.

Then one of the Hurricanes re-appeared, skipping the wave tops as if the pilot was indulging in some reckless game of ducks and drakes. As it neared the convoy it climbed and rolled over to indicate the chase had ended in victory.

'Signal from *Otter*, sir,' called out White. 'Permission to splice the mainbrace to celebrate our duck shoot.'

'Send back "permission refused",' said Paton. 'Only the Sovereign or members of the Royal Family or the Admiralty can order it. But double the issue if you can fiddle the books. Well done . . . and make less smoke.'

Once more *Grey Seal* broke formation and steamed abeam the merchantmen, requesting a fresh breakdown of damage and casualties. It was a depressing recital. One ship was taking water fast, and the vessel which had had its stern chopped off was finding it extremely difficult to make headway. Several more men had been killed or badly wounded. One ship reported that two men had disappeared without trace, presumably blown overboard by the blast. But all their precious cargoes were intact and every ship was confident it could make the finishing line.

Aboard *Grey Seal* the picture was grim. Able Seaman Carter, one of the ratings on duty at the ready-use lockers of the twelve-pounder, had been fatally wounded by a bullet and another had been hit by a piece of shrapnel which had passed clean through the calf of his left leg.

Paton handed over the ship to Carnac whilst he went on another tour of inspection. When he surveyed the damage he was amazed that the ship was still afloat. But he was assured the pumps could cope with the flooding and the wounded sailor was remarkably cheerful, although in considerable pain. The piece of metal had entered and exited without striking bone and it was no longer bleeding. Perhaps the red-hot splinter had cauterized it. Paton ordered him to be carried to his own cabin, where he washed the wound and applied a field dressing and gave the seaman a glass filled with brandy in the vague hope that it would prove a knock out sedative.

Paton returned to the bandstand, surveyed the air and sea and said to Phelp, 'I think we've seen the back of them for a little while at least. Stand the hands down. Issue a tot, then see they try to get some sleep.'

Phelp said, 'Aye, aye, sir,' his eyes straying to the body of the dead sailor, which had been hauled clear of the lockers so as not to impede loading, and now lay like a head-lolling broken doll against a stanchion. 'What about him, sir? Can't leave him like that. He'll upset everybody.'

Paton nodded agreement. 'Have him put in a Neilson stretcher and covered with a blanket. Then get two hands to carry him to the cable locker. We'll give him a decent burial when we get to Scapa. Now nip into the wardroom and help

101

yourself to a stiff one. You've earned it.'

Some of the hands were too weary to bother going below to the mess decks and they slumped against any convenient back rest and dozed on the upper deck, sipping their rum and looking as contented as cats who had got at the cream jug.

Below decks men lay down on their bunks or flopped out on locker tops. Battle-weary they may have been, but when Paton walked through to congratulate them they jumped up and offered him 'sippers' or 'gulpers' from their precious tots.

Paton declined with a broad grin. 'Some other time. I haven't got the head you lads have for that strong stuff.'

In the centre of the mess Jolson was wolfing a plateful of corned beef mixed with rice pudding and tinned apricots. His furiously wagging tail was ample proof that the unwholesome looking mess was a canine banquet as far as he was concerned. 'Good for his coat, sir,' said Morris.

'You'd better get him a life-jacket,' said Paton. 'If he goes overboard with that lot inside him he'll go down like an anchor shackle.'

'Or the Jerry I hit, sir,' retorted the seaman.

In the engine room McIntyre and Ross were squatting on a pile of coal, yarning away like two neighbouring gossips. Reynolds nodded towards them. 'How's that for a turn up for the book, sir?'

When the captain had completed his tour of inspection he returned to the bridge where Midshipman Carnac was standing over the binnacle with all the assurance and self-confidence of an old salt who had been baptised in sea water. Unaware of his captain's presence he was looking towards the slow-moving merchantmen and reciting aloud: 'You dirty British coasters with your salt-caked smoke-stacks and who pulled you from the jaws of death, eh? The jolly old navy.'

Paton coughed and regretted it. A knife turned in his chest. 'You all right, Middie, or are you suffering from the effects of shellshock?'

The young man flushed crimson. 'I didn't know you were there, sir,' he stammered in acute embarrassment.

Paton jerked the midshipman's cap down over his eyes in an impromptu gesture of affection. 'Don't apologize, Mr Carnac. I think we might justifiably claim that we did just that with, of course, a little help from the junior service. But never mind, plucking other men's flowers to salute a grand occasion is forgivable in the circumstances.'

The midshipman looked nonplussed. 'I'm not quite with you, sir.'

'A parody of Montaigne. We regulars don't have just iron in our souls. Poetry is not confined to Hostilities Only.'

Carnac mumbled, 'No, sir,' still completely ignorant of what his captain meant. He had never known him be so intimate or relaxed before; maybe he was the one who was suffering from shellshock. He doubted it. In his eyes Paton was the kind of man he aspired to be: totally unflappable and always in command of a situation.

'Think you can see another hour through, Middie? I'm just about tuckered. You look as fresh as a daisy, but then you've got youth on your side.'

Carnac flushed again and cursed himself for showing his feelings like a ruddy schoolboy. 'I'll see the rest of the watch through if you like, sir.'

'Good for you, but an hour will do. You might have made Masefield turn in his grave, but I think Horatio is sleeping soundly and contentedly. In short, you will do, Mr Carnac.'

A loud and ominous cough emerged from the voicepipe, followed by the sound of Read's voice, 'Wheelhouse, bridge, sir.'

Paton answered and Read said, 'Permission to be relieved, sir. I need to water the horse.'

'Carry on, Coxswain, but put a reliable helmsman on.'

'I'll get one of the trawler lads to do a turn at the wheel, sir. They can steer these ships better with their feet than I can with my hands.'

'You heard that, Middie. She's all yours.'

On the way to his own cabin Paton paused and knocked on the wardroom door where the first lieutenant was sitting back in a chair, his hands behind his head and an untouched drink before him on the table.

'The ship's company did us proud, Number One. I thought you'd like to hear that.' Just as he was closing the door he added, 'You set them a splendid example.'

Phelp downed his drink and clumped angrily up to the bridge. Not a word of praise for the poor bloody Snottie. Well, at least he would put that right.

He was rather surprised to find that he did not have to.

Paton went into his cabin, removed his duffle coat and tunic and pulled up his shirt and vest. There was a dinner plate sized bruise already as purple as a prune discolouring the left side of his chest. He felt around the area gingerly and winced, then coughed on the back of his hand. The pain almost doubled him up, but at least it was comforting to see there was no blood. He hadn't punctured a lung. He had learned enough first-aid to know that there was little more that could be done for a cracked rib until he could get ashore and see a sawbones.

He lay on his bunk and lit a cigarette and immediately regretted it as he started coughing.

It was only then that he remembered the wounded rating. He sat upright and glanced anxiously towards the dark shape on the deck; heavy breathing indicated he was fast asleep. Paton was relieved. He would not have liked him to witness his captain making such a fuss over a knock in the ribs.

As darkness began to descend like a slowly lowered curtain, 'Darken Ship' was piped and the deadlights screwed down over the portholes, the off-duty men began to relax. Only the lookouts and a handful of men remained on duty above. Paton wanted them to get as much rest as possible, for when dawn came it would also bring the possibility of another attack.

The slapping of the waves against the hull and the gentle rolling motion of the ship in a slight swell coupled with the more solid thump of the engine, had an almost lulling effect on the men. They sat and lolled around the stifling mess deck in the clothes they had not taken off since the ship sailed. There had been little time to clean up and the mess had the sour smell of body odour and tobacco smoke. It was as if they could not wait to hear the clang of the alarm bells which would drag them away from the rest they needed so badly.

At one of the tables four seamen were engrossed in a game of 'uckers', from time to time their voices rose to angry pitches as if they were playing for a month's pay instead of matchsticks.

Rhind sat on the edge of his bunk whittling away at a piece of wood that was gradually assuming the shape of a miniature totem pole – an art he had learned from an elderly Indian during his fur-trapping days. It seemed impossible that such huge and clumsy looking hands could work so delicately.

Nearby, Isaac Morris was measuring out with a pencil small squares on an old-fashioned cork lifebelt he had snitched from one of the Carley rafts. Jolson was fast asleep at his feet whimpering and twitching with delight as he slumbered through a dream in which a bitch figured prominently.

'You want to do something useful with that knife, Campbell?'

'I am,' came back the laconic reply.

'No, something *really* useful.'

'Not particularly,' drawled the Canadian. 'I find this relaxing.'

'You could help me here,' said Morris hopefully.

Rhind put down the piece of wood and slowly closed his knife, hoping that this deliberate gesture would impress upon his oppo that his patience was becoming exhausted through the interruptions.

'I am carving something that can bring me good luck, a commodity that is conspicuous by its absence at the moment. So why should I stop?'

'Because it's a matter of life or death. That's why.'

The Canadian made an elaborate show of getting up, sighing deeply and gritting his teeth before he moved and sat alongside his friend. 'Whose life and whose death?'

Morris looked down at the sleeping Labrador. 'His. You realize he's the only member of the ship's company who hasn't been issued with a lifebelt. If we go down, he won't stand a chance.'

The Canadian put a huge hand over his mouth and squeezed his nose, 'Isaac, if this tin can sinks, that,' – he motioned towards the supine dog – 'is the only thing that can be guaranteed to survive. Don't you know anything about Labradors?'

He stretched down and lifted the dog's tail. 'Just like an otter's. Built for swimming. The coat's waterproof. In Newfoundland the fishermen put to sea with one aboard. When they come in they send the dog through the surf with a small line in his jaws so the boat can be hauled in and beached. And you think he needs a lifebelt?'

Morris was adamant. 'I'd just feel happier, that's all.' Rhind reopened his pusser's dirk and without another word removed the life-float from Morris. 'I'll cut the cork into small squares. You couldn't cut a sliced loaf. You take his chest measurement.'

As Morris passed a piece of string gently round the body of the sleeping dog so as not to wake him, Rhind began cutting and shaping and smoothing the cork. When they had the required number of floats the two men drilled through them with a sailmaker's needle and then linked them up with spun yarn. That task completed, they cut a length of canvas to the required shape and got to work with a palm and needle, neatly sewing it into a sausage shape. When they had finished they sewed tapes on the ends and woke Jolson up for a fitting.

In the cramped stokers' mess in a corner that was as near to seclusion as possible, Stoker Danvers and Stoker Cohen were huddled over a table conversing in conspiratorial whispers. Cohen, tall, thin and dark-haired was holding a letter covered with neat schoolgirlish handwriting. Danvers, squat, barn-shouldered with carefully waved hair and boyish good-looks, was studying a small photograph of a pretty girl with tightly rolled curls sitting on the timbers of a breakwater on some - anonymous pebbled beach.

'Read it again,' urged Danvers.

'I've read it twice,' Cohen said dejectedly.

'You sure you haven't missed anything out?'

'Positive.'

'She *really* said all that?'

'She really said all that,' replied Cohen patiently.

'The love and kisses bit too?'

Cohen passed him the letter. 'You can see the kisses bit for yourself,' he remarked irritably. 'Jesus, Bob, it would be a damn sight easier if you learned to read.'

Danvers' eyes registered the hurt he felt and Cohen mumbled a hasty apology. 'I didn't mean that. It's just that I feel as if I'm eavesdropping on something private and personal. What would Maisie say if she knew?'

A hint of anger emerged in Danvers' voice. 'Look, it ain't my fault I was never taught. My old man didn't believe in school. He said Romanies didn't need it. Romany! He's nothing but a bloody scrap merchant *diddacoi* who moved on before the schoolboard people could ever catch up with him.'

'You'll have to tell her some time.'

Danvers shook his head vigorously. 'Not on your nelly. I'd only lose her.'

Cohen thought of his own parents who had almost bankrupted themselves to ensure that he had the best possible education. He remembered, too, his Polish grandfather whose Yiddish was far better than his broken English. He would have been heartbroken at the thought of one of his family signing for his pay with a cross. His thoughts were interrupted by Danvers saying, 'You got time to reply, Lionel?'

Cohen shrugged. 'Sure.' He felt a deep warmth and compassion for his friend. It was probably the nicest thing that had ever happened to him and he dreaded the thought of what might result when the girl, as she inevitably must, found out about the deceit. He went to his locker and returned with a writing pad, bottle of ink and pen.

Danvers leaned forward and said eagerly, 'Say something lovely about the snapshot. You know what I mean, Lionel. Use some of those beautiful words like last time.'

Cohen took the picture, studied it and began to write. Words from Browning's poems and letters tumbled through his mind as the pen raced across the lined paper. The girl's face was blotted from his eyes as it became an exercise to fulfil his own creative urge.

When he had finished it he read it in a hushed voice, and Danvers' face glowed with pride and admiration. 'That makes me want to cry, Lionel. It really is poetry. It's not really lying to her. It really is what I think.'

Cohen put the letter in an envelope and addressed it. He handed it to Danvers unsealed, for it would have to be read by one of the officers before it could be posted. What kind of a shit will they think I am, he thought.

Danvers said, 'You can have my tot tomorrow.'

Cohen shook his head, 'You don't owe me anything.'

'You know you're a bit of a surprise to me, Lionel. How comes a foreigner like you is in the Andrew?'

Cohen bristled, 'I'm not a foreigner. I'm bloody English.'

'How can you be, you're a Jew. I thought you had to be a Christian.'

The dark-haired stoker rose. 'I'm going topsides for a breath of fresh air.'

Danvers said, 'I haven't said anything to upset you, have I? I wouldn't do that for anything. Blimey, you're my oppo. It takes someone with real guts to prefer to work in a stinking stoke hold when he could get a cushy number ashore as a Writer.'

Cohen burst out laughing but the irony of his own remark was lost on Danvers.

5 Paton ducked his head under the chart-table and busied himself with dividers and parallel ruler. He checked the hourly list of figures from the log which was streaming astern recording their speed, took into account the currents and wind, and worked out as best he could by dead reckoning the position of the convoy. Two days and nights had passed since he had been able to fix *Grey Seal*'s position with a sun or star sight, for a deep coastal mist had suddenly rolled over the sea and shut out the sky so effectively that even the top of the mainmast was no longer visible from the bridge. It was a blessing in one sense and a curse in another, for whilst it virtually ruled out any danger of fresh attacks from the air or sea it made navigation very much a hit and miss affair. The ship carried none of the more sophisticated navigational aids found in most warships. Station keeping was an additional nerve-straining hazard, for the ships had to keep within a cable's length of each other or there was a grave danger of them losing contact. Six hundred feet was nothing in a mist-enveloped sea. The swirling mist was like a thin grey drizzle that chilled the bones and made the eyes water, and all over the ship men were stamping their feet and blowing on dead fingers to keep the circulation moving.

The captain straightened up. 'By my reckoning John O'Groats should be about twelve miles off the port bow, Number One. If only this damned mist would clear we could take a bearing on it.'

If he was correct they were passing the most northern tip of Great Britain, which meant they were not far from their final destination, Scapa Flow.

Phelp said, 'I checked our D.R. position before you came up, sir, and it put us in very much the same spot.'

Paton felt relieved; he had the utmost respect for the navigational ability of his first lieutenant and in normal conditions would have readily accepted his opinion. But the safety of the ship was *his* responsibility and one could never dismiss the possibility of human error – therefore he had checked for himself. It would have been grossly unfair telling a court of inquiry that he had hazarded his ship because he had the utmost faith in his first lieutenant. It was no time to pass the buck. Fortunately, Phelp did not seem at all put out at what could have been construed as a lack of confidence.

Paton's own feelings at that precise moment were mixed: he was overjoyed at knowing the voyage was almost over, yet dejected at the prospect of being stationed in Scapa, the most deeply detested base of the hundreds the Royal Navy commanded throughout the world. He had been there as a young midshipman and the painful memory lingered like a bad dream; he wholeheartedly agreed that Scapa was a four letter word. It was the anus of the Admiralty, although the matelots used a far more vigorous word when relating it to the human anatomy. It really was a geographical orifice. The vast, landlocked anchorage, capable of holding the entire navies of the world, resembled a shapeless hole punched in the Southern Orkneys by some vengeful and malevolent fist. In winter the black, barren, blizzard-swept hills in the latticework of seven small islands had an Arctic bleakness about them that froze the soul and numbed the senses. The inhospitable wilderness produced Orkneyitis, a malaise that was recognized by everyone except the Service doctors and which sent men round the bend and made them create a make-believe world in order to shut out the harsh realities of life. Only the hardy Orcadians, the flocks of wheeling, screeching sea birds and the shaggy, weather-hardened sheep which browsed on the sparse vegetation relished the savage environment. But Scapa's strategic importance was beyond question. Measuring fifteen miles from north to south and eight from east to west, it

110

not only provided fast and easy access to the Atlantic and northern waters, it guaranteed control. In theory at least.

For as the convoy steamed towards it, Paton was acutely aware that its much-vaunted invulnerability had already been horribly exposed. Kapitanleutnant Gunther Prien had slipped through the defences in U-47 and torpedoed the battleship *Royal Oak* just six weeks after the declaration of war, and the humiliating disaster had served as a painful reminder of the complacency of many in high places.

Paton had learned from his father that in 1938 at the height of the Munich crisis Admiral Sir Charles Forbes, the Commander in Chief, had taken his Fleet to Scapa and been appalled at the lack of preparation and the loopholes that existed in the defences. But his earnest entreaties had fallen on deaf ears. Such was the confusing state of affairs at the time that the Royal Marines were dismantling First World War gun emplacements while boom defence vessels were preparing anti-U-boat nets for the Second. Ironically, Forbes was somewhat contemptuous of the role the submarine would play and was firmly convinced the war would be won by the guns of the capital ships. It was a view shared by Admiral Sir Dudley Pound, who was to become the First Sea Lord.

This, together with his own early recollections of the hellhole, was passing through his mind when a stiff wind began to rattle the halyards and the mist suddenly began to disperse as if being swept away by some enormous, unseen broom. The shapes of ships which only minutes earlier had been nothing more than indistinct grey blurs now assumed physical proportions and soon afterwards the port lookout reported land, fine on the port bow.

'Bang on target,' exclaimed a delighted Phelp. 'Couldn't have done it better if we'd been on railway lines.'

Paton surveyed the convoy through his glasses; it resembled a line of wounded soldiers limping back from the front, each man with his outstretched hand resting on the shoulder of the man ahead. It was hardly an inspiring spectacle, but apart from the block ship and the sweeper they had come through intact if not unscathed, and he was determined they would enter the Flow like proud survivors and not whipped dogs. He ordered the ships to resume normal stations and make all possible speed.

As *Grey Seal* steamed towards Holm Sound and the entrance to the Flow, 'Hands Fall In For Entering Harbour' was piped over the loudhailer.

The tired but cheerful sailors changed into their number threes and lined the fo'c'sle and quarterdeck. Despite energetic attempts by Phelp to shift him with the toe of his shoe, Jolson insisted on squatting on his haunches at the end of the fo'c'sle party. Paton decided there was nothing he could do, or wanted to do, about it: the dog had become a part of the ship's company.

The defence vessels with bows resembling a crab's pincers began to swing open the boom and provide an entrance through the torpedo nets.

As *Grey Seal* went through, Paton could not help glancing to starboard at Kirk Sound and reflecting that it was through this selfsame gap that U-47 had slipped undetected to inflict mortal damage on the aged but powerfully armed *Royal Oak*. It had been a disaster of catastrophic proportions and one which would take a lot of living down. Morale had nose-dived and Hitler had danced with glee at the news; while many a veteran sailor had wept unashamedly at the needless loss and humiliation. They were not fooled by attempts to minimize the incredible skill and bravery of the German; it was not a case of the hyena skulking into the lion's den and devouring it whilst it slept; it had been a bold and imaginative venture.

Shortly after 1 a.m. on 14th October the surfaced U-boat had fired torpedoes into the massive ship moored a mile off shore in Scapa Bay and within sight of the spire of Kirkwall's St Magnus Cathedral. Unseen and undetected, the German had calmly reloaded the tubes and completed his deadly task.

112

Eight hundred men had gone to their deaths without firing a shot in retaliation. Many were still asleep in their hammocks, others were incinerated.

Paton shuddered involuntarily as a vision of men swinging in tide-rocked hammocks filled his mind. Ghastly stories had circulated and for weeks afterwards a heartbreaking jetsam was washed ashore as a dreadful reminder of the high price of lack of vigilance and preparedness. Islanders picked up items of clothing: caps, jerseys, stockings, shoes . . . and, surprisingly, a load of cabbages.

Not all the details had been released at the time for very obvious reasons, but four hundred men had survived and their bitterness and sense of betrayal soon spread throughout the navy, endorsed by the harrowing tales of those who had witnessed it and scoured the sea in the pitch-dark rescuing the fortunate men who had escaped.

The sky was dotted with barrage balloons and the muzzles of ack-ack guns could be seen on some of the headlands, where frantic efforts were being made to establish batteries and strengthen the neglected defences. They were surrounded by khaki tents which provided totally inadequate accommodation for the army gun crews.

Paton surveyed the depressing scene. When he had first sailed into Scapa the anchorage had been covered as far as the eye could see with huge, menacing warships: battle cruisers, battleships, cruisers and flat-topped carriers. Now it was surprisingly bereft of big ships. There were one or two cruisers and several destroyers and corvettes, but no capital ships. Until the defences were improved and the loopholes plugged the Fleet could not return to impregnable Scapa but would have to operate from Loch Ewe and Rosyth.

Drifters carrying stores, men, mail and islanders scuttled across the sea like waterboatmen on a village pond. They reminded Paton of pining dogs awaiting the return of their masters.

As the merchantmen broke off and headed for their appointed berths, a signal lamp winked from a tower ashore ordering *Grey Seal* and the other trawlers to proceed to Gutta Sound and secure alongside a new jetty which had been erected down the coast from Lyness.

As they steamed slowly between Flotta and Fara, the vast bulk of the *Iron Duke*, Jellicoe's old flagship at Jutland, came into view. How are the mighty fallen, mused Paton as he raked her with his glasses. Too old and antiquated for modern sea warfare, she had now been relegated to the passive and humble role of a depot and transit ship. Two of her five powerful turrets had been removed and the once valiant ship was now a toothless tiger, not floating proudly but resting on a sandbank. Jellicoe's frock coat on display in a glass case in an aft locker was a cruel and mocking reminder of the time when Britannia really did rule the waves.

Three days after the sinking of the *Royal Oak* the Luftwaffe had flown over to rub salt into the open wound. Bombs had cascaded down around the veteran warship, and within minutes the *Iron Duke* had started to keel over and the order 'Abandon Ship' was sounded. Once again the Flow had proved far from invulnerable. The battleship was only saved from an ignominious grave by being towed to safety by a tug and beached in Longhope Sound.

Paton pointed her out to his first lieutenant who felt a deep sense of indignation flood through him as a bugle blared from the old warship and puppet figures began scurrying across the upper deck to form into regimented lines. Impotent, gunless and a monument to shortsightedness though she was, the ceremonial had to continue.

There was an almost smug 'I told you so' look in Phelp's eyes as he turned to his captain. 'If the Germans ever assaulted this place, sir, the band of the Royal Marines could always lull them into a false sense of security with a selection from White Horse Inn while the crew pelted them with holystones.'

'That's quite enough, Number One,' Patton snapped, although he secretly shared his sense of unease and impotence at the way in which some diehards still clung tenaciously to

114

peacetime routines when there was far more important work to be tackled.

The four trawlers tied up in turn alongside each other at the hastily built wooden jetty, and when Paton called out, 'Finished with engines,' he glanced at the dismal scene before him. It reminded him of old sepia prints of the Klondyke when the gold had petered out and the rush had dwindled to a trickle. Rows of ramshackle corrugated iron huts of 1914 vintage sprawled everywhere in a misshapen mess. They were only prevented from being blown away by steel hawsers, passed over the roofs and secured to solid steel bars driven firmly into the ground. Towering above them were enormous fuel tanks. Seamen, soldiers and marines slipped and slithered as they tried to make their way through a quagmire of mud and slush in a desperate race to make Scapa live up to its reputation as a maritime fortress. Others laden down with heavy burdens precariously negotiated the network of duckboards like infantrymen in 1916 Flanders. In contrast to the spick and span turn out of the men on the obsolete battleship, they wore sea-boots, balaclavas, forage caps with the flaps turned down, gas capes and groundsheets . . . anything that would keep out the lancing wind and protect their feet from the slime that oozed through the smallest aperture.

Paton turned to his number one, 'A rather foreboding spectacle, eh? I think it would be appropriate if we hoisted the gin pennant and invited the other officers aboard when they've had time to clean up and change.'

Phelp grinned widely. 'You must be a thought reader, sir.'

A whiplash voice barbed with sarcasm attracted Paton's attention. 'Perhaps I could command your attention when you've finished with your sightseeing?'

He gazed over the bridge wing onto the jetty and saw a wiry-looking figure wearing an immaculate greatcoat with four gold bands on the shoulder straps and a cap with oak leaves on the peak perched at a rakish Beatty angle. 'Permission to come aboard,' he barked in a voice that denied refusal.

'Of course, sir. I'll be right down.'

Paton glanced anxiously along the deck and cursed inwardly; there was no quartermaster on duty yet, which was hardly surprising as the hands had just secured the gangway in place.

He clambered down the bridge ladder and stood at the foot of the gangway and returned the captain's salute as he half-turned and faced the ensign.

'It's customary for a senior officer to be piped aboard, Paton. Not a very auspicious start, eh?'

Paton felt his anger beginning to rise and attempted to explain that they had barely had time to secure the ship before the arrival of the captain. Furthermore, there were injured men needing attention and a dead one in the cable locker. But he was cut short with a brisk gesture that indicated the captain had no time for excuses. 'Perhaps we could go into your cabin?' he said brusquely.

Paton nodded and led the way to his quarters where he asked the four-ringer if he would like to have a drink. He looked at his watch and said, 'A bit early in the day for me, but rules are meant to be broken. In any case, what I have to say to you might not be taken too harshly over a drink.'

Paton wondered what on earth was coming as he poured the drinks. 'I'm Captain Monsey. I'm responsible for the operational activities of the anti-submarine and escort trawlers here. Your group will be serving under me.'

'I'm glad to hear that, sir.'

The captain removed his cap, placed it on the table and fixed Paton with grey unblinking eyes flecked with brown. 'Are you, Paton? Maybe you won't hold the same views when you've got to know me a little better. I demand a hundred and twenty per cent effort from everybody, and what I've seen so far leads me to believe that I'm going to have to do some heavy leaning to get that from you and the other commanding officers.'

Paton was bewildered. 'I'm not sure I understand, sir.'

Monsey leaned across the table and glared. 'I watched you coming in through my glasses. Not at all encouraging.' Paton

116

detected the faint smell of cloves on Monsey's breath and suspected he had already had a drink. It was a bad sign when a man had to disguise his drinking habits.

'Some of the men I saw lolling about the decks looked more like ruddy pirates than ratings in His Majesty's Royal Navy. Football jerseys, caps flat a'back. What kind of rig d'you call that, Paton?'

Suddenly Paton found himself unexpectedly defending his men from arguments which a short time ago he would wholeheartedly have agreed with. In a very brief period of time he had learned the important lesson that there was such a thing as priorities. He tried to explain without sounding rebellious that the cramped and confined conditions in a trawler were not always conducive to the kind of things which were taken for granted aboard a cruiser. Men had to double up at jobs and they had been on the alert most of the voyage with little or no time to spend on appearances. The handful that Monsey had seen had probably emerged from stoke holds and engine rooms to get a well deserved breath of fresh air or were airing their number threes prior to changing before entering harbour. He added that navy life was still alien to many of them and they had to be coaxed into learning it, not driven.

The bradawl eyes of Monsey burrowed into him and stopped him short. 'I don't doubt that there is something in what you say, but it's too easy to fall into their slapdash ways rather than enforce your own. At all times you will maintain the highest standards of dress and discipline. I'm afraid you'll have to sharpen things up, and at the double, if you're to meet with my approval.'

Bridling at the unfair and totally unexpected attack, Paton was stung to retort, 'I'm not unmindful of my duties and responsibilities, sir.' And, against his better judgement, he went into a long and detailed account of the eventful journey to Scapa. His men had experienced their first taste of action and emerged with flying colours. Furthermore, in the squalid conditions in which they lived and with little or no sleep, it was unrealistic to expect them to look like the crew of the Royal Yacht.

Monsey listened attentively and did not halt him, although he drummed silently on the tabletop with his fingertips, as if to suggest that he should get on with it. When he had finished, Monsey leaned back in his chair and said, 'The action – as you call it – Lieutenant Commander, could hardly be described as an unqualified success. One much-needed block ship has gone to the bottom and you've lost a mine-sweeper, while other ships have sustained considerable damage. I would describe it as an abject victory. No more, no less.'

Paton throwing discretion to the wind said, 'I hardly think that assessment bears examination, sir. Two of my escorts are armed with ruddy wooden twelve-pounders. Are they expected to drive off E-boats and aircraft with them? Far from being subject to such unfair criticism, sir, I think they should be commended. In fact, I had thought of mentioning some men for special recommendation.'

'Yourself included, no doubt,' said Monsey sourly. 'But I really don't have time to bandy words with you. I'll read your full report and consider it with total impartiality, although I do hope you'll not dramatise this coastal skirmish into a major naval engagement.'

Paton looked at the sharp-featured officer opposite and wondered what had turned him into such a hectoring bigot.

Part of the answer came as the captain rose to indicate he was ready to leave. 'Let me give you a friendly word or two of advice, Paton. No doubt you're smarting under a sense of injustice. You probably hoped for a fighting ship. Instead you got this.' His eyes encompassed the small cabin. 'Well, I was hoping for something a little better than a shore-based job mothering a load of men who have no idea what the real navy is all about.'

Paton had no desire to start off on the wrong foot with the officer who would control his future actions, but it was imperative that he should indicate that he was not prepared to be browbeaten by a man who formed such nasty and ill-judged first impressions.

'One has to remember, *sir*, that with the passing of time and the longer this war lasts, we're going to have to rely more and more on conscripted men and volunteers to win. So let's not judge them too harshly and prematurely.'

Monsey stiffened, clamped on his hat and glared at Paton with eyes that could not conceal their dislike. 'I think you've said more than enough. I'll overlook your insubordination this time, but bear this in mind,' he wagged a reproving finger, 'the fact that you're the son of a rear-admiral is not lost on me. But don't mislead yourself into thinking that you can skate through this on your backside or your father's name and reputation. That's a suggestion, not a warning.'

'I hope you'll measure me, and my group, on our achievements, sir. I'm more than confident we shall live up to your high standards.'

Monsey grunted, 'I'll see to that, Paton.'

As they emerged onto the deck, Monsey glanced up at the halyards where the gin pennant was fluttering in the breeze. 'I'd haul that down if I were you, Lieutenant Commander. I don't want you to get into the habit of thinking that every time you tie up is an excuse for a booze-up. In any case, I want to see you and the other skippers in my office in an hour's time.' He paused on the gangway. 'One last thing. I don't like to see animals falling in with the men. This isn't a circus.'

Paton clambered wearily to the bridge and hauled down the offending pennant. His action was observed through the wardroom porthole of the *Beaver* where the officers were changing into their best uniforms in preparation for a long and relaxing session. One RNR lieutenant remarked ruefully, 'That's typical of him. Can't make his mind up. Make less smoke, make more smoke. He gets you so confused you don't know your arse from your elbow. Never mind, we'll get tanked up without informing the whole Fleet of our intentions.'

Paton returned to his cabin, finished his drink and poured

119

himself another, even stiffer one. He would turn up at the captain's briefing reeking of the stuff and he wouldn't bother to suck cloves to disguise the fact. He hoped there weren't too many men like Monsey still on the active list. He had met some of them before – fortunately not many. They were the in-between men: too young for the First World War and a bit too entrenched in their ways to contribute much to the Second. They reminded him of men who could not play a round of golf without continually delving into their bag to fish out the rules book.

He remembered in time and before his temper took over Lord St Vincent's caustic rebuke to the officer who blamed his men for his own inadequacies: 'There are no bad sailors – there are only bad captains and bad officers.'

Monsey was not entirely to blame. The navy had to share the responsibility for producing such men. After the First World War the peacetime navy was slow to move with the times and there was an unquestioning acceptance of things that were blatantly wrong and unfair. It was riddled with snobbery and few questioned the belief that the best young officers came from the public schools and the worst from the naval colleges. The ability to play a good hand at auction bridge was considered an excellent qualification for commanding men who, it was automatically assumed, could be relied upon for their loyalty, good humour and lion-hearted courage. Officers seldom queried the decisions or opinions of their seniors, even when they knew they were wrong. And stupid customs became traditions because many lacked the courage to point out that they served no useful purpose. Midshipmen continued to be beaten with the scabbard of a dirk because they had always been beaten. Promotion was often haphazard and real talent often went unrewarded and unrecognized. If you were an average officer aboard a battleship or battle cruiser, you stood a better chance than a more outstanding one serving in small ships. This was for the simple reason that big ships carried more senior officers and you were therefore more likely to catch the eye of someone who could help you up the promotional ladder.

Changes did, of course, come, particularly the Mansell Reforms of 1933, but they were too late for some to alter their attitudes. Monsey was one of them.

Rhind and Morris and the two now inseparable Scottish stokers trudged through the slime and mud cursing loudly and frequently as they lost their footing in the darkness. To protect their well creased bellbottoms from becoming splattered with the yellow filth they had been forced to roll them up above their knees. At first they had laughed and cracked ribald jokes to each other shouting, 'Hold your skirts up, dearie', and sung, 'Knees up Mother Brown', but the joke had quickly worn thin. Only the ruddy Andrew would insist on you dressing up to kill before you were allowed ashore in a dump where even a water buffalo would feel out of place. But like all deep-sea fishermen Rhind and Morris would never have dreamed of staying aboard a minute longer than was absolutely necessary. Going ashore was like drinking your tot even when you didn't feel like it, and you knew you were going to throw it up immediately. It was the done thing. The stokers, on the other hand, had decided that there was no better way of celebrating their new found-camaraderie than with a few pints of beer. Anyway, they wanted to see something of the place which old sweats like Tiger and Reynolds spoke of with bated breath and awesome reverence. They made it sound like a foretaste of hell.

Their thick greatcoats with the collars turned up could not keep out the wind that pierced like a knife and made the lungs ache; while their caps were in constant danger of being blown away and lost in the quagmire even though they had the chin straps secured.

The ship had been berthed a considerable way from the small town of Lyness where the shore base HMS *Prosperine* was scathingly referred to as 'proper swine'. In their exhausting trek to find the 'wet canteen' they had pushed their way into windowless and doorless huts and encountered scenes straight out of an Old Bill cartoon. Men with their feet wrapped in sacking and old mail-bags sat hunched like watchmen over stoves that glowed red-hot; while others slept on the floor like sardines in a desperate attempt to keep each other warm. They were greeted with ribald shouts of 'Welcome to Lyness-on-mud, mates.'

When they eventually stumbled across a canteen their spirits slumped to bootlace level. It was a pigsty of a place which also served as a mess and barracks. The beer which stood in barrels at one end was plentiful but barely drinkable, and there were men reading and writing in hammocks slung from rails in the ceiling. The floor was awash with beer and the stale tobacco smoke formed a deep blue haze that stung the eyes and seered the lungs. A huddled group of men were fast asleep under billiard tables torn and pitted with scorch marks from cigarettes. They were totally oblivious to the raucous voices singing a naval ditty, the words of which were known from Pompey to Port Said: 'Twas on the good ship Venus. Or the ear-shattering bawl of the tombola caller who was trying to make himself heard above the undisciplined choir:

'Number Nine. What the doctor ordered.'
'Eyes down.'
'Seven and six. Piccadilly lady.'
'Marines breakfast.'

Rhind took one look at the place and voted for an immediate return to ship, but Morris deterred him. 'It's the only place in this God-forsaken dump where we can get a drink.'

'I bet the beer's lousy,' grumbled Rhind.

Stoker McIntyre retorted, 'There's no such thing. There's just some beer that's better than others. Right Jamie?'

His oppo nodded in dutiful agreement. 'After four or five pints it'll taste a treat.'

They found a vacant table, tipped their caps back and settled down as Rhind shouldered his way through the solid mass of bodies queuing at the bar to purchase the first round of the evening.

Within an hour they had narrowly avoided becoming involved in two fights with a group of brassed-off pongoes and some equally chokker sailors. But, as men who had so recently peered into the jaws of death and not liked it, they believed there were far more important things to get angry about than losing your place in a queue or having beer slopped over you. And so they grinned at their challengers, swallowed their pride, and invited them to pull up a chair and join them in a pint.

They quickly discovered that the antagonism was the result of sheer unadulterated boredom and envy of men who were at sea fighting a real war, while they were stuck ashore in conditions in which no self-respecting farmer would house his animals.

One of the seamen, happy to confide his moans to a fresh and attentive audience, said, 'I told my officer that my billet wasn't fit for a pig to sleep in. Know what he said? "Yes it is."'

Another butted in, 'Wait till you meet Monsey! He's a real bastard. We're working on the new base they're setting up for you trawler blokes. We're up to our charm pits in mud and he expects us to look as if we're turning out for the Spithead Review.'

Understandably they were embittered and resentful, and lack of communication made them feel they were being held responsible for the gross neglect of the past. They were simple, pathetically naive men who had enlisted to fight Hitler, although they would have had great difficulty in expressing themselves very coherently. They would have been embarrassed to talk about abstract things like freedom or democracy.

One man shook his head drunkenly. 'It's not right for men to fear their officer more than the bloody Jerry.' The hurt and bewilderment was evident in his voice for he could not explain what was so self-evident to him: why did some men have to drive willing men who only needed to be led? A pat not a kick up the arse got more from a dog, and the same applied to sailors.

The only consolation for the disconsolate ratings was that they were minimally better off than the 'brown jobs' sitting opposite. They too had their Blimps and they had to suffer them in even more primitive conditions. They were forcefully reminded of this by a particularly forlorn looking soldier who was living in one of the canvas villages. There was almost a hint of pride in his voice, as if he found some masochistic pleasure in proving the navy were living like pigs in butter in comparison with the soldiers.

'You've got nowt to bellyache about. We're stuck in a place surrounded by water yet it's rationed. You ever had to shave in what's left of your morning tea?'

They had, he went on, a weekly supply of water delivered in a tank on the back of a lorry by the water fatigue. It was the colour of brown windsor and was foul tasting. Keeping clean was a real problem for it was too rare a commodity to be issued in large quantities, and they had to share what was poured out each morning into the outdoor rows of enamel bowls. 'And another thing,' he said dismally, 'you don't have to perch on a pole like a bloody canary and do it into a slit trench. You try that and keep your balance after a night out on this,' and he held his glass aloft to emphasize his point. When one of the sailors tried to interject he silenced him with a frosty stare. 'I'm not finished yet, Jack. On top of that we have this berk of an officer who inspects your buttons and cap badges every morning and expects your puttees and webbing to be spotless.'

'Stop swinging the lamp. You shouldn't've joined,' said McIntyre, which was the navy way of terminating all arguments.

When the gaitered shore patrol finally strode through the canteen waggling their sticks and reminding everyone that it was time to be back in their billets or aboard, the four men from *Grey Seal* were tight enough to feel they were living high off the hog. And as they stumbled through the mud and

124

darkness to where the ship was tied up alongside they no longer cursed and swore. It was almost as good as going home.

Paton sat before the small writing desk suffocating under a blanket of self-pity brought about by too many whiskies. He was still smarting from the memory of the briefing in Captain Monsey's headquarters. Headquarters! The description was laughable. It was no more than a draughty wooden shack with a blackboard on one wall listing the movements of ships. A trestle table with a telephone on it served as a desk and there were half a dozen filing cabinets lining the walls. Yet Monsey had acted as if it were an operations room in the Admiralty. But what had upset him was Monsey's apparent determination to offend everyone. As soon as the officers had seated themselves on the hard benches he had adopted the attitude of a hectoring master admonishing wayward pupils. He had produced a handwritten list in which he had itemized all the faults he had noted in the extremely short time between the trawlers entering the Flow and tying up. He had dealt with each ship individually, ticking off every item as he disposed of it, and ending with a comment on each of their commanding officers. His remarks had been scathing and personal and to Paton's mind totally unreasonable. Some of the skippers had risen to defend themselves, and more importantly their ship's companies, but they had been ruthlessly cut short. 'I want results not explanations,' Monsey had said icily.

His final words of dismissal had summed up the whole tenor of the meeting. 'Well, gentlemen, you have heard my views, and I hope you're in no doubt as to what I expect. This unit will not muddle through. I don't share the view that it is an Englishman's prerogative and that the last battle is the only one that counts. Anyone who doesn't measure up to my requirements will be relieved of his command – and sharpish. I trust I have made myself clear, gentlemen.'

And with that he had stalked out.

On the short walk back to the ships Paton had sensed the intense anger smouldering inside the trawler skippers who were not the kind of men who could be bullied or intimidated. And as for the threat of being relieved of their command, they were more than likely to tell Monsey just what to do with their ships if he rode them too hard. And so he had invited every officer in the group aboard *Grey Seal* for a session that had only one stipulation: no shop.

Now he was halfway through a letter to his mother in which he realized he was expressing aloud his personal thoughts in an attempt to clarify his own feelings. He read what he had written:

> I know you detected I had misgivings about my first command and I'm taking this, the first opportunity, to put your mind at rest. I don't mind admitting that I have become quite attached to *Grey Seal*. Not exactly the *Hood*, but she'll do. The ship's company is small enough for me to have got to know most of them personally already. I like the intimacy, although at the moment I'm still remaining a little aloof. Too much familiarity too early on would defeat my object. I want a ship's company that is proud of *Grey Seal* and I can only achieve that by building up a strong team spirit. While we may all be pulling together on the same rope there is a tendency at the moment for some of the lads – and officers – to pull in different directions. The RNR men are superb seamen who have always done things their own way and are a little resentful of change. What I must avoid at all costs is to create a division of 'them' and 'us'.

He paused and re-read what he had written, then tore it into small scraps. Why bother her with my personal problems?

He took up a fresh piece of paper and began to write a jolly, chatty letter which contained more questions than answers. How were the neighbours? How was his father? How was Bosun? How was Lesley? He overstressed his own good health, and said they had just arrived in a place that was renowned for its invigorating air, beautiful landscapes and high living. It was the kind of letter a mother liked to receive and loved answering. He made no mention of his aching ribs although he realized he could not postpone a visit to the base hospital for much longer.

Before breakfast the following morning he sat down and wrote out a long report to Captain Monsey. It was detailed, factual, fulsome in its praise for the officers and men, and highly critical of whoever it was who had sent ships to sea in such a deplorable state of unreadiness. In the past Britain may have relied on its wooden walls defending it from the enemy, but wooden guns was a laughable arrogance. He knew that Monsey would be outraged, but there was nothing he could do about it. It was his duty as group leader to bring shortcomings to the attention of higher authorities, and Monsey, a stickler for the book, would have to forward on the report. Something might be done before *Grey Seal* and the other trawlers were ready for sea again. The damage they had sustained would take at least a week to put right. Plenty of time for someone to sit up and take notice. And he did not give a damn if Monsey claimed all the credit, as no doubt he would.

When the routine for cleaning ship was completed the ship's company assembled on the jetty, spick and span in their number ones. As Paton stepped ashore the first lieutenant called them sharply to attention. 'Ship's company ready for inspection, sir.' The captain walked along the two lines, stopping before each man and casting an appraising eye over his appearance. You did not hurry past men who had made so much effort, leaving behind the impression that it had all been a waste of time. A bosun's pipe warbled and the three hands under Guns Jenkins, armed with .303s, presented arms with much stamping of feet and slapping of butts. Paton and his two officers saluted as the coffin of Able Seaman Carter, draped with the Union flag, and borne by two stokers and two seamen, was brought ashore.

The coffin was loaded into the back of a lorry which had

been loaned by the transport officer and the officers and men of *Grey Seal* clambered in after it.

As the lorry bumped and bucketed along the uneven road, men crashed against each other and only managed to remain upright by being supported by those clinging precariously to the steel struts securing the canvas roof. The pallbearers had to use their combined weights to prevent the coffin from moving about like a cargo that had broken loose in the hold of a storm-lashed ship.

'It's an incentive for staying alive,' muttered one seaman cynically, to be silenced immediately by the young and emotionally susceptible midshipman who thought the whole affair bordered on the sacrilegious. He could not shut out from his mind the picture of the dead man being jolted up and down in the plain wooden coffin as if some unseen hand was trying to shake him awake.

In the driver's cabin Phelp remarked drily to his captain, 'We should have buried him at sea, sir. At least he would have gone with a little dignity.' He had had the unenviable task of filling in the necessary form in which he had written 'Dead' against the blank space marked: Reason for discharge. Immediately afterwards, he had sent a signal to base head-quarters requesting replacements for the dead man and the wounded sailors who were now in hospital.

In the small, hillside cemetery they stood bareheaded around the open grave as a padre romped briskly through the burial service. The wind blew a mournful requiem and the sailors' bellbottoms flapped noisily against their thighs. It was no time for unnecessary hanging about. A volley of rifle shots was fired overhead and the ship's company piled back into the lorry, silent and subdued, as they returned to the ship to carry on where they had left off. 'If that's a hero's farewell, you can stuff it,' muttered Morris.

Back aboard, Paton sat staring at the blank sheet of paper in front of him. It was the first time he had written to a dead man's next of kin and he was at a loss for words. He knew very little about the dead man, but was desperately anxious to

128

avoid the stilted cliches usually associated with such letters. In any case, Carter's parents would have already received the dreaded official telegram. He wanted to say something that would make his family realize that their son was more than just a name, rank and number. He summoned Hall, the steward, and asked him to tell the coxswain he was wanted in the captain's cabin.

Tiger Read knocked and entered, his cap tucked smartly under his arm. 'You wanted to see me, sir?'

'Sit down, Coxswain. I'm trying to drop a line to Carter's family and I hoped you might be able to help.'

Read scratched the top of his grizzled head as if trying to locate some sensitive spot that would trigger off a flood of memories. 'He was a nice kid, sir. Popular in the mess. A good shipmate, you could say. Bit of a roving eye for the ladies. One in every port I'm told.' But he too seemed at a loss for words. 'Perhaps it might help, sir, if I had your permission to open his locker and bring up his ditty box and any other personal belongings. His family are entitled to them, sir.'

When Read returned he placed a small brown fibre suitcase on the table and said, 'I think you ought to open it, sir. Makes me feel a bit like a Peeping Tom.'

Paton lifted the lid and looked at the pathetic collection of items that represented all that was near and dear to the dead man: a snapshot of a girl wearing a fixed camera smile, another of his mother and father, a small bundle of letters held together by an elastic band, his pay book, some bars of nutty, a small Bible, and a mouth-organ.

So Carter was the instrumentalist for the mess deck singsongs.

'Not much, is it Coxswain?'

'Poor little sod didn't really have much time to collect a lot, did he, sir?'

When Read had gone Paton wrote his letter. He told the boy's parents that their son had died very bravely in action and that they could be extremely proud of him. He tried to conjure up the dead man's face but it eluded him. John – he had never used his Christian name before – had been one of the most popular members of the ship's company and he would be deeply missed by his messmates who, in the short time they had been together, had come to respect and admire him.

When he had finished, Paton felt slightly ashamed of himself; the words seemed so glib and transparent. He hoped that in their grief his parents would not notice. He also hoped that he would not have to write many more similar letters. He recalled Read's words about Carter's weakness for the opposite sex and some second sense made him unfasten the elastic band round the bundle of letters. It was just as well that he did, for one half were from a girl in Portsmouth, the other from another in his home town of Huddersfield. Even from the most cursory glance, it was clear that both considered themselves engaged.

Paton put the bundle from the girl in Huddersfield into the large envelope he was sending to his parents. The others he sent to the address in Portsmouth along with a short letter from himself. At least Carter had made a little hay before the sun stopped shining for him.

There was a knock on the door and the quartermaster entered and handed him an envelope. 'Hand signal from ashore, sir.'

It was from Captain Monsey: In the interests of economy and to conserve much needed small-arm ammunition, firing parties will be dispensed with in the event of any future burials ashore.

When 'Stand Easy' was piped, Tiger Read let it be known that he wanted all hands to muster in the seamen's mess deck.

As they crowded together wondering what on earth he wanted, Tiger announced in a voice that brooked no argument, 'Right, we're going to have a ship's auction of the dead man's kit. Everyone's got to have something and you've all got to dig deep in your pockets. Right! What we raise we'll send home to his folk.'

Jerseys and collars that would never be worn or used, caps, uniforms, shoes, razors, brushes and sea-boot stockings, were purchased for sums the men could ill-afford. But they willingly parted with the money.

They raised £14.15s, and each man signed his name to a short round robin letter of condolence. When Read put the money in an envelope he insisted on having it witnessed. He didn't want anyone suggesting he had pocketed it.

'This will become unofficial routine if anyone else is unfortunate enough to cop it. Now back to your work you lazy beggars.' He hoped that the crew replacements wouldn't be too green. Everyone was settling down fine now and he didn't want to start wet-nursing all over again.

Next morning a convoy of lorries and a powerful-looking crane mounted on caterpillar tracks trundled along the metalled road and halted alongside the trawlers. As men piled out of the backs a gunnery petty officer clutching a sheaf of official looking forms strode aboard *Grey Seal* asking for 'Jimmy the One'.

Lieutenant Phelp was ashore on ship's business and Midshipman Carnac was O.O.D. When he appeared on deck the gunner looked at him, pursed his lips, and grunted in a manner that suggested that if no one else was available the boy would just have to do.

'Morning, sir. Eight Oerlikons trawlers for the use of.' Carnac wondered whether he was trying to take the mickey but realized he wasn't; he was simply reading what someone had written down. 'Two for *Grey Seal*, two for *Otter*, two for *Beaver*, two for *Vole*.' He thrust three forms into the midshipman's hand. 'Sign all three sir, and keep one for yourself. The rest of the ships can sign for their own.'

The petty officer glanced round the deck. 'If you've got any gash hands loafing around with nothing to do, sir, I'd be grateful if they could be detailed to help. I've brought the armourers, chippies, welders and what have you for the skilled work, but I could do with some odds and bods to do a little heaving and hauling.' Clearly such mundane chores were not for his team.

Carnac summoned Read and then went off to inform the captain of the unexpected delivery.

Read stood gazing at the scene before him with a look of consternation on his rugged features. 'And just where do you think you're going to put them, PO? As it is, there's not room topsides to swing a cat round.'

The gunner consulted his papers. 'Midships. One port, one starboard. Bolted to railway sleepers. Not exactly how I would mount a gun, chief, but *they* seem happy to settle for anything these days.'

Read had no idea who *they* were but from the tone of the petty officer's voice he did not think very highly of them.

By the time Paton emerged on deck the crane had hoisted two heavy sleepers aboard and the air was filled with the penetrating sound of hammering and drills biting into metal as a group of men from the armoury began securing them to the deck.

To the annoyance of the petty officer, Guns Jenkins had clearly decided the new weapons were his babies and he was not slow in offering advice and suggestions. Both men with crossed gun badges on their arms, short-cropped hair and rigid backs, looked as if they had been cast in the same mould and they were warily eyeing each other like two proud beasts determined to defend their territory against any encroachment. Paton was just in time to prevent the petty officer from blowing his top and telling the stroppy 'killick' to get out from under his feet.

'To what do we owe this unexpected treat, Petty Officer?' Paton asked with a disarming smile.

'Don't ask me, sir. Mine's not to reason why. Someone must have put a flea in someone's earhole because orders came direct from the admiral's office. Someone up *there* apparently did his nut when he heard what you'd got to fight with.' He made *there* sound as if it were some celestial location.

With the aid of Read and a group of sweating seamen working the blocks and tackles with the added power of the capstan, the guns were hoisted into the air, and after much shouting of 'avast hauling', 'hoist away', 'handsomely', 'belay there' and 'ease away, gently', the guns were lowered and secured to their primitive mountings. When the job was completed *Grey Seal* had to slip out and let the trawler on the outside move in to the jetty.

As the long dark nights came early and quickly in Scapa, the work had to be abandoned with two of the ships still waiting to be fitted with their new armament. But the working party was back at first light and the task completed before 'Up Spirits' was piped.

The gunner's mate surveying his handiwork with the distaste of the craftsman who had been compelled to do a bodged-up job, turned to Paton and said ruefully, 'They'd go spare if they saw that little lot at Whale Island, sir. Still, the ruddy things will fire and that's all they seem to expect these days. Which reminds me, sir. For God's sake don't fire them till we've welded on some guard-rails to limit the field of fire. Otherwise you'll shoot up the bridge, blow the mainmast down, and demolish your funnel.'

Paton said, 'They may not instil you with a great sense of pride, but believe me they're like manna from heaven to us. At least we'll be able to give a reasonably good account of ourselves next time we run into trouble. Who cares what they look like!'

The gunner who had spent his service life alongside guns mounted in streamlined turrets or on placings specially designed for the job, looked at the sleepers which had been purloined from a stretch of unused railway track, and grunted. 'You *might* have something there, sir. As I used to say in my green and salad days, "You don't look at the mantelpiece when you poke the fire".' The aphorism was not particularly apt but Paton got the meaning.

The sound of a car engine revving madly followed by the grinding of gears being savagely changed filled the air, and the

133

petty officer glanced towards the metalled road. 'You've got company, sir. Captain Monsey's Jeep, if I'm not mistaken.' He emitted an exaggerated long-suffering sigh. 'He won't exactly dance a hornpipe when he sees my efforts. More than likely hand me a bottle.'

The blue Jeep slewed to a halt and Monsey was almost out of the vehicle before he had switched off the engine, striding with quick determined steps towards the ship.

'Quartermaster at the double. Standby to pipe the captain aboard,' hissed Paton. Monsey was moving so quickly that he suspected he was trying to beat the quartermaster to it.

As the two officers exchanged salutes, Monsey nodded to the newly-mounted Oerlikons and their primitive sleeper-mountings. 'Bit like wearing a cloth cap at Divisions, Paton, but you can always put the covers on in harbour.'

'Appearances can be deceptive, sir. Look at the old *Iron Duke*. Looks formidable but couldn't say boo to a goose.' He saw Monsey's jaw begin to tighten and decided it would be tactful to change the subject. It was clearly no time for jocularity. 'Care to join me in a drink, sir?'

Monsey glanced at his watch. 'A bit. . .' he left the sentence unfinished. 'A splendid idea. We'll wet your new babies' heads.'

Monsey drank his first whisky as if he were a desert traveller who had stumbled upon a long sought-after oasis, and as Paton refilled his glass he said, 'I read your report, Paton, and was most impressed. So was the admiral. I might have been a bit churlish in my first reaction but I wasn't fully in the picture.' Paton reflected silently that in that case it was a pity he hadn't bothered to see what it was before blowing his top, but he said, 'That's very good of you, sir.'

'As a matter of fact the admiral is considering putting your name forward for a decoration, along with anyone else you might think is deserving of the honour.'

Paton said, 'I'm not particularly interested in gongs myself, sir, but I think it would do wonders for the morale if the lads knew their efforts were appreciated.'

Monsey pushed his empty glass across the tabletop. 'There's only one point on which I would cross swords with you, Paton. There really wasn't any need to stress quite so strongly the inadequacy of your armament. I trust it wasn't a rather unsubtle way of going over my head. I had it all well in hand. And as you can see, I acted pretty promptly.'

'Thank you, sir.'

'That's quite all right, but one should avoid giving the impression of a bad workman blaming his tools.'

Paton suppressed his annoyance. You couldn't cross swords with Monsey; you would have to arm yourself with a bludgeon. 'I'll have no cause for arousing that false impression in the future, sir. Thanks entirely to you.'

Monsey smiled with all the warmth of cold steel. 'My job. By the way the admiral – I mean I – have also given instructions for the two trawlers with the dummy guns to be fitted with the genuine article.'

When Paton escorted Captain Monsey to the gangplank the remaining whisky was level with the bottom of the label, but he wasn't at all perturbed. He's welcome to all he can swallow, thought Paton. With a bit of luck we'll have him pensioned off with cirrhosis of the liver.

But as he watched Monsey go ashore he realized that would take a very long time and an inordinate number of visits; his step was as spry and steady as it had been when he stepped aboard and he almost vaulted into the driving seat as if it was the saddle of a mettlesome charger. God, he thought, he must get through a heck of a lot of cloves.

Paton stood studying the hospital sign board erected at eye level on the concrete road that led to a group of Nissen huts linked together by a spider's web of narrow paths. Wards were listed numerically with arrows pointing to their location. There was a Pathology Lab, a Blood Transfusion Centre, the Senior Medical Officer, Nurses Quarters, Mortuary and X-Ray Unit. It was some time before he was able to pick out the Casualty Department. He followed the arrowed signpost through a labyrinth of pathways until he found the half-circle corrugated iron hut. At the trestle table which served as a reception desk a nurse in a starched white cap and a heavy blue cape was sitting as close as possible to a small paraffin heater, her feet encased in fur-lined boots.

'Can I help you, sir?'

Paton noticed that she was wearing blue woollen mittens, and hoped sincerely that his aching ribs would not necessitate a stay. The hospital was quite obviously not given preferential treatment when it came to fuel. He had delayed visiting the quack for as long as possible, hoping the pain would go away, but it had persisted. If there was something seriously wrong he ought to find out; it wasn't fair to the men otherwise.

'I'd like to see the MO, nurse. Nothing serious. A precautionary visit really.'

'How can you be sure of that?' she said archly. 'Are you a doctor?' He shook his head. 'Then let us be the judge of that. Name, please, and rank.'

Paton dutifully provided the details and as she filled in a stiff, ruled card he found himself apologizing. 'I got a nasty bang in the ribs and I thought I'd better get it looked at before I went back to sea.'

She looked at him, pen poised. 'Drunk?'

'No, I bloody well wasn't! I got thrown against a compass binnacle by a bomb that fell too close for comfort.'

'Tut, tut,' she said. 'I was only joking. Don't say we've lost our sense of humour. Most of the injured sailors who call here say their wounds are the result of too much grog. It's become a standing joke.'

Paton mumbled an apology and the nurse smiled forgiveness. 'If you'll take a pew in there, sir, I'll send in a young nurse to keep you warm while I call the doctor.'

Paton grinned appreciatively and went into the waiting room. Gazing out of the window was a woman wrapped in an enormous fur coat. He said, 'Excuse me,' and when she turned he found himself looking at the face which had stared at him from the posters and photographs in the foyer of many a West End theatre. The heart-shaped face topped by a crown of glorious blonde hair looked rather pale and jaded and there were dark rings under the heavy-lashed eyes. She was puffing anxiously at a cigarette in a long holder.

'Aren't you Cecily Grey? *The* Cecily Grey?'

The woman performed an exaggerated curtsy and said hoarsely, 'None other. The famous star of stage, musical comedy, screen and radio. Please don't stare at me like that. I feel bloody awful.' She brandished the cigarette holder like a conductor's baton. 'This isn't theatrical. I'm an incurable addict and I'm just trying to limit the damage to my tonsils. A present from the admiral. I'm bunged up with cold, I've lost my voice and I've done nothing but puke since I arrived here.'

Paton was totally disarmed. 'I'm one of your admirers,' he said clumsily, 'but even I must admit that you don't look as gay and vivacious as you did from the circle of the Coliseum the last time I saw you.'

'I don't feel it. I just hate the idea of letting the boys and girls down. A group of us flew up to Rosyth two days ago and put on a show for the Fleet. Then we took a boat to some God-forsaken hole and put on another for the ack-ack lads. But I'm no sailor. I just want to crawl away into some corner to curl up and die. And there's another show at Lyness this evening. Unless your quack can give me something I won't be able to sing a note.'

'You don't need to sing, just stand there. That'll be more than enough for the lads.'

'Flattery, young man, will get you everywhere with me.'

Paton could hardly believe his good fortune; he had admired her so often from a distance and here she was standing just a few feet away and looking very human and extremely fragile.

'You might as well sit down. Navy hospitals have a deserved reputation for slowness. They like to keep you waiting for as long as possible to deter the malingerers. Then if you're still alive when the sawbones is ready to see you they reckon you're entitled to treatment.'

137

When she sat beside him on the bench he noticed that she was wearing a long, low-cut evening dress. Her eyes followed his and she burst out laughing. 'Don't imagine I like traipsing around the Arctic Circle dressed like this, but quite honestly I couldn't even be bothered to change. I just wanted to die. I haven't felt so bad since I faced my first audience, and I was a kid of eight then.'

They sat chatting for half an hour, during which Paton learned more about her than anything he had read in countless newspaper interviews. Her costermonger father had been a drunkard and her mother a woman who had scrimped and scraped to bring up a family only to die young of tuberculosis.

'I got to the top by hard work, not lying on my back. I had a good natural voice and what little I earned I spent on singing lessons and elocution,' she said defiantly.

'Good for you,' said Paton.

'It's odd you should say that. But do you know, while I'm proud of it, my publicity agent insists that that side of my life shouldn't be exposed. Bad for my image. Ever heard such nonsense?'

Their conversation was brought to an abrupt halt by a surgeon-lieutenant entering and saying, 'Miss Grey? If you'd like to come through I'm sure we can find something to settle your stomach and relieve your cold.' He looked at Paton and said coldly, 'I hope the lieutenant commander hasn't been telling you we deliberately keep people waiting. Some bright idiot decided to roll over a ten hundredweight and we've been stitching up the victims. Must get you on top line for this evening. Wouldn't be the same show without you, Miss Grey.'

She winked at Paton, then turned to the doctor and said, 'How awfully sweet of you, darling.'

If Paton had not been talking to her alone for so long he would have cringed at the over theatrical language. As it was, he knew she was laughing to herself. When she reappeared Paton asked her how she had got on and she replied, 'That young doctor should do well in Harley Street. Told me to cut

138

down on the smoking, avoid unnecessary boat travel, wrap up against the cold and take two of these every three hours.' She rattled a tube of tablets. 'Aspirin, I hope, and not your dreaded cure-all Number Nines.'

'I don't suppose,' said Paton hesitantly, 'that there's any chance of you putting a ticket for tonight's show my way? I really am a fan.'

She rummaged in her handbag, produced a small packet of tickets and handed him one. 'If you don't mind sitting beside the admiral surrounded by more gold braid than I've had hot dinners, you're more than welcome. But don't expect too much from an old corn crake.'

Paton was kept waiting a further ten minutes before a nurse appeared and enquired, 'Lieutenant Commander Paton?' He nodded although there was no one else present in the room, and she said, 'The surgeon will see you now.'

The examination was short but thorough, and the surgeon assured Paton that although it was extremely painful he had nothing more to worry about than a cracked rib, and all it needed was strapping up.

Paton left feeling on top of the world and wondering how he could get a message back to the ship that he would be late returning aboard. He was already anticipating the great pleasure he would get, assuming the opportunity arose, from telling Miss Grey that the doctor did in fact have a peacetime practice in Harley Street and they were aspirin tablets.

The wet canteen converted by willing hands into a makeshift theatre was so overpacked that men were even sitting on their haunches in the aisles. The rough and ready stage was no more than planking supported on empty oil drums and heavy wooden crates. There were no curtains and the lighting was a collection of hastily improvised spotlights, attended by a couple of signalmen who provided variation by holding sheets of different coloured cellophane over the fronts. Crude it may have been, but the atmosphere was more in keeping with a West End premiere. Men who had been starved of live enter-

139

tainment for so long were in bubbling high spirits and determined to enjoy themselves. While the entertainers, who had endured considerable discomfort to be there, were equally determined to put on a show that an impresario would have needed an overdraft to back. And they did it for nothing.

The cast, carefully balanced to meet all tastes, performed with a zest and enthusiasm fitting for a Royal Command performance; as if the audience before them were wearing dinner jackets instead of blue uniforms. The virtuoso violinist who had performed in nearly every major city throughout the world appeared on the wobbly stage in white tie and tails and played as if the crude building was Carnegie Hall. Despite the objections of his insurance broker he had insisted on bringing his Stradivarius – nothing but the best would do for the navy. To the delighted roars of the assembled sailors, he had even invited requests and proved that his priceless instrument was capable of swinging it with the best of them. The two comedians had taken immense trouble to rewrite their material in order to give it a local flavour, so that all their jokes and repartee were linked to Scapa Flow and its better known environs. Instead of making cracks about prominent politicians they referred to senior officers on the base, much to the delight of the audience who felt they were getting their own back – if only at second-hand. Even the much abused band of the Royal Marines proved that they were capable of playing something other than 'A Life On the Ocean Wave'. Paton enjoyed it, but his mind and attention was not entirely with the performers; he could only think of Cecily Grey.

There were loud cheers, piercing wolf whistles and a deafening thump of boots on the floor when she strolled casually onto the stage to be transfixed in the centre by an enormous searchlight. She bowed so deeply from the waist that for one moment it looked as if her hair would touch the floor, then as she straightened she gave a comic salute and blew kisses into every corner of the huge hall. She was wearing a dazzling black and white evening dress that was divided diagonally across her body and clung so tightly it revealed

140

every contour of her shapely figure. Her face bore none of the signs of fatigue that Paton had noticed earlier.

Someone had rustled up a battered piano from somewhere or other and she gave a slight nod to her accompanist who played a few opening bars before she began singing 'These Foolish Things', which filled the massive hall with a deep sense of nostalgia. She performed for more than half an hour with barely a pause, singing request after request for a brief moment transporting lonely men back home to their loved ones. Then she jumped down lightly from the stage, grabbed the admiral's cap, put it on her head at a jaunty angle and began to sing, 'All the Nice Girls Love a Sailor'. She moved along the crowded rows of seats sitting on laps, kissing cheeks and ruffling hair. The men went wild with delight. As she neared the end of the song she moved to the front row and sat on Paton's lap, and to the intense amusement of the audience began to sing in a low seductive voice, 'I Can't Give You Anything But Love'. Paton's obvious embarrassment delighted the servicemen, and when she finished she planted a kiss firmly on his lips. There were deafening shouts of: 'You lucky old so and so', and the sense of fun was so infectious that when she rose to return to the stage Paton stood and acknowledged his good fortune with hands clasped above his head like a champion boxer. Only Captain Monsey sitting to one side of him did not seem to think it was very amusing. He muttered from the side of his mouth, 'Don't make a clown of yourself, Paton. Tomorrow you'll be expecting them to show respect.'

Cecily stood in the centre of the stage and bowed time and time again as the audience roared and cheered and chanted, 'More, More'. She held up her right hand and when the din subsided she turned to the pianist, nodded and began to sing, 'Keep the Home Fires Burning'. She held her arms wide open as if embracing the audience, then invited everyone to join in. Paton felt a sharp stinging at the back of his eyes, and when he glanced around to see if anyone had noticed he observed that his eyes were not the only ones that were moistened.

When it was over the entire cast walked on to the stage, linked hands, bowed, then waved and walked off stage.

Paton felt dejected. Tomorrow she would be sitting on someone else's lap singing the same song.

'I've invited a few people back for drinks to meet the cast and just say thank you on behalf of everybody. Perhaps you'd like to join me, Paton.'

He jerked himself back to an awareness of his surroundings and realized he was being addressed by the admiral. 'I beg your pardon, sir. I was miles away.'

'Understandably too. If I'd had that young lady on my lap singing sweet nothings in my ears I'd be in the same state. But the invitation still stands. In any case, it'll give me the chance to ask you how things are shaping up.'

Paton could scarcely believe his good fortune at this further opportunity to meet her.

He stood against a blacked-out window shaking his head as a succession of stewards hovered in front of him with trays covered with sandwiches and sausage rolls. The glass in his hands was almost empty and when a steward passed by with a tray of drinks he helped himself to a fresh one. Paton wondered how many more he would need before he could pluck up enough courage to walk across the room and interrupt Cecily Grey who was surrounded by the group of officers who had monopolized her since she arrived in the room. Not once had she glanced in his direction, seemingly more than content with the company she was keeping. From time to time she stopped talking to sign an autograph. Paton noticed that her glass was empty and decided to take the plunge. He excused his way through the crowd until he was standing by her side. 'They're all so busy talking they've neglected your drink. Can I top you up?'

'They've been plying me with drinks,' she said, and placed a hand over the top of the glass. 'But I can't keep pace with you sailors. Anyway, I keep thinking of another boat trip in the morning, and I don't think the two will mix. Still, I'm very pleased you came over. I thought perhaps you might be angry with me.'

'Angry?'

'For making you look silly in front of all the men. The captain in the corner was a bit stuffy about it.'

'If you promise to do it again I'll arrange for the entire Fleet to be present.'

'Well, now you're here perhaps I'll have a small one to keep you company. I thought for one minute you were never going to come over and rescue me.'

'It took some time to summon up the nerve.'

'You don't sound at all like the hero the admiral was describing.'

He coloured and said, 'What on earth has he been telling you?'

'Oh, nothing much. Just how your intrepid little band of trawlers fought off E-boats and the might of the German Air Force.'

'We didn't really have much alternative,' he replied lamely.

'Let's go and find that drink,' she said, and Paton realized that she was anxious to move away from the crowd.

When they had found a relatively quiet corner he said, 'I can't tell you how much I've enjoyed meeting you. It would be very nice if I could console myself with the thought that we might meet again. I suppose this kind of thing often happens in wartime. Like ships passing. You must get used to it in your profession. Lots of animated and adulatory talk, then you move on and realize you don't even know a person's name.'

'But I do, Crispin. I asked the admiral. So you see we actresses aren't all empty talk and insincerity.'

Paton was anxious to hear about her, but she kept steering the conversation back to him and he found himself reluctantly telling her about *Grey Seal* and her ship's company.

When the party began to show signs of breaking up, Cecily glanced at her watch and said, 'I really must tear myself away. We're off at the crack of dawn. I really have enjoyed meeting you, Crispin. Wait there till I've said goodnight to the

143

admiral, then you can see me home in the dark.'

They walked through the blackout to the dormitory where Cecily had been provided with a bunk for the night. At the doorway she paused and said, 'Those poor girls in there! It's so cold they sleep with their clothes on, often two in a bed. Even their face cream gets frozen solid. When I think of what I'm going back to when this trip is over – clean sheets, plenty of warmth – I realize how lucky I am.'

'Alone?'

'Very much so, apart from a rather lovely old lady who looks after me. What did you imagine? Black satin sheets shared with a matinée idol? You mustn't believe everything you read about theatricals. I haven't even had one husband yet.'

'Is there any chance of meeting you when I get leave?'

'I'd love that but I really don't know what my plans are. No one seems certain what the theatres will do. It depends, I suppose, on the air-raids and how many of these shows I'm asked to do. But hang on a minute.' She disappeared through the door and returned with a sheet of paper which she pressed into his hands. 'There's my telephone number and address in London. Keep in touch. Now I must get some shut-eye. Keep your feet dry for me, Crispin.' Then the door closed.

The long walk back to the ship passed unnoticed for Paton was too engrossed in thoughts of Cecily Grey. He wasn't, he told himself, acting like a silly teenager. She was the most exciting woman he had ever met and not at all like the conventional picture he had always had of people in the entertainment world. She seemed natural, unaffected, and he had only heard her address one person – the surgeon – as *Darling*. He wondered what the admiral would say when they next met; he had a right to be angry at being given the cold shoulder. But for the moment Paton was past caring.

6   Although it was still only mid-afternoon, the sky was a
     fierce tangerine and the placid water glowed from the
     reflection of the sun which was sinking like a crimson
ball behind Burray to the west. Phelp stood on the bridge
surveying the land and seascape through a pair of binoculars.
For the first time since their arrival at Scapa the wind had
dropped to what was no more than a gentle breeze that
scarcely rippled the surface of the water, and huge flights of
seabirds – guillemots, skuas, puffins and fulmars – were
heading for their clifftop colonies before darkness descended
with the abruptness of a curtain being lowered. He picked out
shags skimming low over the water with fast beating wings and
herring gulls wheeling and gliding with effortless ease, their
raucous mews sounding a non-stop lament. In the distance he
could see small fishing boats, so motionless they could have
been painted on the surface of the Flow, and less than a
hundred yards away the dark blob of a seal's head as it popped
up to survey the area with round, soulful eyes. It seemed
totally indifferent to the presence of the fishermen, as if aware
of the Orcadians' belief that the selkies should never be
harmed because they were drowned sailors who had returned
from their watery grave. There could be something in that
superstition, he thought, for he had read somewhere that they
often formed close attachments to the men who manned the
warships and always appeared when a ship returned from sea
as if guided by some form of telepathy.

    Phelp was enjoying the unexpected tranquillity. It was a
rare treat to be able to escape from the claustrophobic con-
fines of the wardroom without being buffeted and chapped by

the unremitting wind and spend a few moments alone wrapped in silent contemplation.

If only Scapa could be like this most of the time it would be an ideal place in which to be based, he thought. As a professional sailor he had the utmost respect for the elements, and although not a devoutly religious man, he never ceased to marvel at the way in which nature manipulated its awesome forces. A savage gale could within minutes be subdued and replaced by a zephyr, and the Old Grey Widow Maker could suddenly become as comforting as a mother. It was as if the Almighty was indulging in conjuring tricks and treating the deep, land-locked expanse of water as if it were a top hat.

Leading Wren Lesley Paton stood on the jetty and studied *Grey Seal* and lamented: 'Poor Crispin! He really must be down in the dumps. She's certainly nothing worth writing home about.'

Battered, ugly and ungainly the *Grey Seal* was a maritime mongrel that would be out of place among the names so proudly recorded in the family home. Her eyes were attracted by a sudden movement on the bridge and she looked up to see a young RNR lieutenant sweeping the Flow with his glasses. Cupping her hands over her mouth she called out, 'Permission to come aboard, sir.'

She saw him turn and savagely ram the glasses into the case suspended round his neck as if irritated at being disturbed.

When Phelp looked down he did not at first realize it was a woman on the jetty; the shiny, black ankle-length oilskin with up-turned collar almost obscured her face so that for an instant she resembled an ordinary sailor.

'What do you want?' he demanded brusquely.

'I was hoping to see Lieutenant Commander Paton.' The voice was rather low, almost husky, and he immediately recognized his error and modified his tone. 'I'm afraid he's ashore. Can I help?'

'Would it be possible to come aboard and wait? It's a heck of a cycle-ride for nothing otherwise.'

'I don't see why not.'

146

Phelp clambered down the ladder and returned the girl's smart salute as she stepped onto the deck. It was such a long time since he had spoken to a woman that he did not even bother to consider the impropriety of inviting a female rating into the wardroom.

As he led the way into the cabin he nodded towards a row of hooks in the small alcove outside which held an assortment of oilskins and other sea-going gear. 'Hang your coat up and take a seat. Not exactly three star, but you can get used to living in a cupboard very quickly.'

The girl sat down and removed her cap, patting her hair as if to make sure that there were no unruly strands which needed coaxing back into place. It was an involuntary movement, for her light brown hair was drawn tightly back over her head and plaited in a neat bun at the nape of her neck. It seemed to Phelp that she had gone out of her way to hide her femininity behind an unnecessarily severe hairstyle. Even so, there was no hiding her attractiveness, and Phelp, who had enjoyed many a romantic but casual encounter in ports throughout the world, could not recall a woman who had made such an immediate impact. She was, in naval parlance, 'a bit of all right', although that was not a phrase he would have used aloud in her presence. She possessed what he could only describe, for lack of more appropriate words, as poise. Not that she was beautiful in the classical sense, but she had a wide generous mouth, good bone structure, and big, warm brown eyes.

He became aware that she was conscious of his close scrutiny and said hastily, 'Drink?'

'Should I? I'm sure there's something in KR and AI about officers drinking with ratings?'

There was a total lack of concern in her voice which nullified her own query and encouraged him to sound recklessly defiant. 'Probably is. There seems to be a clause to cover just about everything, but I never read them. I just wait until my attention is drawn to them.'

'In that case I wouldn't say no to the tiniest of gins. I got

147

quite cold cycling here,' and as if to demonstrate that it was not just an excuse she gave an exaggerated shiver. 'Unlike the sailors we don't get a rum issue. Just lime juice. Hardly the drink for this place.'

The first lieutenant shook the merest drop of angostura into the glass, swilled it gently, added the gin, topped it up with water and took the opportunity of studying her more closely. She wore very little make-up, but maybe that had something to do with regulations. He wondered what her legs were like, for they were hidden by the table. It was fortunate the captain was ashore and the midshipman with him; given the time and once the ice was broken he would try and arrange a date ashore. Not that he rated his chances very high, for from what he had heard females were so scarce in Scapa that Wrens had the pick of the Fleet and they aimed their sights a little higher than RNR lieutenants.

'What do you want to see the captain about?' he enquired casually.

The girl smiled disarmingly and said, 'Nothing very important. A social call really.' Phelp experienced a sudden feeling of disappointment. He's got in first. When and how though, God only knows.

'Are you old friends?' he asked, trying hard not to sound particularly interested.

'We've known each other all our lives. Why do you ask?' she replied with a mischievous smile that made Phelp wonder why she was being so annoyingly vague.

'Sorry, I didn't mean to sound so inquisitive. Just making polite conversation,' he said rather gruffly. And feeling he had been rebuffed and told to mind his own business he began to indulge in small-talk which he detested in normal circumstances.

'What made you join the Wrens? I'd have thought you could have landed a soft number in some ministry or other, chauffering a VIP around instead of being stuck in this dump.'

'Oh, it's not so bad on a day like this. In any case, it never occurred to me to join anything else but the Senior Service.

148

Apart from that, I think blue suits me,' she said with a chuckle. 'I love these thick windproof stockings and the black-outs that go with them.'

'I didn't realize there were any Wrens on Hoy; I thought the Admiralty considered it too primitive.'

'There aren't many of us. A couple of dozen. We came over from Kirkwall a week ago. There'll be more following though when they've sorted out the accommodation problem.'

Before Phelp could question her further she deftly turned the conversation: 'Isn't it a trifle unusual for an RNR officer to be serving under a straight-ringer in such a small ship? I thought most of you skippers had your own commands.'

Phelp bridled; surely she wasn't one of those toffee-nosed people who had a thing about the shape of the rings on a man's sleeve. 'I'm not a fisherman. I was with a well-known shipping line,' he said sharply. 'We used tubs like this to carry our provisions. But to answer your question, it is rather unusual but *Grey Seal* is a group leader and I suppose that might have something to do with it. Frankly I don't concern myself with such side issues. We're all in the same war and the enemy doesn't manufacture special ammunition which singles out straight, wavy or square rings.'

Lesley said, 'Oops! I've touched you on a sore spot. But don't get cross, I agree with you. I'm H.O. too, remember, and don't agree with regulars treating us as some kind of second-class citizen. I think there are far too many fuddy-duddy RN men who think of fighting the war in terms of rugby. You know: the RN are Union and the others League. Not quite gentlemen.'

The first lieutenant chuckled loudly. 'I know what you mean, but it hardly supports my argument. I happen to be a Union man myself; yet I'm still on the wrong side of the tracks. If you wanted to make a sporting analogy I'd say it was more like cricket with its gentlemen and players. They just stop short though of having different doors for men doing the same job.'

'Does your captain see it that way?'

149

'I'm afraid he does. He's a superb officer and I've already learned to admire him tremendously, but he and I will never see eye to eye. He's Dartmouth and I'm Merchant Navy at heart, and he doesn't believe the twain can ever meet. Remember, it will still be his navy when this lot is over and the rest of us have to go back to earning a crust.'

'Maybe he'll learn to modify his views and not be so arrogant.'

'I honestly don't think that's the right word. He's been indoctrinated since boyhood into believing the navy way is the best and only way. He'd prefer we learn that.'

'You don't agree?'

'How could I? I can appreciate honest rivalry but not antagonism or worse, condescension. I have no time for a system that grades a man according to his accent or the way he pronounces his vowels.'

Again the teasing laugh echoed round the cabin. 'Surely you can't mean that! You're just being bilious. I once met an admiral who sounded like a caricature of Long John Silver.'

'Maybe I was overdoing it,' said Phelp grudgingly. 'It isn't really a question of background. There are some things that my practical training tells me are sheer nonsense.'

'Such as?'

'Well, a captain going down with his ship and all that kind of stuff. It seems crazy at a time when there is such an acute shortage of experienced officers. It would be far better to ignore the tradition and live to fight again in another ship.'

The girl shook her head in mock solemnity. 'My! You really don't understand the navy. You've got it all wrong. It's not mock heroics that make them remain on the bridge. It's the thought of a court of inquiry and all the papers they will have to fill in. The thought's so daunting that some of them regard it as a fate worse than death.'

Somehow he detected that she was pulling his leg. 'It's a waste of time trying to express a logical point of view to you.'

Again there was the rippling laugh with the merest hint that he was taking himself too seriously. 'I can assure you,

Lieutenant Commander Paton won't disappear beneath the waves saluting the ensign. When you get to know him a little better, you'll discover he is not all that hidebound.'

Opportunity would be a fine thing, he thought.

Lesley studied the man opposite without making it blatantly obvious. He was a big man who moved easily, with strong capable hands, steady eyes and craggy features which looked as if they had been tempered by hot suns and chill winds. What the other Wrens in the dormitory after lights out would describe as good-looking, handsome or more tritely, smashing. Although she came from a naval family in which the Service was the overriding factor and topic, she had escaped its tentacles when she had gone to work in the City office of a multinational concern where results counted far more than pedigree. Some of this had rubbed off on her and she found she could sympathize with the young lieutenant who wore a chip on his shoulder like an epaulette. As the war progressed men like her brother and Phelp would have to learn to compromise. She was confident they would. The real danger lay with the older officers: men like Captain Monsey, under whom she worked, who would break rather than bend.

But she had no time to express her views; there was a loud rap on the door as the quartermaster announced, 'Captain heading back aboard, sir.'

Phelp rose, put on his cap and said with more than a tinge of envy, 'It'll be fun just seeing his face when I tell him you're aboard. What name shall I give?'

'Wren Paton, sir.'

Phelp could have kicked himself. Something had niggled vaguely and tantalizingly at the back of his mind while they had been talking. Now it slotted into place: the photograph of the girl in Paton's cabin. Was she his wife? He couldn't remember noticing a wedding ring. It was the hair which had fooled him. The girl with the cat did not have the same severe style; she had obviously adopted it when she enlisted. He felt himself flush at the thought of what she might tell Paton when they were alone.

151

Phelp went to the gangway, exchanged salutes and said, 'You have a visitor, sir. A Wren.' He deliberately omitted to give him her name because he wanted to be present at the encounter. 'I've put her in the wardroom, sir. Thought it was a little more spacious than your cabin.'

'Thanks, Number One. That'll brighten my day after another encounter with Captain Monsey.'

When Paton opened the door he paused on seeing the girl who had hastily put on her cap and was giving him an exaggeratedly smart salute.

'Lesley! Why the devil didn't you warn me? And you can cut out the leg pulling. In any case, you don't salute an officer when he's bareheaded.'

Phelp witnessed it with a grim unsmiling face, but when they embraced and kissed each other on the cheek he had some consolation in noticing that the greeting was affectionate more than passionate.

'I suppose my sister has introduced herself, Number One?'

'As a matter of fact, sir, she hasn't.' To his annoyance, Phelp found himself grinning.

Paton grimaced in mock indignation. 'Typical of her. I expect she wanted to hear your opinion of me without any softsoap. Right Lesley?'

Once again the small cabin echoed to her laughter. 'Right. And it lived up to my expectations. Now make what you can of that.'

Paton said, 'Lesley, meet Brian Phelp my right arm. I don't tell him that too often. Naturally. Now why don't we just pull the door to and have a noggin', Brian.'

The first lieutenant realized that it was the only time he could recall him using his first name. He looked guiltily at the two empty glasses and said, 'I'm afraid I took the liberty of inviting your sister to have one while she was waiting, sir. But I honestly thought she was your wife.'

'Spare me that,' said the captain, holding up his hands in mock horror. 'She'd be telling me how to run my ship. Lesley, I regret to say, is an emancipated female. A condition not to be encouraged in wives of naval officers.' It was said in such a bantering tone that Phelp was left in no doubt that they were extremely close to each other.

'He was a bit worried that you'd keelhaul him for breaking KR and AI, Crispin.'

'I would have if he hadn't.'

Phelp said, 'Wouldn't you prefer to go to your own quarters, sir? I'm sure you've a lot to talk about without me being present.'

'No, please stay,' she urged. 'Once I start gossiping there's no stopping me and Crispin will soon get chocker with that.'

Phelp could barely suppress a smile; it was surprising how quickly she had fallen into the habit of using naval words.

Paton went to the door, summoned the quartermaster and told him to tell Midshipman Carnac he was wanted at the double.

'I want Lesley to meet him. Then I'll show her round the ship and introduce her to the men.' He winked broadly at his first lieutenant. 'Who knows, she may be able to use her persuasive influence in the Wrennery and line up a few dates for the lads.'

They spent an enjoyable hour together with Steward Hall, immaculate in a white coat, fussing over them as if they were in a West End bar. After being shown round the ship, Lesley joined her brother for a private 'natter', then indicated that it *really* was time for her to go. 'We have a regulating officer who checks us in and out like pawnbrokers' parcels. One minute adrift and she's screaming rape.'

Phelp helped her into her oilskin, borrowed the quartermaster's torch and walked ahead of her, carefully shining the hooded beam on each individual strut on the gangway.

'I'm very flattered, but I don't really need my hand held,' she said with a light teasing laugh. 'I really *can* find my own way.'

When they reached the jetty and Phelp had located her cycle resting against a bollard, he said, 'It would be a bit of a lift up for the lads if you could persuade some of your friends to meet them. We could even lay on some big eats aboard.'

'That shouldn't be too difficult. Although I ought to warn you they get inundated with invitations. You might have to wait your turn in the queue.'

'The anticipation will only serve to increase the pleasure.'

'And what about the officers? Don't tell me you're all mysogynists?'

'Far from it, but the welfare of the men comes first.' His teeth gleamed in the dark and she knew he was not being stupidly pompous. 'If I thought for a moment I wouldn't be wasting my time I'd suggest meeting you. It would save joining the queue.'

'I'll give it a thought,' she said as she checked the visored rear and front lights. It was a sturdy, cumbersome ladies machine, a relic of bygone days, with no crossbar, a metal shield covering the chain and a fan shaped pattern of strings radiating from the hub of the Sturmey Archer gear to the rim of the back mudguard, to prevent the hem of a skirt becoming entangled in the spokes.

'If you're free next Sunday pick me up. Make it early, the days are so short,' she said.

She made it all sound so matter-of-fact that Phelp could hardly believe his good fortune. 'I'll be there,' he replied enthusiastically.

He watched the red rear light veer from side to side as the cycle gained momentum; then it steadied and gradually disappeared from view.

Although he never seemed to have a spare minute, time passed incredibly slowly for 'Jimmy the One' of *Grey Seal*. When the repairs were completed the ship had to put to sea to make sure everything was working efficiently and there were regular exercises and shoots to enable the Oerlikon gunners and loaders to get accustomed to their new weapons. In addition, the new members of the ship's company had to be wet-nursed until they fitted in with the rest of the men.

As Sunday approached, Phelp asked his captain if it would

be possible to have the day off. He did not volunteer the reason and he was grateful that Paton did not ask; instead he simply agreed that he deserved a break.

After a snatched breakfast he set off along the metalled road wearing a white rollneck sweater, thick serge trousers and a windproof golf jacket. Resting snugly in his hip pocket was a flask of whisky. His impatience made the journey seem interminably long and he was thankful when the driver of a passing army lorry halted for the thumb that was jerked, more in hope than anything else, in the direction of Lyness. As Phelp climbed into the driving cabin he said, 'Thanks a lot. I'm in a heck of a hurry.' The lance-corporal did not take his eyes off the road. 'Can't imagine anything in this dump worth hurrying for,' he said sourly.

The soldier dropped him at the main gates leading to a cluster of Nissen huts containing the Wrennery. 'I can see the reason for your hurry, mate. Some buggers have all the luck.' He winked. 'Don't do anything I wouldn't do. Still, you won't need any more scope than that.'

Lesley was already walking down the path and waving. She was wearing bellbottom trousers, a reefer jacket over an Orkney genzel, and a woollen hat. A haversack was slung over one shoulder. 'Special dispensation being allowed ashore like this. Against all rules not to be in uniform. But I spun a cock and bull story about being a keen ornithologist.' She led him towards a hut surrounded by whitewashed stones.

'You'll have to sign for me at the regulating office,' she said cheerfully. 'Just like a registered parcel.'

When that had been completed and Phelp warned by a severe looking matronly petty officer that he was responsible for seeing that his charge was returned on time, Lesley took his elbow and said, 'I've got a nice surprise in store for you.'

She walked him to an asbestos-roofed cycle shed and pointed to a battered looking machine. 'I hired that from a messmate for a bar of Palmolive. You can't imagine what a sacrifice it was. If you can cope without a crossbar we'll ride across the island.'

He fell off twice much to her amusement, but remounted each time with all the grim determination of a rodeo cowboy who had been tossed from a bucking bronco. 'I haven't done this since I was a kid,' he grunted, 'but they say you never forget. I'm beginning to doubt the wisdom of that observation,' he added ruefully as he dusted himself down.

They set off with much bell ringing and exaggerated hand-signals along the narrow, flint coast road towards the northern tip of the island and the impressive bulk of Ward Hill, the highest point on the rugged island. Gutta Sound was so placid the V-shaped wake of the eider ducks was clearly visible. The treeless landscape was dotted with grazing cattle and the occasional rambling stone-built houses of the crofters. Some came to their doors and waved at the strangely attired young couple who were blatantly defying the long established customs of the Sabbath; a day in which little was done except those tasks which could not be neglected, such as the feeding of animals and milking of cows.

At Pegal Hill a circular patch of lush emerald grass six feet across reminded them of the rigidly held views of the islanders. Buried beneath the grass in unconsecrated ground were the remains of Betty Corrigal, an unmarried mother who had died in childbirth. It was the price demanded in a society where if one whistled on the Sabbath it had to be a hymn. They paused for a brief rest at the Dwarfie Stone and leaned their cycles beside the sandstone tomb while they ventured inside to explore the Neolithic burial chamber. They felt like children who had been let out from school early.

At Radwick they left their cycles at the small post office and journeyed on foot along the cliff top to where the Old Man of Hoy towered 450 feet above the sea like a giant sentinel. They ate their sandwiches and hard boiled eggs beneath its wind-sheltering bulk and poured the contents of the hip flask into the thermos of scalding tea. Then they lay quietly on their backs, gazing up at the wheeling birds and listening to their mournful calls. Their silence more eloquent than any words.

Phelp stretched out with his hands resting behind his head

wondering what Lesley would say, or do, if he moved towards her and did something that would quite clearly indicate that the outing could not remain on a purely platonic level, but he feared rejection and the quite understandable reminder that they hardly knew each other.

There was a slight movement and he turned and saw Lesley resting on her elbows and gazing intently at him. 'A penny for them.'

'You could have them for nothing, but I'm scared of sounding half-baked,' he said.

'Let me guess,' she replied. 'You're wondering if there's such a thing as love at first sight or if it's just the war. And if emotional attachments are formed in a desperate hurry because every day seems so precious because it could be the last. Does that sound half-baked?'

'Not when you say it. It does when I think it.'

She suddenly turned her head and gazed out at the rolling expanse of the Atlantic. 'It's hard to believe there are men out there drowning. There might even be some who are dying with unanswered questions in their minds and bitterly regretting they lacked the courage to put them.'

'Perhaps they couldn't face the possibility of getting the wrong reply.'

'But how much nicer to have got the right one,' she said. She moved towards him until her breasts were resting on his chest and Phelp could feel their soft resilience beneath the heavy jacket. He drew her head towards his and as they kissed he slipped his hands beneath the jacket and cupped her breasts in his hands. 'I'm hardly dressed for this kind of thing,' she said with a soft laugh. 'Anyway, let's not rush it.'

To his own amazement her reply delighted him. They lay together happily, content just to talk and plan a trip to the small cathedral city of Kirkwall as soon as an opportunity arose.

Time did not stand still for them, it raced by and they realized they would have to set off on the return journey. As they passed one of the farmhouses a small boy in his Sunday best came running towards them. He halted in front of them more breathless from excitement than exertion and blurted out in his lilting brogue, 'My Dad and Mum asked if you'd like tea.' Then he scampered off without waiting for them to reply.

They walked towards the squat, stone-built 'but and ben' through a gaggle of honking geese and a woman emerged from the doorway, smiled and beckoned them inside. The low-beamed room with whitewashed walls was filled with the rich odour of a peat fire and an oil lamp burned dimly from one of the rafters. The spinning wheel stood idle in the ingle; the one day in the week when it was not in use. A row of cuithes and sillocks were drying above the fire. The man of the house rose from his straw-backed chair and gestured towards the table. 'We're always happy to see fresh faces.'

It was a typical crofter's home, spotless and comfortable but primitive. A large, wooden ale kirn stood near the fire and there were home-cured hams and sides of bacon hanging from the beams. The woman carefully laid out plates and knives and forks and poured tea from an enormous pot. Then she started a seemingly endless to-ing and fro-ing from the stove until the table was covered with piping hot bannocks and mealie puddings.

She watched with evident pleasure as they tucked into the food which was such an enjoyable change from the monotonous Service fare and it took Lesley and Phelp some time to convince her that they really had eaten their fill.

As they relaxed round the fire the crofter asked them about England and Scotland, which he had never visited, and his wife sat quietly in her canopied straw chair more than content to just sit and listen whilst her husband and child revelled in the rare pleasure of having strangers to talk to. The father and son sat wide-eyed as they heard about things they had only seen in picture books: steam locomotives, buses, underground trains and majestic buildings. They were extremely reluctant to let their guests depart, and it was almost dark when they reached the Wrennery. The regulating officer made no attempt to hide her displeasure: Scapa Flow was no place for a young girl to be roaming around in the dark with a man – even if he was an officer.

As Phelp made his way back to *Grey Seal* he considered whether or not he should tell Paton that he had spent the day with his sister. He decided against it, telling himself that it was a personal matter. But he knew that he had made the decision for a totally different reason: he feared that Paton might raise objections.

When he got back aboard he found the captain sitting with the midshipman playing a quiet game of chess.

Carnac said, 'Can I get you a drink, Number One? I thought it was daft me sitting all alone in here and the captain on his own in his cabin so I invited him down.'

'I'm glad of that,' said Phelp. 'It's always struck me as being a bit silly us living a separate existence in a ship this size.'

'If you're both agreeable we could make it a permanent arrangement,' said Paton.

To his great relief Paton did not question him about his trip ashore; he simply confined his interest to asking him if he had enjoyed it. And this Phelp was able to answer honestly and enthusiastically.

The next morning *Grey Seal* and the rest of the group were ordered on the Northern Patrol.

7 The Northern Patrol! Nothing could describe the sheer horror the words conjured up in the minds of the men in *Grey Seal*. They had tackled the gruelling patrol that ran between the Faroes and Iceland a number of times now and there seemed no respite. Paton could not be sure of the exact number – four or five. It was hard to recall. The monotonous soul-eroding routine never seemed to vary. They slipped and sailed through Hoy Sound and headed at full speed for the Atlantic and the most detested spell of duty in the navy with only one thought in mind: to get back in one piece. And the more trips they did the worse the conditions seemed to become. When they felt they had taken and survived all the Atlantic could throw at them the mighty ocean produced something fresh, as if to show there was no limit to its might. They felt they had become totally isolated from life for when they returned to Scapa they wanted to do nothing but sleep. By the time they had recovered a collier was alongside and they were off to sea again.

Only Phelp made the effort to go ashore. He had an incentive. But his meetings with Lesley were all too brief and fleeting. Even so, they were long enough for them to know they were in love.

Paton stood on the bridge and surveyed the heaving grey-green mass where the horizon was barely distinguishable from the sea. It was their fourth day out and he had never experienced weather like it. One minute the bows seemed to be pointing heavenwards, the next they seemed to be diving almost vertically like a pelican plunging for food. The whole ship juddered from stem to stern as the bows crashed down with a force that jarred from toe to head. Tons of icy water cascaded over the fo'c'sle, sending up great torrents of bubbled spray that swamped the open bridge.

Even with lifelines rigged fore and aft it was a precarious business moving from one part of ship to another. Men hurrying to their action stations suddenly felt the monkey's fist they were grasping so tenaciously torn from their hands, as an angry wave lifted their feet clear of the deck and tossed them into the overflowing scuppers. The freezing spume stung like a million needles and no matter how much clothing they wore the cold always managed to get through. And there was always the risk of being swept overboard with no possible hope of rescue. The ship would not turn back and search: it was a waste of time. The estimated time of survival in the icy water was only three minutes.

Paton's jaws were aching from the cold and, although he was wearing thick stockings of oiled wool inside his sea-boots, he had no feeling at all in his feet. The hood of his duffle coat was pulled over his head and he had wedged himself tightly into a corner of the bridge, which he had discovered was the only way to remain upright. He felt an immense pride in his men, who put up with the unremitting hardships with such good-humoured tolerance and resignation. The mess decks were constantly awash with water that ebbed and flowed with the movement of the ship so that at times it was often three feet deep at one end. The bulkheads dripped with condensation, the deadlights were always screwed down and the air was foul with the fetid smell of unwashed bodies. As the hands were working four on and four off, there was always someone sleeping while others were eating. Wooden fiddles were fitted to the tabletops to keep plates in position but they were of little use in counteracting the violent movement of the ship. Plates and bowls containing an unappetizing mixture of tram smash – the navy slang for tinned tomatoes – soya links, rice pudding, dehydrated potatoes and fruit salad – there was never enough time to serve separate helpings – were lifted bodily to shower their contents on the men sitting on either side of the long benches. Knives, forks and spoons clattered

161

noisily onto the deck as men slid along the benches, as if the seats of their trousers had been greased. Men slept fully clothed in a motley assortment of gear; putting on a sea-boot stocking could take an interminable ten minutes. It just wasn't worth the effort.

But worse of all was the unadulterated boredom. Day after day, night after night, the ships steamed slowly at seven knots along clearly defined patrol lines searching for neutral vessels which might be carrying contraband. They also had to keep a look-out for enemy surface raiders and report their presence to shore, as well as seek out the U-boats which were claiming a mounting toll of merchantmen. Sometimes they caught sight of a homeward bound convoy with decks lined with enormous crates containing much-needed aircraft. But more often than not, whole patrols passed without another ship being sighted.

But they invariably returned to base with some harsh and grim reminders that the savage area they often patrolled so diligently but uneventfully was also the graveyard of countless brave men: a drifting lifeboat with a frozen corpse still clutching the tiller, an airman in a rubber dinghy. They hauled in lifebuoys with ship's names on them, planking, spars and Carley rafts containing packs of untouched emergency rations and kegs of fresh water. All scrupulously salvaged, often at great personal risk, for possible identification later.

The Northern Patrol had at first been carried out by armed merchant cruisers, but these were being gradually withdrawn as they were incurring such tremendous losses. Cruisers had also been used in the initial stages, but these were now more urgently needed elsewhere. Destroyers lacked the endurance to remain at sea long enough and so the task was gradually being handed over to the tough, coal-burning trawlers which could stay at sea for three weeks if necessary. And, unlike the big ships, they were expendable. A stark reality when the losses were totted up. Some were sunk by gunfire, some hit by floating mines, others were torpedoed or simply vanished from the surface of the sea; dragged to the bottom by the weight of the black ice which had formed on the rigging and upper deck.

And if they did spot any surface raiders slipping out to plunder the convoy lanes they were expected to send an urgent signal, then turn towards the enemy and certain oblivion.

It was the nautical equivalent of a bayonet charge against tanks. To make matters worse, the twelve-pounder was often little more than an ornament. Salt water crystallized on the sights making accurate laying almost impossible and an improvised heater was placed under the breech block to prevent it freezing solid.

Steward Hall clambered up the bridge ladder with the skill of an Alpine goat, one hand clutching the guard-rail, the other balancing an enamel mug of hot cocoa. 'Thought you'd like some ki, sir. Just brewed.' He cut an incongruous figure with his cap secured by its chin strap over a balaclava. Surveying the angry sea he enquired, 'We didn't turn turtle last night, did we, sir?'

Paton looked at him, but the face was solemn and unsmiling. 'Not that I'm aware of, Hall. Why?'

'When I woke up after getting my head down for a spell my hammock lashings were all twisted.' Whereupon he burst out into a roar of uninhibited laughter which Paton could not help joining.

It was astonishing how men could retain their sense of humour and laugh at the appalling conditions. 'It was rough, but not that rough. You must have turned over too sharply.' Such moments of informality and leg-pulling were rare and therefore much more precious, for although very little might be happening the patrol was a tremendous strain, demanding perpetual vigilance. They were always in a near trance-like state of total exhaustion and fatigue which made clear decision-making extremely difficult. The simplest of tasks demanded abnormal concentration when fingers were frozen stiff. A single lapse and the skin could be stripped off the hand if one inadvertently touched bare metal.

But much as the men suffered it was far harder for the captain who was rarely able to leave the bridge.

'The weather may be foul, Hall, but it has its consolations. If it's bad for us it's the same for Jerry and he can't do an awful lot of damage in these conditions. Even the U-boats will have to keep well down, thank God.'

The words were no sooner uttered than a deafening explosion echoed across the sea and a giant column of white foam erupted on their port side, so high it dwarfed the waves. There was an orange glow in the heart of the mushroom-shaped explosion which was rapidly turning black. It rose high in the air until it resembled a storm-cloud. Then it began to rain lumps of coal and dust. The port lookout screamed, 'I think it's *Otter* that's copped it.'

Paton's right hand reached as if by instinct for the glasses dangling round his neck, while his left hand jammed down hard on the alarm bells. He moved swiftly across the bridge and bellowed down the voicepipe, 'Hard a port. Full ahead.' Lifting the cover of the engine room whistle pipe he summoned Reynolds. 'Give me maximum revs, Chief. I think *Otter*'s in trouble.' The lumps of coal thumping down on *Grey Seal*'s deck indicated the ferocity of the explosion by the distance they had been hurled.

As the clamour of bells echoed through the mess decks men abandoned half-eaten meals, grabbed their oilskins and steel helmets and raced for the ladders leading to the upper deck. Men swung from their hammocks and rolled off bunks in the mad scramble to get topsides and find out what was happening.

The towering column of coal-clogged water had subsided as quickly as it had erupted and Paton called anxiously to the lookouts. 'Tell me as soon as you see anything.'

A breathless Phelp arrived on the bridge, followed immediately by Midshipman Carnac. The blinding spray which lashed into their faces as the ship turned sharply towards the explosion made observation extremely difficult.

'Ease to ten,' called Paton.

'Ten of port wheel on, sir.'

The swinging ship's head began to slow down as the helm was eased. 'Midships.'

From the wheelhouse Tiger Read called back. 'Midships, sir. Coxswain on the wheel, sir.'

Read needed all his strength to handle the wheel and keep the ship on a steady course in the heaving sea. He patted his chest to make certain that his pension book, carefully sewn inside an oilskin pouch and tied round his neck with a piece of strong tape, was still there. It was all he had to offer his missus if anything happened to him. Next to the engine room, the wheelhouse was the worst possible place to be when there was a spot of action. It was as tightly sealed as a tin of pussers' herrings. One could only hear noises and imagine what they indicated. And the imagination always made them more terrifying.

Paton shouted to make himself heard above the pounding of the engine and the howling of the wind. 'I've no idea what's happened, Number One. Get some hands midships ready to lower the scrambling nets and release the Carley floats.' He turned to Carnac, 'Have the boats' crews standing by. We might need everything that's capable of floating.'

The explosion had also been spotted by one of the escorts, for it violently altered course and headed in the same direction as *Grey Seal*. As it topped the peak of a green mountain an Aldis blinked from her bridge. Signalman White called out, 'Message from *Beaver*, sir. "Am seeking survivors".'

'Acknowledge and say "good luck",' snapped Paton.

The sodden men stood in the waist of the ship clinging to any available piece of equipment which would prevent them being washed overboard: davits, hawsers, gun rails, guard-rails. They kept throwing anxious glances at the bridge in the hope that some encouraging news would be relayed to them, but neither Paton nor the lookouts could see a thing.

Rhind volunteered to climb up to the crow's nest in order to get a better view, and Paton reluctantly gave his permission.

The Canadian had proved on more than one occasion that he possessed phenomenal eyesight which enabled him to spot objects long before men armed with powerful binoculars. Paton watched anxiously as he climbed up to the barrel-shaped eyrie and lashed himself to the mast; a black shape in glistening oilskins.

In the engine room, Chief Reynolds was trying to coax more revolutions out of the straining engine and urging it on with quiet words of encouragement as if the pipes, valves and thrusting pistons were capable of responding to his exhortations. 'Come on you dozy old cow. You can do better than this. Get your skirts up. Imagine you're bein' chased by a randy matelot.'

Nearby, the stokers worked in a demented frenzy as if they were firing the furnaces of hell.

Reynolds watched approvingly. 'Burst the old girl's bloomers at the seams, lad. Captain Monsey will do his nut, but we might get a spot of refit leave out of it.'

'Masthead lookout, sir. Object dead ahead.'

Everyone's head turned in the direction of the crow's nest where Rhind stood with one hand shielding his eyes.

Paton called down for 'Slow Ahead' and scanned the sea for a glimpse of the object Rhind had sighted. Whatever it was, it was too small to be a ship. Then he picked it up. It was either a wooden door or a hatch-cover with two spread-eagled men clinging to it as it slid up and down the surface of the waves like a toboggan.

Paton realized that the slightest miscalculation could end up with the small object being smashed to smithereens and the two men pulped to a bloody sponge. He was grateful to have someone like Read on the wheel; he was as dexterous as a rally driver.

Paton manoeuvred the ship until it was abeam the drifting makeshift raft watching the waves which were sweeping them towards the men waiting amidships with boathooks and heaving lines with mounting anxiety. One seaman carried the line-throwing Lee Enfield, but it was not needed. Paton's superb ship-handling had put the floating men within reach of the heaving lines.

As the cork-buoyed scrambling nets were tumbled over the side, Phelp shouted, 'Let go the heaving lines, and for God's sake don't miss.'

The monkey's fists, coated with red lead and with a heavy iron nut in the centre to give them added weight, shot out across the stretch of water which had narrowed to less than twenty yards. Most fell well short but two of them straddled the floating object which everyone could now recognize as a door. 'Grab hold and hang on. We'll haul you inboard,' yelled Phelp.

One of the men seized a heaving line and, although pounded and frequently submerged, managed to tie it round his chest. 'Heave away,' bellowed the first lieutenant, and the man was hauled through the water like a human torpedo. The other man, petrified with fear, refused to let go of the door which, to his tormented mind, offered greater safety than the line lying a few inches away. Voices screamed out angrily, urging him to grab the rope and assuring him that everything would be all right.

By the time they had hauled the rescued man inboard the door had drifted to within ten yards of the almost motionless ship but there, for some inexplicable reason, it remained as if anchored. They could quite clearly see the look of abject fear on the face of the young man on the door who stubbornly shook his head when they urged him to take hold of the heaving line. In exasperation Morris clambered down the scrambling net, one hand grasping it, the other extended towards the door. As the water drenched him he realized that unless the sailor acted immediately it would be too late. The cold was so intense he would not be able to cling on to the door much longer.

Watching from the bridge Paton realized that it was impossible to lower the whaler; it would be smashed to pieces against the hull. Then to his utter dismay he saw Morris tie a line around his waist and plunge into the turbulent sea and strike out towards the door.

Phelp bellowed, 'You daft bugger. If he wants to stay there and drown, let him.'

Morris felt the cold seize him in a vice-like hold that sent a bolt of pain through his chest as he hit the water. He opened his eyes but could see nothing. He struck out blindly in what he hoped was the direction of the door. Then he received a fearful blow on the head which forced him to swallow a mouthful of water and he realized he had come up under the door. For a moment he was consumed with total panic, then he reached up and clawed his way to the edge of the door and lifted his body until half of his torso was on the wood.

'Get off, get off,' screamed the sodden man. 'There's not room for two.'

Morris edged his way towards the petrified man and held out his hand, 'Grab hold, before it's too bloody late.' The effort of speaking was almost too much for him. The sailor slowly released one hand and grabbed hold of Morris's. 'Now the other.'

The sailor said, 'I can't. I don't want to drown.'

The man clung ferociously to Morris with one hand but retained a clamp-like grip on the door with the other.

Phelp watched the drama with mounting fear. 'Haul them inboard. There's no point in losing one of our own chaps as well. If he hangs on to Morris all very well, if he doesn't there isn't anything else we can do.'

The sailors in the waist of the ship began to haul away and Morris felt himself sliding off the door. At the same time he felt the grip of the man who was holding his hand slowly relax until he slipped completely from his grasp. He heard the sailor scream, 'Mum. Mum. Help me.' Then there was silence.

Morris felt himself dragged at what seemed a tremendous speed through the water and his head struck the hull with a thump that literally made him see flashes of light. When he was hauled inboard he felt as if his lungs had burst, although there was no feeling in the rest of his body. He could *hear* his teeth chattering but that was all. He glanced over the side and saw the door floating away empty.

Phelp shouted, 'Wrap him in a blanket and get him below. Give him and the survivor a tot and something hot to drink.'

Rhind almost lifted his friend off his feet in his anxiety to get him to the relative warmth of the mess deck. 'For a guy who's determined to get through this lot with his skin intact, you're going about it in a very odd way,' he muttered in a voice that could not conceal his admiration.

Paton stood gazing at the drifting door, then called for 'Full Ahead' and the men on the upper deck stood by in the hope of finding more survivors.

They searched for two hours, but there was no sign of *Otter*. Apart from some floating balks of timber and deck planking she might never have existed. *Beaver* signalled that had she recovered two bodies and Paton advised her to abandon the search: there was no possible hope of finding anyone alive. It was then that three dark shapes were seen floating face-down in the water, kept afloat by their lifebelts. The bodies were recovered and laid out on the deck in the shelter of the cable locker and covered with blankets.

As Paton signalled to the group to resume the patrol, he reflected on the small item of news that might or might not be broadcast on the BBC: The Admiralty regrets to announce the loss of His Majesty's trawler *Otter*.

That would be all, for no one knew what had sent her to the bottom: a U-boat, a floating mine, or even an internal explosion.

Phelp went down into the mess deck to speak to the sole survivor and to see that Morris was all right. Both men were sitting at one of the tables, wrapped in blankets and wearing an assortment of clothing provided by a hasty whip-round by members of the ship's company. Grasped in their cupped hands were steaming cups of ki which gave off an aroma of rum. Jolson was sitting on his haunches at Morris's feet and repeatedly putting up a paw and scratching his knee, as if trying to explain in dumb language how happy he was that his master was still alive.

The survivor said, 'Thanks a lot, sir. I really thought I'd had it.' He turned his head towards Morris. 'He told me the lad didn't make it. Poor little beggar. It was his eighteenth birthday. Not much of a present, was it?'

'When you feel up to it, the captain would like to speak to you. There's three of your lads who will have to be identified.'

The rescued man nodded. It was a task he did not relish, but it was one that could not be avoided. He could help Paton with that, but he would not be able to say anything helpful about the sinking. He had been on the bridge counting the minutes until he was relieved when the ship had literally disintegrated. He could only vaguely recall struggling to the surface to find himself clinging to the door, then being struck by a lump of coal and thinking indignantly: What a way to go! Stoned to death!

The first lieutenant put a hand on Morris's shoulder. 'That was a bloody silly thing to do, Morris.'

'I know, sir. I'd changed my mind as soon as I hit the oggin, but it was too late. Bit like jumping out of a window.'

Phelp smiled and removed his hand. 'Still, it was a very plucky thing. We're all proud of you. We'll make a pusser sailor of you yet.'

As he climbed up the ladder he thought: You're beginning to talk like the captain. You patronizing so and so.

When daylight came a watery sun was trying to break through the clouds and the sea was moving gently, like the breast of a sleeping giant exhausted by the exertions of a bitter battle and gathering strength before renewing the onslaught. The wind no longer howled through the rigging and the smoke from the single stack was only being carried astern by the speed of the ship. The monotonous ping of the Asdic could be heard on the bridge like an audible pulse beat.

The first lieutenant glanced to port and starboard; *Beaver* and *Vole* were clearly visible. It was the first time since they had left Scapa that such a happy situation had existed. He deliberately ignored the absence of *Otter*. It was no good

170

dwelling on it, nothing could bring her or her ship's company back.

Paton appeared on the bridge with nothing over his uniform. The customary white jersey had been replaced by a collar and tie, and he carried a prayer book. 'Provided we don't see or hear anything suspicious, Number One, we'll hold a short burial service. The coxswain is attending to the bodies right now. We'd better muster as many hands as we can spare. It's the least we can do.'

He walked for'ard towards the cable locker where Read, Rhind and two other seamen were busy with palms and needles sewing the dead men into their canvas shrouds. They had all been fortified with an extra tot before starting on their gruesome task. The three bodies lay stiff and almost peaceful-looking; they bore no facial injuries and no one had bothered to look for any bodily damage. There was no point. What personal belongings they had been carrying when they died had been carefully removed and placed inside thick envelopes along with the brown identity tags hanging round their necks. Two fire bars from the boiler room had been placed at their feet to make sure they sank quickly.

As the first corpse was sewn up one of the seamen asked, 'Shouldn't you put the last stitch through the bottom of the nose, Cox? I heard they always did that to make sure they're dead.'

Tiger Read paused and snapped angrily, 'That's an old superstition, lad. These men are all past making any protest. Now let's get on with it. It's bad luck to have dead men aboard.'

The bodies were carried midships where everyone who could be spared stood in silence on either side of the three planks which had been laid out on the deck. Paton removed his cap and nodded to the first lieutenant on the bridge. The clang of the engine room telegraph was heard as the order to 'Stop Engine' was rung down. Read barked 'Off caps,' and the men stood bareheaded as the captain began to hurry through the burial service. The planks were lifted onto the gunwale and tilted. As the bodies splashed into the water and disappeared beneath the surface, Paton replaced his cap and saluted.

Read barked, 'Hands dismissed. Right lads, there's work to be done.'

The weather remained reasonably fine as the small force steamed on day and night until the dark foreboding shape of Iceland appeared ahead.

Only then did Paton order the group to turn and retrace the course they had laboriously followed for so long.

Every man aboard passed his brief off-duty spells in a different way. Rhind carved more totem poles and Morris spent his time teaching Jolson all kinds of new tricks. Some read, others wrote letters. For Stoker Cohen it became a labour of another man's love. Danvers pestered him non-stop and tempted him with bribes of a tot or a bar of nutty to write, 'Just one more' to the girl who was no more than a name and a photograph to him. Danvers was deaf to his warnings that one day he might not be around to act as his ruddy secretary: he might get drafted, promoted, or shoved in jankers. Anything. Then what would he do? But Danvers brushed aside all objections.

Phelp carefully plotted the progress of the ship, for each nautical mile they steamed carried him nearer to Lesley and the ever-present contemplation of the long-delayed visit to Kirkwall. Surely a spot of shore leave would be granted? *Grey Seal* was in desperate need of a boiler clean and that would take at least four or five days. Even Captain Monsey would have to recognize that you could drive men and ships too hard. Something would crack otherwise.

Midshipman Carnac thought continuously of the explosion that had sent *Otter* to the bottom. He was worried sick at the thought that *Grey Seal* might go down as quickly and unexpectedly and he would die without ever having had a woman. His horizon was bounded by the fear that he would die, what the men disparagingly referred to, as 'a cock virgin'.

Paton dwelt on the ship and the men in his care. If, when he

172

lay with his eyes open on his bunk, the face of Cecily Grey appeared he shut it from his mind. It had been a wonderful brief encounter that would not be renewed, and he ought to face up to it.

When they had been at sea for eighteen days and nights, Paton gave the order 'Full Ahead', and as *Grey Seal* surged forward as if released from restraining bonds men in every part of ship let out a loud spontaneous cheer. The signal indicated that they were heading for home. Home wasn't much in anybody's language, but at least it was preferable to the cold inhospitable Atlantic. It meant a hot bath, a shave, a change into clean dry clothing, big eats, and a good sleep. But even more important – mail: the one link with the outside world and a reminder of why and what they were doing out there on the vast rolling expanse of ever-changing sea.

8 The dark, sullen mass of Ward Hill standing 1,565 feet above the sea was the first reported landfall, and soon afterwards the Old Man of Hoy became visible. Further northwards, the memorial column on top of Marwick Head, erected by local people to mark the nearby spot where Kitchener went down with HMS *Hampshire* appeared. Phelp took a cocked hat fix on the three landmarks and carefully plotted the ship's position on the chart. It was merely a routine piece of navigation for even the thickest seaman who could not distinguish latitude from longitude knew exactly where they were by then. Nevertheless, the information was meticulously recorded in the log book. He then ordered a slight alteration of course which put the ship's head in the direction of Hoy Sound and the run in to Scapa. The senior boom defence vessel flashed a challenge signal and when Chalkie White had responded and identified the trawlers Phelp sent down for the captain.

When Paton arrived on the bridge to take over the ship for entering harbour he noticed that more changes had taken place since their comparatively short absence at sea. Soon after the outbreak of war Winston Churchill, the new First Lord, had hastened to Scapa to re-acquaint himself with the Fleet and address an audience of officers and seamen from a capstan on the quarterdeck of *Iron Duke*. Something he had done twenty-five years earlier. He had again hurried back to Scapa following the sinking of the *Royal Oak* to confer with Admiral Forbes and work out an emergency plan to strengthen the defences. In accordance with Winston Churchill's orders, more anti-aircraft sights were now visible all round: near Stromness, Graemsay and on Hoy.

174

Every return to base heralded subtle changes. More block ships had been sunk, more torpedo nets erected, more patrol craft scouted for the enemy. Batteries of powerful searchlights were mounted to sweep the surface of the water for nighttime invaders. And work had already started on what was to become known as the Churchill Barrier – thousands of blocks of solid concrete piled on top of each other in order to seal the entrance through which U-47 had slipped in. Plans were also well in hand for a fighter base on the mainland.

The Flow literally bristled with guns in the form of shore batteries and anchored flack ships. And there were so many barrage balloons that one got the impression that if their mooring wires were cut and the balloons set free the islands would sink below the water. The three ships steamed down Bring Deeps leaving Cava to port, then passed between Fara and Lyness heading towards their usual berth. When the signal lamp on the tower instructed them not to tie up along-side but to secure to a trot of buoys a mile off shore, there were groans of disappointment throughout the ships. It was obvious to everyone that they were in line for another long spell at sea.

Almost before the whaler was hoisted inboard and the buoy jumpers back aboard, Paton saw a small motorboat approach-ing from the shore. The most cursory glance through his binoculars confirmed his worst fears: Captain Monsey was on his way. 'Christ, he might have given us time to make the ship a little more presentable,' he grumbled to the first lieutenant. 'Stand by to pipe him aboard,' he added dejectedly.

Paton hastened to the waist of the ship and prepared to welcome the unheralded, unexpected and unwanted visitor. The spick and span pinnace glistening with fresh paint and bone-white ropework reduced speed about fifty yards away, and Monsey emerged from behind the canopy immaculate as ever in greatcoat and kid gloves as he clambered onto the bow. The boat's crew were perfectly drilled and there was only the slightest of bumps as the pinnace came alongside. Monsey waited until the bow was lifted by the swell before grasping the rope ladder and clambering nimbly aboard.

Monsey said brusquely, 'May we proceed to your quarters, Paton?' He sounded like a man with a lot to say and very little time in which to say it.

Paton produced a bottle, glasses and an unopened tin of fifty cigarettes. It had become such a commonplace routine that he did it automatically, not even bothering to ask Monsey if he wanted either. As Monsey lit a cigarette and took the first gulp of his drink, Paton noticed that his hand was shaking perceptibly and his face had a taut, drawn appearance.

'Sorry to hear about *Otter*. It'll be the deuce of a job trying to get a replacement. We're building and requisitioning ships as fast as we can, but the losses are almost outstripping production. We'll just have to be that much more careful.'

Paton raised his eyebrows; it seemed such an insensitive remark to have made. 'I don't think the skipper and his men were exactly negligent, sir. They never knew what hit them.' He could detect the bitterness in his own voice and waited for Monsey to administer a rebuke.

'I'm not suggesting any lack of vigilance, Paton. Although that is what your tone seemed to imply. Maybe I misheard you. I hope so. Of course everyone values his own skin. It would be unnatural to expect otherwise. All I'm saying is that we owe it to the navy and the country to be just that bit more wary.'

As Paton refilled the captain's glass he gave him a verbal run down on the patrol mentioning Morris's heroic but unsuccessful rescue bid. 'I would like to think that his act would receive some kind of recognition, sir.'

Monsey rocked back on the rear legs of his chair. 'I'm sure you would, Paton. It was a very brave thing. It was also rather stupid and foolhardy. It emphasizes what I was trying to say a moment or two ago. We must learn not to take unnecessary risks. In this case you could have had two dead men instead of one. Substitute ships for men and you'll see what I'm aiming at.'

'I don't suppose that Morris considered it too carefully, sir.

176

Otherwise he might not have risked his own life,' said Paton sourly. 'A bit remiss of him.'

'Exactly,' said Monsey, as if he had at last made his point sink home. A small smile of satisfaction flickered across his face to indicate that although it had required a great deal of effort it had been well worthwhile.

There was a lot that Paton would have liked to say in reply but he knew it would have been a sheer waste of time; in any case, there were items of more immediate importance that he wished to discuss.

'I was a trifle surprised when we received orders to secure to a buoy, sir.'

Monsey's eyebrows arched. 'Why?'

'Well, all three ships are long overdue for a boiler clean, sir. We've been at sea almost non-stop since we arrived. Apart from that, the men are beginning to feel the strain. They deserve a break.'

Monsey stared at him as if he could not believe what he was hearing. 'Are you seriously suggesting that cruising up and down for a couple of weeks is placing an undue strain on you, Paton? If so, I suggest you put it in writing and maybe you can be replaced by someone a little more resilient.'

Paton bridled. 'I wish you would not twist words, sir. I never mentioned myself. I'm talking about the men. They aren't cracking. They're simply dog-tired. They'll be able to perform their duties that much better after a short break.'

The captain rose and began to pace up and down the small cabin, his head nodding slightly as if conversing with himself. Then he straightened and directed his gaze at Paton. 'I ought not to have to remind you that we are at war, but it seems I must. If you cast your mind back, Paton, you will know that it is not so long ago that officers and men of the Royal Navy spent months, not *days*, at sea without whining. You haven't exactly had a hard time on patrol. I've read all your reports and I can't recall any occasion when you've actually engaged the enemy. You're not suggesting are you that your men are lacking in moral fibre?'

'That's a most uncalled for remark, sir. The morale of the men – and officers – is remarkably high. But they are *tired*. So are the ships.'

He realized that his words were having no visible effect on the captain, so began to explain as patiently as possible all that the Northern Patrol entailed. The fact that you didn't see the enemy did not lessen the strain. Men were not clockwork machines who could be wound up when they got run down. A senior officer should not need reminding of that, he thought.

A nervous tic appeared below the captain's eye and Paton realized he had overstepped the mark. 'Perhaps it might not be such a bad idea if you had a few days in the Flow. It's not been a bed of roses here. Whilst you've been cruising up and down complaining about wet feet we've been subjected to a series of air-raids. While your guns have been silent ours have been extremely busy.'

Then as if on cue, sirens began wailing across the wide expanse of water followed immediately by the staccato crack of anti-aircraft guns. The alarm bells jangled throughout *Grey Seal*. It was a blessed relief for Paton who brought the conversation to an abrupt halt by racing up to the bridge. The gun crews were already closed up on the twelve-pounder, the Oerlikons and Lewis guns although the latter were purely ornamental at the moment: the enemy aircraft were out of range of the small-arms.

The sky was pockmarked with black and white puffs of smoke as the shells exploded high above. The din was deafening as shore batteries, flack ships, destroyers and trawlers opened fire. The pompoms on the deck of the stranded *Iron Duke* joined the cacophony. Even so, the steady drone of the aircraft engines was clearly audible. Paton searched the sky and spotted the high-flying bombers approaching in perfect formation, seemingly happy in the knowledge that they were out of range of all but the biggest guns. They were so high he was unable to identify them. Suddenly black blobs began to tumble from the bellies of the aircraft and the air was filled with the shriek of falling bombs as the wind raced through their fins. They seemed at first to be falling in slow motion, then they became lost to view and great spouts of water rose high in the air as the bombs exploded. Some fell perilously close to ships, but when the sea resumed its calm all were seen to emerge unscathed. The planes flew out towards the Atlantic until the throb of the engines could no longer be heard. An uncanny silence filled the Flow as the 'Orkney Barrage' ceased.

But a few minutes later the unmistakable drone once more filled the air, becoming louder and louder as the planes got closer. This time the bombers came in much lower and Paton was able to identify the cigar-shaped fuselage of the Heinkel III. Having witnessed the ineffectiveness of their first high-level attack they had obviously decided to run the gauntlet of steel. Once more the barrage opened up with such intensity that the islands seemed to shake. *Grey Seal* joined in with her entire armament and the ship juddered as the twelve-pounder blasted away. Precise gunnery was not all that important; so much metal was being hurled skywards that it seemed as if the Germans were trapped in a mesh of shellfire. Black smoke began to billow from one of the engines and it rapidly lost height, to explode in an orange ball of fire on one of the islands. Another plane disintegrated in mid-air, a third pancaked onto the water in a spume of spray, then slowly slid below the water. Bombs fell noisily but harmlessly into the water. It ended as quickly as it had started. The planes re-grouped, strained to gain height, their engines labouring heavily, then disappeared in the direction of the North Sea. A few desultory rounds were fired, then the Flow was silent once again. The birds reappeared and the puffs of gunsmoke slowly dispersed from the sky.

When Paton returned to his cabin Monsey was sitting slumped over the table, an empty glass clutched in his hand. There were small beads of sweat on his brow, and as he reached out for the bottle Paton noticed that his hand was shaking violently. 'See what I mean, Paton? It can be pretty grim here. Give me a sea-going job any time.'

The bottle rattled against the glass and Paton realized why he had not ventured out on deck during the attack: his nerve had gone. The captain looked up as if he had been reading his thoughts. 'You're wondering why I stayed here, aren't you? Well, it wasn't cowardice. What use would I have been? I had to take into account the importance of my job here. It would have been foolish of me to have gone out and been hit by a stray piece of shrapnel. Don't you agree? It's what I was trying to explain earlier.' There was a note of urgent pleading in his voice.

Paton nodded and said, 'I'll tell your pinnace you're ready to go ashore, sir.'

Monsey straightened and snapped, 'Don't be so bloody patronizing. I haven't finished with you yet. I'll let you know when I want my boat summoned.'

It was with some relief that Paton heard the trawlers would not be sent out on the Northern Patrol immediately; instead they were to relieve the small force which regularly patrolled along the boom defences off Holm Sound and Water Sound to make certain there was not a repetition of the U-47 incident.

He watched the departing pinnace with mixed feelings. He had come to dislike Monsey with an intensity that made him feel ashamed, for he realized his feelings were not due entirely to the captain's total lack of understanding (that could be excused if one accepted that he was merely doing his duty as he saw it), but he knew that Monsey was fighting a deep inner battle against cowardice. Instead of loathing he should have felt pity. But he did not. No one knew what made one man a hero and another a coward. It was as incomprehensible as trying to decide why one man was seasick and another wasn't. Real courage was being able to face up to your limitations and overcome them. He wished Monsey well but could not suppress the feeling that he would have preferred him to win his private battle elsewhere.

Paton took the unusual step of clearing lower deck to explain to the ship's company why the long-awaited boiler clean would have to be delayed even longer. The humdrum chore they had been assigned to was like the Northern Patrol: a necessary evil, and he reminded them of the fate of the *Royal Oak*. If they could prevent a recurrence then they would have more than justified their existence.

'Now go below and have a bloody good drip about me, the navy, their Lordships, and Adolf Hitler. Anyone or anything you fancy. Tomorrow I want to see you all with happy, smiling faces and singing your hearts out when we coal ship.'

Grey Seal's ship's company took him at his word and for the next half an hour the mess decks rumbled with oaths and growls of discontent. But it was short-lived. Guns Jenkins put it back in perspective. 'Think of the extra money we'll have saved by the time we do get leave. Anyway, being out there'll be a holiday. We won't have to keep looking down the heads to see if we've brought up our own anus.'

They steamed up and down the boom defences non-stop for eighteen long weary days and nights, keeping a watchful eye open for the signal flares on the torpedo nets to light up indicating a U-boat had become enmeshed, probing with the Asdic and scanning the horizon for surface attackers. But they heard nothing below water and saw nothing above to indicate the presence of the enemy. They felt very much as if they were a village constable with a beat in an area where nothing ever happened; hating the prospect of trouble yet looking forward hopefully to anything that would relieve the monotony. But it all passed uneventfully.

When *Grey Seal* led the group back through the boom, the onshore signal tower flashed the message they had all been longing for: proceed to Mill Bay for a boiler clean. Everyone knew what that meant. The fires would have to be drawn in order for the boiler tubes to be cleaned and that in turn meant at least five days' rest and shore leave.

9 As the ship's company of *Grey Seal* lined up on the quayside ready for inspection, every man knew exactly how he was going to spend the well-earned spell ashore. Some were going to Stromness, the picturesque fishing village of gable-ended houses jutting out over the water, others to Kirkwall, the tiny capital of the Orkneys. Both held promises of good food, plenty of beer and comely wenches. Their accumulated pay was already burning holes in their money-belts. There were, of course, exceptions. Rhind had pestered his oppo Morris to take a trip to civilization, but Isaac had stubbornly refused: he could not leave Jolson alone. Instead he would go ashore every day and let the dog stretch his legs and chase rabbits or anything else that took his fancy, while he himself would get well tanked up every night, safe in the knowledge that there would be no officers aboard to give him a rollicking when he got back legless. Very reluctantly Rhind was forced to fall in with his plans. He could not envisage enjoying a spell of shore leave without his opposite number.

Paton inspected them and was delighted at the turn out. Their number ones were neatly pressed and their lanyards glowed as white as freshly laundered sheets. If the weather stayed fine they would have a jolly good time. They had earned it and he did not give a damn what they got up to so long as they reported back in one piece and kept clear of the law.

When they were dismissed they clambered into the back of the lorry which would take them to Lyness and the drifters which ran a ferry service to Stromness and Kirkwall.

Back aboard in the wardroom, *Grey Seal*'s officers sat around the table relaxing and drinking pink gins. Paton

182

looked at Carnac and said, 'What are you aiming to do, Terence?'

The midshipman grimaced. 'I'm not sure, sir. I know what I'd like to do. I'd like to sacrifice my virginity to some strapping island girl. But I suppose I'll have to settle for Kirkwall.'

'And you, Brian?'

The first lieutenant felt a slight flush mounting his cheeks and hoped it wasn't noticeable. 'I planned getting the second boat over, sir. I thought it would be a nice change to get out of uniform and just wear civvies. Provided, of course, that's all right with you?'

'I've no objections whatsoever. I plan to do the same thing. Nip over to the golf course and see if I can borrow a set of clubs and cadge a couple of balls. But I'm afraid I'll have to follow on behind you. There're still a few things to sort out here.'

Phelp experienced a surge of relief. As his captain would not be travelling on the same boat, he had been saved from telling him that he had arranged to travel over with Lesley. As soon as he had learned about the boiler clean he had asked the rating who had been despatched to collect the mail to deliver a message to the Wrennery and get a reply on the way back. To his immense delight he had learned that Lesley had been able to get permission from Captain Monsey to go ashore. There was little or nothing to be done at the moment, for those trawlers which were not at sea were either refitting or having their boilers cleaned.

Phelp changed into a heavy tweed jacket, grey flannels and a windproof Burberry. Carnac put on his best uniform in the optimistic hope that it would enhance his chances with any female he might encounter. Both carried small suitcases containing their pyjamas, shaving-kit and a change of clothing.

The upper deck of the tall funnelled drifter was already jammed with sailors and islanders when they reached the pier, and it took some time for Phelp to spot Lesley and shoulder his way through to her. When she saw Carnac following close behind his first lieutenant she expressed surprise at meeting him. 'What a happy coincidence. Is Crispin with you?'

Phelp was acutely conscious of Carnac's interest and wondered if he had spotted the white lie, but he seemed to have no suspicions at all that the meeting was prearranged and was totally oblivious that the remark had not been made to him. 'No, I'm afraid he has a couple of chores outstanding before he can leave the ship. Perhaps we could have a drink together?'

'That *would* be nice,' she said.

Phelp cursed inwardly; the last thing he wanted was the Snottie hanging round his heels. Her eyes flashed cheekily and Phelp recognized that she was rather enjoying his discomfort. 'Don't you agree, Lieutenant?'

Phelp felt like saying: No, he damn well didn't. It seemed so long since they had last met that he had almost forgotten how beautiful she was. She was wearing a suit of brown corduroy that fitted snugly over her hips and accentuated her full bosom. Her feet were encased in a pair of stout brogues and although the stockings she wore were aimed more at keeping her warm than enhancing appearance, there was no mistaking their shapeliness. Resting on the deck at her feet was a small zip bag with a raincoat on top. 'I've brought that,' she said, 'just in case, although I'm keeping my fingers crossed I won't need it.'

Carnac said admiringly, 'You look absolutely smashing, Miss Paton. How did you manage to swing it?'

She looked nonplussed. 'Swing it?'

'Get permission to wear civvies. I thought it was against the regs.'

She smiled with relief and tapped the side of her nose with a forefinger. 'Influence and bribery. Bribing to be more precise. A pair of precious silk stockings, a share in a bottle of Chanel, and the promise that I won't do it again.'

Phelp was in a quandary of anxiety. For weeks, when his mind had not been engrossed by other things he had thought of little else but this excursion to Kirkwall and had worked it out with meticulous care. Now a crop of seemingly insurmountable problems that had not occurred to him before flooded through his mind. How on earth in wartime, when one had to produce identity papers, possibly a marriage certificate, and certainly a ration card, would he convince any hotelier that Lesley was his wife? God, the manager had only to look at her left hand to realize the truth.

Surprisingly, in view of her background, it had been Lesley who had first suggested that this was how they should spend their leave. Phelp had been more than content to wait. But she saw no point in that. Although he had made only brief references to life at sea in a trawler, Lesley had heard from others what a terrible ordeal it was and that every trip could well be the last. And so she had struggled against her long-held belief that lovemaking should be withheld until marriage and said quite simply, 'We must take our happiness while we have the chance.'

He heard Carnac's voice say, 'Excuse me, sir, but you seem all at sea. And I don't mean that as a feeble pun. Miss Paton and I have been talking to you for a good couple of minutes and you haven't heard a word.'

He brought his thoughts back to the drifter and their company. 'I'm awfully sorry. I was *miles* away.'

Lesley's peal of laughter echoed across the crowded deck and several heads turned in her direction. 'Perhaps Lieutenant Phelp has problems. Maybe he's wondering if all the hotels are booked up.'

He felt his face flush crimson and thought: Hell, the woman can read me like a ruddy book. Am I that transparent? When he did marry her he would certainly have to watch his step. He wouldn't get away with a thing. It was uncanny; just like that mystical form of communication which existed between twins. When one had toothache the other experienced the pain too.

'As a matter of fact,' he said rather testily, 'I was simply thinking how pleasant it was to be sailing along without having to worry that the deck might disappear beneath you any minute.'

185

Midshipman Carnac said, 'Once we've had a few drinks and a good meal together, sir, you'll have forgotten the Northern Patrol ever existed.'

The remark made Phelp realize that there were more immediate problems to be faced up to once the drifter berthed than the one of fooling an hotelier. Getting rid of the Snottie without being too obvious being the most pressing.

As the drifter approached Kirkwall the top section of the mainmast of the ill-fated *Royal Oak* could be seen jutting from the water like an accusing finger. Some people crowded to the side of the boat to get a better look, others averted their eyes. Attitudes varied so much in wartime. Phelp thought of the fleshless bodies rocking gently in hammocks and was reminded of Lesley's words as they lay together beneath the shelter of the Old Man of Hoy. He would not, he vowed, let this opportunity slip away simply because he was frightened of making an idiot of himself over a simple matter like booking a room.

As they approached the small stone pier the boat's crew lowered the old car tyres which served as fenders over the side to cushion the shock. To many of the men who had been at sea almost non-stop, Kirkwall represented civilization: real houses, real streets, proper pubs, and a real warm, dry bed that stayed where it was throughout the night.

As the liberty boat bumped alongside, the ratings stood dutifully aside to let the officers ashore first, then there was a mad scramble as servicemen and civilians raced to get a seat on the one bus that travelled into the centre of the town. Kirkwall was carefully divided into 'Uppies' and 'Doonies' to indicate on which side the inhabitants played in the traditional street game of football called 'Up the Gates' and 'Down the Gates'.

Some preferred to stretch their legs and walk up the steep streets, aiming for the spire of St Magnus. Phelp and Lesley decided on this course and joined the long procession, and to their annoyance Midshipman Carnac followed them like a faithful dog.

The queue gradually diminished as men darted off into small cafes for a meal of sausages and eggs, bacon and hot fried bread washed down by strong tea. Many weren't even hungry, it was simply the sheer pleasure of sitting down at a table covered with a cloth where the food was served on spotless plates and one asked for the butter to be passed and not the 'flippin slide'. Others more cautious with their money hastened towards the 'Fourpenny Bash' – a service provided by the women of Kirkwall where you could eat your fill of every conceivable kind of bun, bappie and homemade cakes and scones.

Phelp turned to Carnac and said, 'Look Terence, we thought we'd do a bit of sightseeing. Visit the cathedral and so on. Not much fun in that for a lad with his eye on more important things. So if you want to nip off we'll understand.'

To his annoyance the midshipman indicated that nothing would suit him finer than to accompany them. The thought had occurred to Phelp quite out of the blue, and he now found himself committed to a tour of the cathedral. He and Lesley half-listened to the story of the martyrdom of Magnus and became bored with the sound of their footsteps echoing through the empty church as they dutifully followed a local guide. Finally in desperation they suggested a drink together.

They had three, and it was only when Lesley announced that she would like to go shopping that they were able to slip away. The thought of popping from one shop to another was too much even for the adhesive midshipman.

They meandered through the narrow streets looking for a suitable hotel and passed The Big Tree, a sycamore skirted by iron railings and such a rarity that it was rumoured that the locals took it indoors every night and replanted it every morning. They paused at a number of places but did not enter. They were too big. They wanted some small place where they could relax like honeymooners and enjoy a good dinner without being the object of scrutiny. Finally they came across one in a side street off The Quadrant.

They went into the lounge where a large coal fire was

187

burning. Phelp lowered his voice and confided, 'I've been worrying about how I'm going to tackle this, Lesley.'

'I know. You're already beginning to look furtive.' She chuckled aloud. 'I bet you were thinking of calling us Mr and Mrs Smith, or perhaps Brown to be a little more original.'

He joined her laughter. 'No, I'm just dead scared that someone will ask for papers and so on and then order us out, or worse call the police.'

Lesley stood up, took his hand in hers and said, 'We'll do it together.' She winked and said, 'Just you leave it to me.'

The reception desk was deserted when they went into the small foyer and Lesley banged a small brass bell to attract attention. A dark-haired woman in her early fifties emerged from a door wiping her hands on her apron. 'Can I help?' she asked with a welcoming smile.

Lesley beamed a return smile and said, 'Do you have accommodation for a couple of nights. We're not really fussy. Two singles or a double will do.'

The woman's eyes glanced quickly at Lesley's left hand and saw the single gold band on her third finger. 'We've got both. So you can have your pick.' Her voice had the attractive lilt of the Orcadian.

'In that case we'll have the double.' She turned to Phelp. 'It'll be more like home, won't it darling?'

Emboldened by her complete self-assurance he said, 'What about ration coupons and so on?'

The woman lowered her voice. 'You hang on to them. We're not really short of anything here. If you want something special for dinner just tell me.' She pushed a register across the top of the counter. 'Now just sign the book and I'll show you your room. I'm sure you'll find it more than satisfactory.'

The room was at the top of the house overlooking roof-tops on which were perched large gulls seeking warmth from the smoking chimneys. It was small but spotless with a large bed covered with a hand-knitted quilt. A jug and china basin stood on a washstand in the corner. Lesley eyed it approvingly. 'It'll do fine. It's lovely in fact. We've been apart for so long it'll seem like the bridal suite.'

The woman smiled knowingly. 'You just make the most of what time you have together.' She closed the door behind her and winked very broadly.

Phelp took her in his arms and kissed her, and he felt Lesley tremble slightly. She returned his kiss with an unexpected passion as she whispered, 'I really wish this was our honeymoon, Brian. Or is that rushing things?'

He pushed her gently away and looked at her with eyes that could not disguise his love. 'No, I want nothing more than to marry you. But let's do it properly. You'll need to tell your family and I'll need to tell mine.' He paused. 'And there's your brother to consider.'

Lesley sensed the concern in his voice but decided not to pursue the matter. They had three or four days alone together and there was no point in spoiling them by discussing imaginary hurdles.

'That was very smart of you to get a wedding ring,' he said.

'I didn't. I just put my signet ring on my wedding finger and turned it round. Not that it matters, darling, she knew right away. She's a lot shrewder than we gave her credit for.'

When they had washed and unpacked they went downstairs and ordered a meal from the proprietor's wife, Mrs MacGregor, who asked them if seven o'clock would suit them as she was very shorthanded; her husband being away at sea while some of the waitresses had got more lucrative jobs elsewhere. They said that time was no object as far as they were concerned; in any case, they wanted to see a little more of the town.

They explored the harbour front and watched the crabbers and herring boats arrive and unload their catches. The liberty boats gradually filled with sailors, soldiers and marines who had only managed to get a few hours away from their ships, bases or gun emplacements and now had to return. Some of them were slightly tipsy, others noisily drunk. 'They'll be for the high jump,' said Lesley.

'I doubt it. Most officers adopt the same approach as we do in *Grey Seal*. If you're vertical and can salute the quarterdeck you're sober,' he replied.

Darkness had shrouded the outlying islands and the narrow unlit streets required careful negotiating when they decided to return to the hotel. They ordered two whiskies and Mrs MacGregor produced a bottle of malt whisky from one of the island's two distilleries. 'You've never tasted the like of that before,' she said proudly. 'It's the peat water.' And they hadn't.

They drank slowly before the roaring fire until Mrs MacGregor poked her head round the door and called, 'Dinner's ready when you are.'

She did them proud, producing a meal fit for a royal couple: thick steaks of local beef, roast potatoes, braised leeks, sprouts, with tingling horseradish sauce, followed by treacle tart and cream. Phelp leaned back in his chair and rubbed his stomach, contented and exhaled. 'It's a long time since I had a meal like that.' Mrs MacGregor beamed happily as she cleared away.

They lingered slowly over their coffee and it was Lesley who made the first move. 'Give me five minutes, darling.'

Phelp smoked a cigarette and immediately lighted another, putting off until the last moment what he had dreamed and hoped for for so long. Then he rose, called, 'Goodnight' to Mrs MacGregor and went upstairs. He knocked gently and called out, 'You decent?'

Lesley replied mockingly, 'God, I hope not. I didn't come all this way for that.'

She stood in the centre of the room and revolved slowly. 'Like it, darling?' Phelp drew in his breath; he had never seen anyone so beautiful. She was wearing a transparent nightdress of aubretia blue through which he could see the dark outline of her nipples, and as she turned he had a glimpse of tall, long slender legs and a dark smudge of pubic hair.

'One of the girls got it for me in Stromness. She had to hunt high and low to find it.' She completed another pirouette, then slipped quickly between the sheets which she drew up until only her head was showing.

He quickly changed into his pyjamas, put on his raincoat, rummaged for his toilet bag and hurried along the passage to the bathroom. When he returned he slipped in beside her and she immediately embraced him and sought his mouth. Phelp was swept away on a wave of desire so deep and intense he felt he was drowning. His lips brushed her hair and his hands moved up and undid the bun until her hair tumbled down like a silken veil. His hands sought her breasts and he felt the nipples harden in love. Her hands began to explore his body with the same urgent tenderness.

He entered her carefully and gently and she was amazed that such a powerfully built man whose body had been hardened by the unremitting demands of life at sea could be so sensitive. The consummation of their love was fierce and turbulent; all clashing symbols and the tumultuous roll of drums.

They parted and lay looking into each other's eyes and whispering all the things they had stored away during the long, long period of waiting for this moment.

Filled with a contented languor they fell asleep in each other's arms.

They awoke to the hoot of ships' sirens and the raucous cries of the wide-awake seabirds. Phelp parted the blackout curtains to let in the first glimmers of daylight and he saw Lesley's face lying sleepily on the pillow framed by the gorgeous halo of her hair. He returned to her side and traced his fingers over her eyebrows and lips, whispering, 'I love you, Lesley. I've never said that to any woman before.'

She sat up in mock indignation. 'I should hope not. What else could you say to a girl after you've stolen her most precious possession.' The sheets slid down to reveal her alabaster breasts and she held out her arms.

If their first act of lovemaking had been the tempestuous climax of a Wagnerian overture of love, the second was an idyllic slow movement of strings and heart-rending emotion.

At breakfast Mrs MacGregor fussed over them like a mother hen as she placed plates heaped with bacon, eggs, fried bread and grilled tomatoes before them. She glanced at Lesley with open admiration. 'My, my! You look all peaches and cream. I've never seen anyone happier or lovelier.' Lesley's eyes were indeed glowing with contentment and joy. Mrs MacGregor glanced at Phelp and said more curtly, 'You don't look too bad yourself, young man.'

Three days passed in idyllic happiness. They rose late, ate like fighting cocks and explored some new part of the mainland. At night they made love with ever-growing pleasure and mounting passion.

In the morning they were stopped on the way to the dining room by Mrs MacGregor who said rather anxiously, 'Another couple stayed here last night. You'd gone up by the time they arrived. Inquisitive so and so. When he signed the register he seemed very interested in knowing who you were. Maybe the name meant something. Nothing to worry about I'm sure, but I thought I ought to just mention it.'

They exchanged puzzled glances and shrugged simultaneously. 'Can't imagine who it could be,' said Phelp.

They soon knew. As they entered the dining room and took their seats at their customary table they saw Captain Monsey sitting at a table with his back to the window. He was in uniform and sitting opposite, erect in her chair, was a tall woman in a thick knitted woollen dress, the severity of which was only relieved by a single string of pearls. Sharp-featured, with a tight querulous mouth, she gave them an icy glare, then returned to surveying the menu.

Monsey said coldly, 'Morning Lieutenant Phelp. Morning Wren Paton,' then he too lowered his head and consulted the menu.

The woman muttered aloud but as if to herself, 'It's positively scandalous. Sordid.'

Lesley murmured, 'Good God, of all the luck.' But she looked across the room, smiled and said with a cheerfulness she did not feel, 'Good morning, sir. It looks like being another nice day.' Phelp also muttered an embarrassed greeting, but if Captain Monsey heard he chose to ignore them.

Breakfast was finished in an atmosphere of stoney silence and chilly disapproval, with Lesley and Phelp talking in lowered voices as if they were conscious that Captain Monsey was trying desperately hard to overhear every word they exchanged.

Captain Monsey rose and then held the back of his wife's chair as she left the table. They walked out of the room without giving them a glance or exchanging a word.

Phelp mumbled dejectedly, 'Well, that's clearly put the cat among the pigeons. We would have to choose the one place used by the captain and his lady.'

Lesley lapsed into the language of the mess deck to express her indifference and indignation. 'Captain Monsey can get stuffed as far as I'm concerned. I'm certainly not letting him or that sour-faced old crone spoil the last day. In for a penny in for a pound, I say.'

Phelp gently put his hand under her chin. 'That's my girl. I bet he's already thumbing his way through KR and AI to see what he can throw at us.'

When they went into the foyer, Mrs MacGregor was leaning on the counter of the reception desk looking extremely dejected. 'What on earth did you say and do to upset her like that? She insisted on having the bill and mumbled something about not sharing the same roof as a wanton. A wee bit melodramatic, but my word, she was angry.'

Phelp said, 'I'm sorry, Mrs MacGregor. I owe you an apology for this. Perhaps I ought to explain. You see . . .'

Her hand stopped him short. 'I don't want to hear another word. Least said soonest mended. I know what you were going to say and I don't give that much,' her fingers snapped loudly. 'Come again if you have a wish to. You're more than welcome.'

They shut Captain and Mrs Monsey out of their minds like a bad dream that is too painful to recall, and that night their loving was bolder and more adventurous with an element of tragic desperation, as if some dark shadow endangered their love.

The following morning, when they embarked aboard the drifter for the return trip to Hoy, they stood at the stern and watched Kirkwall slowly recede behind them as if they were saying farewell to something in their lives that had been lost for ever. Their melancholy was only relieved by the unexpected appearance of the exuberant Carnac who looked and acted like a boy who had lost sixpence and found a shilling. His incessant chatter was laced with vague innuendoes of a sexy nature and he whispered to Phelp, 'You know, Number One, the next time we go out I won't be so worried about dying.' But his voice belied the words: he sounded like someone who had found a new reason for living. He tried hard to make them ask him the reason but they seemed too wrapped up in themselves and he had to relive again in his memory the three hours he had spent in the company of a rather plain girl he had met at a local dance. During the interval she had allowed him to take her outside for a breath of fresh air. In the darkness he had clumsily embraced her, kissed her and slipped his hand beneath her blouse and fondled her breasts. He was no longer the odd man out. He could stand on the deck of *Grey Seal* and no longer blush when the crew talked about sex. If Phelp or Lesley had expressed interest he would, of course, have embellished it a bit.

Lieutenant Commander Paton returned to a *Grey Seal* that rang with the sound of steel against steel. It was so clamorous it seemed as if the ship was one great anvil. Bits of equipment and piping littered the deck, but the supervisor in charge who greeted him as soon as he stepped aboard assured him that the work was almost completed and the ship would be ready for sea quicker than anticipated. Paton said jocularly, 'Come and have a drink and we'll discuss ways of holding it up.' The joke was lost on the man who had expected the captain to express his thanks and sound appreciative.

It was only when he was assured that it was a leg-pull that he

194

accepted and as he mellowed with the drink he said grudgingly, 'I suppose you can't be expected to want to rush out there, but we get tired of the leg pulling from the sailors. They think we have a soft number and are dodging the column. They don't realize that without us the bloody navy would grind to a halt.'

Paton commiserated, poured him another drink and convinced him that sailors were renowned for their caustic humour and that none of them would swap places with men who had to spend their working hours crawling around the insides of boilers and cleaning furred-up pipes.

He was in an expansive and placatory mood: the three days away from the ship had been a real tonic and he felt thoroughly refreshed and ready for anything. He had managed to borrow a set of hickory shafted clubs and make a regular four ball consisting of an army major, a local doctor and a retired boat-builder. His golf had not been all that wonderful, but the company was congenial and the boat-builder had insisted that he should be his house guest. Even more important, the house had a telephone and he had managed to get through to Cecily. He had tried several times without success; each time there was no answer and he had almost given up hope when he heard her voice at the other end. She had sounded genuinely pleased to hear from him and asked him when he was due for a long leave to make sure he looked her up if he was in London. Before he rung off she asked him if he had received the photograph she had sent, and when he replied that he hadn't she promised to send another if it failed to turn up.

He was suddenly reminded of this as he made a short tour of inspection, and remembering that some of the men had preferred to stay behind and live aboard, he leaned over the mess deck hatch and bellowed, 'Below there.'

Morris's head appeared at the foot of the ladder, and when the captain asked if there was any mail he said there was a whole pile of it he was hanging on to. When he clambered onto the upper deck he handed Paton several letters: one from his mother, another from his father, a couple from old service friends, and an envelope with a stiff cardboard back. It was the first he opened when he reached his cabin. Staring at him was a studio portrait of Cecily with the words, 'Love – Cecily' written across the bottom, and enclosed was a letter which smelled faintly of perfume. It recalled their meeting and said how much pleasure it had given her. Since then life had been one mad whirl of service concerts and now she had settled down in a new show that everybody confidently predicted would outlast the war. 'I'd be more than happy if the curtain came down after a week if it would mean the end of this horrible business.' There was a PS reminding him of his promise to look her up. He re-arranged the pictures of his parents and Lesley to make space for his new acquisition. He knew he was being foolish and making far too much of what was really no more than a casual encounter. She probably sent similar photographs to every serviceman she met and enclosed the same stereotyped letter. But he did not give a damn; as far as he was concerned he was something special in her eyes.

With time on his hands he went up onto the bridge and hoped everyone would return aboard as contented as he was. From what he had heard over the radio, the war at sea was intensifying and the losses had reached alarming proportions. A really tough task lay ahead in which *Grey Seal* would be called upon to play an increasingly prominent role.

From the corner of his eye he caught a glimpse of a familiar blue Jeep and his spirits slumped: Monsey! Christ, I could have done without him until tomorrow.

He saluted the captain as he stepped aboard, and Monsey said curtly, 'I want to have a word in private, Paton.'

Paton went to his drink cupboard and produced a bottle and held it up. The captain nodded, 'Please. I'll need a stiff drink in order to say what I have to.'

Paton looked puzzled. 'Not trouble I hope, sir.'

Captain Monsey took the proffered cigarette and studied the end before lighting it. 'It's something I don't relish, but as it affects the efficient running of your ship I am duty bound to

196

say something.' He looked at Paton's astonished face and said, 'I see you know nothing about it, so you're clearly not guilty of complicity. My wife joined me in Kirkwall for a brief spell of leave and unfortunately we stayed in the same hotel where your first lieutenant and your sister – a member of the service too, I might remind you – had booked in as man and wife. We were faced with no alternative but to leave.'

'I'm sorry about that, sir.'

'Sorry! I'd have thought it required some stronger reaction than that mild expression.' The vein throbbed above his eye. 'God damn it, man. My wife was acutely embarrassed, more than that, insulted. There was this couple sitting opposite and acting like honeymooners!'

Paton tried to blunt the angry side to his voice. 'I know my sister extremely well, sir, and I have got to know and respect Lieutenant Phelp. I am absolutely certain, sir, that they will have formed a real and genuine attachment.'

The words sounded empty and vaguely pompous, but in his anger he said the first that entered his head.

'It could hardly be that, otherwise they would have spoken to you about it, surely. Instead they just sneaked off for a sordid bout of unbridled lust. I wouldn't even dignify it with the description of an affair.'

Paton saw a red haze before his eyes and he was unable to constrain his fury. 'I won't listen to another word, Captain Monsey, unless you moderate your tones. You *are* talking about my sister. In any case, I really don't see what it has to do with you or me. They are both adults and unless it affects the way they do their work I don't see that it should concern either of us. God Almighty, we would be extremely naïve if we thought that this kind of thing wasn't happening all over the ruddy country. Now if you will excuse me, sir, there are lots of things that need attending to.'

The captain leaned forward, his lips drawn back in a smile that lacked sympathy or understanding. 'It's *because* of the deleterious effect it could have that I have taken the trouble of coming here to speak man to man. I have taken no official

197

action – as yet. Whether or not I do depends entirely on you. You must surely see, Paton, that an impossible situation has developed. How on earth can you run an efficient ship if the number one is sleeping with the commanding officer's sister. Quite impossible! She could exert an unbearable pressure on you while he might feel that he is no longer subject, owing to his privileged position, to your discipline.'

'I think you're underestimating the strength of their characters. My sister would never do or say anything that would deter a man from his duty. And I know my first lieutenant well enough by now to recognize that he would ignore her even if she did.'

Monsey rose. 'I shall have a word with Wren Paton. You will, of course, speak to your number one. I know it will be unpleasant, but don't think I enjoyed having to speak to you like this.'

You enjoyed every minute of it, you sadistic bastard, Paton thought. 'I'll give it careful thought, sir,' he said aloud.

'You'll do more than that, Paton, if you value your command and the reputation of your family.'

Paton saluted the captain and saw him ashore without saying another word. Back in his cabin he sat at the table in utter dejection. He pounded the top with a clenched fist and cried out: You stupid couple of idiots. Why on earth did you have to pick the one place where that vindictive swine was staying? He pondered on Monsey's thinly veiled threat. Just what could he do? That was simply answered. He was capable of just about everything. If his mother heard about it she would be heartbroken. She came from an old school that could forgive but never condone immorality. His father wouldn't exactly jump over the moon with delight either. He tried to collect his thoughts and think with clarity: what offence had they committed? He had to admit he did not know. Could Phelp be charged with conduct unbecoming an officer and removed from the ship, and Lesley be kicked out of the WRNS?

The ship's company returned one by one or in small groups,

all proudly sporting their gains: plucked and trussed chickens and ducks, boxes of fresh haddock and kippers, eggs carefully resting on a bed of straw. One man carried a squawking hen by the legs, confident that he had solved the problem of fresh eggs at sea.

It seemed hours before Phelp arrived back aboard with Midshipman Carnac. Paton went to his cabin door and called out, 'Number One, could I have a quick word with you?'

When the first lieutenant stepped into his cabin he said, 'Sit down, Brian, and have a drink. Captain Monsey paid me a private visit this afternoon.'

Phelp pursed his lips. 'I had a feeling he might, sir.'

'In which case there's not much point in repeating everything he said to me. You must admit it was rather indiscreet of you both.'

'I hope I'm not going to get a lesson on morality, sir.'

'No. Morals are not my strong suit. All I'm saying is that I've been pitchforked into a situation where I can't ignore it. Even if I did the captain wouldn't. He knows the slightest breath of scandal would upset my parents and he is mean-minded enough to stir things up.'

'You mean it would look bad if it became public knowledge that the daughter of an admiral was linked with that of an RNR lieutenant. The master of the house and the maid in reverse situation.'

'Don't be so bloody silly, Brian. My parents would willingly give their blessing if it was what Lesley wanted. I'm talking about something quite different. I honestly don't know what Monsey can or will do. But it would hurt them terribly if she was kicked out in disgrace. It wouldn't help you either.'

'What you're saying is that the Service comes first?'

'I suppose I am.'

'I would not have expected any other answer from you, sir.'

'Only because there isn't one, Brian.'

'There is, sir, but it would be a waste of time giving it. But I want to make this clear. This isn't some nasty little hole in the corner thing as you seem to be implying.'

Paton interrupted him. 'I wouldn't insult either of you by suggesting it was. But it doesn't alter the facts.'

'Is that all, sir?' Phelp was already on his feet.

'Yes. But I'd like to know what you intend doing.'

'I'm afraid you'll just have to wait and see.'

Phelp stormed out of the cabin seething with rage. All right, so Monsey had put Paton in an awkward situation, but he didn't have to go along with him so readily. Hell, if you punished everyone for going to bed with someone – in his case it was significantly more than just that – the Services would be facing a manpower crisis. He could, of course, have told him that they planned to get married, but he would only have thought that was a last minute excuse. It was the same old story: men like Paton and Monsey were totally blinkered. He didn't give a tuppenny cuss for Monsey, but he was disappointed with Paton. Just when he was beginning to alter his opinion of him, he had to prove the old adage about the leopard and its spots.

Paton had his dinner sent up to his cabin that night; he could not face the prospect of sitting opposite Phelp in sullen silence. And it had recently begun to look as if he had at last achieved his objective and convinced his number one that there was only one navy and they were all part of it. . . . The steward served the meal with aggravating cheerfulness. It was, he kept saying, a very special meal: freshly killed lamb. 'Morris and Rhind went in for a little sheep rustling, sir. So make the most of it. It might be some time before they get another opportunity.'

Paton devoutly hoped that their next spot of leave would be in the very dim and distant future, for no other reason than that it would keep Lesley and Phelp apart. For by then the problem might have sorted itself out.

Hall watched the captain push aside the half-eaten meal and thought: Ungrateful so and so. Rhind and Morris would have been lynched if they'd been caught. When it comes to sheep, the crofters are a bloody sight worse than the cattle barons of the old Wild West.

Paton lay on his bunk tossing and turning, unable to sleep and wondering what his reaction would be if he had been Phelp and Lesley had been Cecily. In peacetime he would have resigned his commission; but it wasn't peacetime, it was wartime, which meant that personal interests had to be sacrificed for bigger and more important things.

Two days later, *Grey Seal* and her sister trawlers sailed for another spell of duty on the Northern Patrol – which at least permitted Paton to shut out the problem for the time being.

10 Vice-Admiral Sir Horace Beynon, VC, DSO, sat behind his desk in the wooden chart-lined hut which served as his headquarters, tapping a signal folder with the butt of a silver pencil and gazing at Captain Monsey who was sitting opposite. Except for the two of them the room was deserted. Beynon had sent his secretary out on some specious errand in order that their conversation could be as informal as possible and very much 'off the record'.

'I've read your memorandum, Tom, and frankly I'm pleased you made it confidential. My own reaction, and I hope you will agree, is to forget the whole messy business. What possible good will it do making an example of two youngsters who are only doing what goodness knows how many others are doing?'

Monsey was visibly agitated. 'I'm sorry, I just can't see it that way, sir.'

Beynon looked at the man opposite and thought: Thank the Lord I didn't have a senior officer like you when I was a randy young sub. He cast his mind back many many years to when he was in Malta and he had spent a delightful night ashore in the arms of the wife of a fellow officer, who preferred the fleshpots of The Gut to his wife's bed. The navy hadn't fallen apart at the seams. But then he hadn't been caught. That was the cardinal sin.

'Why don't we just sit on this for the time being, Tom. I know Admiral Paton very well and he's got more than enough on his plate to be worried with things like this. I know I would not like to be a convoy commodore with my mind distracted by domestic problems. The fate of a lot of men rests on his decisions.'

'I respect your sense of loyalty, sir, but I honestly think

202

you're oversimplifying the issue.' Beynon was conscious of the thinly veiled innuendo but chose to ignore it and let Monsey have his way. 'I too am responsible for the safety of a considerable number of men, sir, and if this kind of thing is encouraged discipline and morale could go to pot. In normal circumstances I might choose to ignore it. But this is a powder-keg situation.'

The admiral grimaced. 'Come on, Tom, don't over-dramatize it. You'll be telling me next that Nelson should have been drummed out because of Lady Hamilton.'

Monsey kept his hands in his lap for he was having trouble controlling them; he could feel his fingers beginning to twitch alarmingly. He badly needed a drink. 'With the utmost respect, sir, neither Paton nor Phelp are in the same category. And I must say I don't share the accepted view, in my opinion Nelson should have been dismissed from the service.'

God, the man was an insufferably unctious, sanctimonious sod, thought Beynon. He's determined to try and force my hand.

'Look at it objectively for just a moment, sir. There's no great love lost between Paton and his first lieutenant. There never is between a naval officer and a reservist . . .'

The admiral interrupted, 'Do you know this from personal knowledge, Tom, or are you just surmising? I've read all Paton's reports and they hardly convey a lack of confidence or respect in any of the officers under him. Damnit, don't let's manufacture grievances. If Paton wanted to get rid of his number one he could have done so easily by recommending him for his own command. With Phelp's experience and background plus the acute shortage of men capable of doing the job, it would have been accepted. Hell, I've got rid of a lot of troublemakers in my time – officers I mean – by putting them up for promotion. It's accepted practice.'

Monsey realized that he did not have a shred of evidence to back up what he was saying, but some inner compulsion forced him to continue. It occurred to him that having started something he was reluctant to back down and admit he had reacted somewhat overhastily. 'Paton wouldn't do that, sir, for very obvious reasons. He would get no satisfaction from that, but he'll get a lot from riding Phelp, and Phelp in turn will get back at him through his sister. We can nip that potential danger in the bud right now. He should be removed from the ship and the girl kicked out.'

Beynon was becoming more and more impatient, but he restrained himself. 'Tom, I've known young Paton since he was a cadet. He's served under me. There isn't a mean streak in him. He won't let this incident affect his judgement in any way. If anything, he'll go out of his way to convince his number one that it makes no damn difference to him what they do so long as it doesn't affect the running of the ship.'

'But it will,' insisted Monsey. 'It must.'

'I think we should sleep on it. The problems you envisage may never arise. If they don't, all well and good. If they do, we'll act.'

Monsey was startled to hear the edge to his own voice. 'You seem to have overlooked one very important and significant aspect of this case, sir.'

Case! thought Beynon. It's hardly that. It's a problem. But he left his thoughts unspoken and said, 'And what's that, Tom?'

'The girl was in civilian attire which is an offence. Furthermore, in wearing them she revealed it was a carefully planned escapade.'

The admiral sighed. 'Well, you'd hardly expect her to advertise it from the rooftops. But I take your point. Now just leave it with me. Meanwhile, let's talk about you.'

'Me, sir?' The astonishment was genuine.

Beynon stood up and walked over to the window, presenting his back to Captain Monsey. 'I've been thinking, Tom. It's time you had a good long spell of leave. You haven't really had any, and you deserve it. How long have you been up here now? Six, seven months?'

'Nearer eight, sir. I came up well before the start of hostilities.'

'Too long without a break. I know your wife has been able to come up on the odd occasion, but that's not enough. You'll end up with the dreaded Orkneyitis.'

The tic started in Monsey's temple and he could feel the sweat clammy in the palms of his hands, his knees began to jerk spasmodically and uncontrollably. Was it really so noticeable? 'There's nothing I'd like more, sir, but I have so much to do.' He ended rather lamely, 'It's just not on.'

'It is, Tom. Just leave it to me. You're doing a grand job but I'm not going to drive you till you crack. There's a safety factor in every human just as there is in a bridge. You just can't keep piling on the work load.'

Monsey began to regret the words as soon as he started speaking, but again the same mad impulse made him continue. 'It's not really the way to solve the problem, sir. Finding a scapegoat never is.'

The admiral swung sharply round from the window and stared at the man sitting by his desk. 'What does that mean?' His voice was harsh and threatening.

Monsey's voice rose to a near hysterical shriek. 'Getting me out of the way so that you can protect old friends.'

Beynon walked slowly towards his desk and sat down. 'I'll pretend I never heard that. It's unworthy of you, but I'm serious about leave. You're on the brink now, I don't want you to topple over. If that happens it will become a medical matter.'

'I didn't know there'd been any complaints or adverse comments,' said Monsey quietly. 'Although I'm not unaware that I arouse enmity in some of my colleagues.'

'No one has uttered a word. Probably through that sense of loyalty which you seem to despise so much. So let's put the record straight.' He lifted his braided sleeve and tapped the single broad band surmounted by two thinner ones. 'Contrary to what people may think, you don't get these by arse-licking or belonging to some mythical old boys network. You get it because you know men and can command their respect and get them to follow you because they have faith in your decision. And just as important, you care about them.'

Monsey nodded dumbly and wished he had never raised the subject of Paton's ruddy sister. 'Tear up my memo, sir, and we'll forget it ever existed.' He pointed to the desk top. 'Do it now in front of me.'

A look of total incomprehension clouded the admiral's face. 'Now listen very attentively, Tom, because we seem to be at cross-purposes. I don't give a fart about this report. The girl may have a bun in the oven for all I know, which will mean automatic dismissal. Phelp may be blown to kingdom come. It's a fifty-fifty chance where he is right now. Then there'll be no problem. But you'll still be here getting sicker and sicker – unless I step in before it's too late.' He opened his cigarette case, took one out, lit it and pushed it across to the captain. 'I've been watching you, Tom. I've noticed little things at conferences and briefings that were not there before. You argue when there's nothing to argue about. You raise objections when everyone else is in perfect agreement. It's as if you're scared that someone will think you're not contributing. But that's not all. There are other signs that you might be losing your grip.'

'Is that all, sir?' The tone was acrimonious.

'Not quite. The cloves or peppermints or whatever they are don't fool anyone, Tom.'

'I've never been unfit for duty through drink, sir,' Monsey protested.

'There you go, Tom. I never accused you of that. I want you to go on leave and think of it as a breather in between rounds. You'll come back refreshed for the fray.'

Monsey rose. 'I'll make arrangements to hand over, sir. I suppose things might have worked out differently if I'd got what I wanted, a sea-going posting.'

Beynon knew that the question had never been seriously considered by their Lordships; Monsey possessed the necessary qualifications for commanding a ship but not the qualities. But he was conciliatory.

'Do you think I like sitting on my backside? I'm a sailor too.

206

But they put us where they think we can serve the navy best.'

The captain opened the door and paused as a sudden thought occurred to him. 'I'd be grateful if you'd grant me one favour, sir. I'd like to go to sea with Paton's group before I go on leave.'

'I don't think that's an awfully good idea, Tom. I can't allow it.'

'I'd just like to see my fears were groundless.'

'You'll find out either way without going to sea,' said Beynon brusquely.

'It would help me to make amends. Simply going off as you suggest, sir, will give rise to all sorts of rumours.' He was almost pleading.

Beynon remained silent, deeply in thought. 'It's against my better judgement, Tom, and I may live to regret it. But go ahead. And good luck. Just promise me one thing, Tom. Let things follow their own course, don't stir them up.'

'You have my word on that, sir.'

The captain closed the door behind him and Beynon walked over to the window once more and gazed out across the vast expanse of the Flow. Statistically Monsey was just another casualty of the war, but he had served the Service and his country well, and he was entitled to the benefit of the doubt. If he went to sea in *Grey Seal* with malice in his heart then he was putting a noose around his own neck. Although Monsey had four rings, Paton was still master of his own ship, and if he was anything like his old man he would clap Monsey in the cable locker if he jeopardized the safety of the ship.

He returned to his desk, picked up the confidential memorandum, gave it an imaginary weighing, then put it in a drawer and locked it.

11 *Grey Seal* returned to Scapa looking like a candidate for the scrapyard. Although it had been another nerve and energy sapping patrol free of incident, she had taken a fearful pummelling from the weather. Her hull plates and superstructure were bare where the sea had stripped off the paintwork, and the funnel was scorched and pitted with holes from red-hot cinders. She was also minus a whaler which had broken free from its davit and been swept away before there was a chance to secure it. But the vicious weather had brought its compensations; it had kept the ship's officers so busy that there had been no time at all for relaxation. They relieved each other on the bridge, took up their action stations, then went below to wolf down a quick unappetizing meal before tumbling, totally exhausted, into the bunks to snatch an hour or two of merciful sleep. While the growing sense of isolation had begun to tell on Midshipman Carnac, it had been a blessing for Paton and his first lieutenant who were saved from mentioning the one subject that occupied their thoughts on those rare occasions when they had time to think of something other than the ship. And for that they were both extremely grateful. Both were desperately anxious for time in which to allow the problem to sort itself out, or, even better, the arrival of some unexpected and blessed solution. Paton was totally convinced that all would be well for the patrol had proved one thing; neither of them had allowed anything to affect the efficient running of the ship, which had certainly made Captain Monsey's fears seem unfounded. If only he would leave them alone, the problem would vanish as suddenly as those sea mists which they had become so accustomed to on the Northern Patrol.

Within two hours of securing alongside in their customary berth, Paton knew that was not to be the case; a messenger arrived with a hand-signal informing him that as soon as *Grey Seal* had provisioned and coaled she would sail with the group on yet another Northern Patrol. The significant difference was that Captain Monsey would be taking passage.

Paton flung the signal onto the table in disgust and cursed aloud. Monsey was like a ruddy terrier with a bone. Well, there was nothing he could do about it; Monsey would not be the first senior officer who had decided it was his duty to go to sea with the ships he controlled to discover how they operated at first-hand. He sent for the first lieutenant and, when he entered the cabin, he silently handed him the signal. Phelp read it with an expressionless face, then returned it. 'I'll see to it that he finds no cause for complaint, sir.' His voice was remote and coldly formal.

'Sit down, Brian, and have a drink,' said Paton irritably. 'None of this was of my seeking, or yours for that matter, so don't let it get on top of us. We can't go on acting as if we're ruddy strangers.'

The first lieutenant sat down and waited patiently while Paton poured the drinks before he spoke. He was still politely remote. 'I ought to point out, sir, that nothing Captain Monsey says, or does, will alter the situation between Lesley and me. If he's determined to break me there's not a lot I can do about it. If you support him, there's nothing I can do about that either, sir.'

Paton grinned. 'Good for you, Brian. It's the answer I would have expected. I don't, as you put it, support him; he's a pain in the neck. But that doesn't mean he'll stop being vindictive. You can't have helped noticing he's a sick man who's not really accountable for his actions. All we have got to do is give him no possible cause for thinking he's right. And, by God, he'll be looking for every opportunity to prove he was. If we can get through the patrol without any trouble I don't think we'll have to suffer his company again. I'm sure I wouldn't go there if I had the choice – and he does.'

Phelp interjected dismally, 'With him sharing your cabin he'll have ample opportunity to pour poison down your ears.'

Paton shook his head. 'He won't. I've already decided to move in with you and the Snottie. He can't bitch at that. It's a courtesy any captain would extend to a senior officer.'

The first lieutenant shook his head in bewilderment. 'It baffles me entirely, sir, why he should get so worked up about it. I suppose one way out of it would be for me to get transferred to another ship.'

'Forget it. Why should I get rid of the best Jimmy-the-One I could ask for, just to pander to the imaginary fears of an ailing man. In any case, it wouldn't achieve anything. I suspect Captain Monsey would not accept that solution anyway. He wants blood. Don't ask me why. Petty-minded tyrants don't need reasons. Something's snapped in him and the only way he thinks he can survive is to hide behind a veneer of super efficiency and adhere strictly to the book.'

That evening, for the first time since Monsey had issued his warning, *Grey Seal*'s officers sat down together again at dinner. Carnac was beside himself with pleasure and talked incessantly over the meal. He had no idea what had caused the sudden undefinable friction between number one and the captain, but whatever it was he was jolly glad it was over. Both had been acting like a couple of women with the curse!

After provisioning and coaling there was no time left to do anything more than replace the whaler, carry out patchwork repairs and slap red lead over the bald patches on the side of the ship. When this had been completed Paton suddenly observed that the Flow was in the process of being transformed before his eyes. Ships seemed to be mooring at every available buoy. The Home Fleet was returning from its period of enforced exile. A jubilant thrill surged through his body and he raced up onto the bridge to get a good look at the remainder of the vast armada approaching from seawards.

He quickly picked out the impressive shape of HMS *Hood*, the largest ship in the Fleet and the pride of the Royal Navy, and watched as the booms opened in welcome and lines of majestic ships steamed through to secure at their moorings. It was a magnificent and awe-inspiring spectacle that brought a lump to his throat. Soon afterwards a buzz swept through the mess decks, carried by that invisible network of communication unique to the navy, that 'Winnie' had personally arrived ahead of the main force through Switha Sound – the tradesmen's entrance – aboard a destroyer. It was rumoured that he had intended to arrive in a style befitting the first lord, but had been thwarted. He had sailed from Rosyth with Admiral Forbes, the C-in-C, aboard his flagship *Nelson*, but a warning that aircraft had laid mines near Hoxa had forced the admiral to stand off until the channel was swept. But Churchill was so impatient to be in Scapa to greet the Fleet he had transferred to a destroyer and nipped in through Switha. Winnie's pride would not permit Hitler to put one over on him or his beloved navy. Now he was safely aboard *Hood*.

It was an extremely emotional occasion for the Royal Navy. There had been an overriding feeling of shame that one brave and enterprising U-boat captain had forced the greatest Fleet in the world to vacate in haste the base from which it proudly boasted it ruled the seas. Now it had returned as every man-jack afloat had prayed it would. They were even prepared to accept the rigours of Scapa in preference to further humiliation.

From the corner of his eye Paton caught a glimpse of the familiar blue Jeep of Captain Monsey travelling fast along the bay road leading to the trawlers' base. If the return of the Home Fleet had filled him with pride the arrival of Monsey filled him with a deep sense of despair and depression, and he tried desperately hard to conceal it as he hurried down to the gangway to receive the unwelcome visitor.

Monsey's face looked taut and sunken with fatigue as he stepped aboard, saluted and snapped, 'If you'll tell me where to stow my belongings, Paton, I'll get the two ratings to bring it aboard.' Paton glanced over Monsey's shoulder and groaned inwardly as he saw two seamen unloading the Jeep;

he seemed to have brought enough gear for a round the world cruise.

'I'll have someone show them to my cabin, sir. It's at your disposal. I'll move in with the other officers.'

Monsey dismissed the suggestion with a brusque wave of his hand. 'I don't want to turf you out of your quarters. I've brought a camp bed. If it's agreeable to you, I'll put it up at night and sleep on the deck.'

'There's really no need for that, sir. I've already had my stuff shifted. It'll be far better that way, and no hardship I assure you. Once we get to sea I seldom set foot in my cabin. There's no day or night for us out there. Apart from that, you'll be able to get a night's uninterrupted sleep if I'm not there.'

Monsey retorted tartly, 'I don't intend to spend my time getting my head down, Paton. That's not the object of the exercise at all.'

Paton was in no frame of mind to argue, neither did he intend to change the arrangements he had made. He simply turned to Steward Hall and said, 'Take the two ratings to my cabin and show them where they can stow Captain Monsey's gear.'

Before the captain had a chance to remonstrate, Paton said cheerfully, 'I don't know about you, sir, but I'm ready for a drink.' It was an invitation he knew that Monsey would not decline.

There was a tangible air of tension in the small wardroom that evening as the four officers sat down to dinner. Captain Monsey had rejected the offer to have his meal served separately in his cabin, saying he preferred to meet the other officers, and as a result of his unwanted presence conversation was polite but stilted and revolved entirely around the return of the Fleet and other general topics of Service conversation. Phelp could hardly wait to excuse himself and leave the table; he even declined a cup of the real coffee Monsey had brought aboard, saying he had one or two urgent tasks to attend to.

Monsey stirred his coffee aimlessly, staring intently at the swirling liquid, and without looking up said, 'Is he always so surly and uncommunicative? His attitude is hardly conducive to a happy and contented ship, which if I recall rightly is your paramount objective.'

'It is, sir, and I like to think I have achieved it. Lieutenant Phelp is always preoccupied with last minute details just before we sail.'

Monsey said tardily, 'I'm not in favour of last minute rushes myself. I prefer to have things ready well in advance. I fail to see how you can expect the men to be on their toes if the first lieutenant hasn't got a grip on things. But it's your ship.'

Paton chose to ignore the jibe, but rather unwisely Midshipman Carnac tried to ease the mounting tension by interjecting, 'Wait till we get to sea, sir. You'll see that everyone gets on like a house on fire.'

Monsey fixed him with a glassy stare. 'Not a very apt metaphor. If that is the best you can do I'd prefer to do without your unsolicited opinion. In any case, I'm not blind. I prefer to see for myself. That, after all, is the purpose of my visit.'

The shamefaced Carnac buried his head over his coffee and mumbled miserably, 'Sorry, sir.' He looked so utterly dejected and deflated Paton feared the lad was close to tears.

'Don't be so ruddy cringing, Snottie. Can't you see I was only joking?' said Monsey placatingly. He wondered what on earth had made him suddenly turn on the boy; he had no quarrel with him. What mad impulse was it that made him say things which he immediately regretted. He had hardly been aboard a dog watch and he had already created an atmosphere and alienated the youth. He reminded himself that his intention in coming aboard had not been motivated solely by a need to prove that his fears about Phelp were justified, but more as a personal test which would convince Admiral Beynon that he had been premature in writing him off. He secretly admitted that there was a grain of truth in what the admiral had said; he was a trifle jittery and he did reach for the bottle a little too readily. But he had not reached the stage where he should be packed off home without a chance to redeem himself. Neither was he material for the trick cyclists. On reflection he may have been over hasty in rushing to Beynon about the couple; but he was absolutely convinced he would be proved right in the long run. Not that he intended precipitating a crisis. He would be scrupulously fair and let events follow their natural course. There was no question of him being vindictive. He was fighting for survival. The thought of being beached terrified him.

He tried to sound jocular. 'How about a spot of brandy to round off an excellent meal, Paton? We're going to be sitting on each other's laps for the next couple of weeks, so let's get off to a good start. And please send a hand to ask the first lieutenant to join us.'

Monsey lifted his glass. 'A toast. A safe and successful patrol.'

Their glasses had scarcely reached their lips when a breathless Phelp burst into the cabin. He was so excited and overawed he could hardly get the words out. 'You'd better come out at once, sir. We've got VIP visitors, and I really do mean VIP.'

Paton mumbled a hasty, 'Excuse me, sir,' grabbed his cap from the hook and hurried out onto the open deck. In the shrouding darkness he could just make out the tall imposing figure of Admiral Beynon, but he could not identify the short, portly figure beside him.

Beynon boomed jovially, 'Hope I haven't caught you with your pants down, but the First Lord insisted on visiting a trawler. After the *Hood* he wanted to see how the Harry Tates lived.'

A voice that Paton recognized immediately growled, 'Good evening, Captain. Let's go somewhere we can see each other.'

Paton, his heart palpitating furiously, led the visitors into the wardroom, completely overwhelmed and still finding it hard to believe that Winston Churchill was paying a personal visit to *his* ship.

As he stepped into the cabin Paton saw he was wearing the

familiar peaked cap set at a jaunty angle and a reefer jacket; an unlit cigar was clamped tightly between his teeth. The First Lord looked more pugnacious than he did in the countless photographs he had seen in the newspapers.

Steward Hall, who was clearing the table, was so surprised he dropped several cups and saucers which shattered into pieces and Captain Monsey shot out of his seat as if he had received a sudden and powerful electric shock.

Churchill glanced at the table, removed his cigar and stabbed it at the bottle of brandy. 'I see, Lieutenant Commander, that you were anticipating my call.'

Paton invited the visitors to sit down and sent Hall off at the double to rustle up more glasses. Then he introduced Monsey and his own officers to the man who personified the navy to everyone from the lowliest OD to the highest-ranking admiral. 'It's a privilege to have you aboard, sir.'

Churchill waved his cigar and the gravelly voice replied, 'The privilege is mine. I am not unmindful of the great and gallant work you have been performing. The absence of the Fleet may have made you feel an unfair burden was being thrust upon you. Now the Fleet is back. But I must warn you that your burden will not be lessened by its return. You will set out to sea and see them riding majestically at their moorings and perhaps wonder when they are going to join the war. My answer to that is be patient. As in the First World War it may be months before the Fleet has the opportunity to put to sea and engage the enemy in a mighty battle which could well be the turning point.' He lifted his glass. 'Gentlemen, to the return of the Home Fleet.'

For the next three-quarters of an hour Churchill plied Paton and his officers with questions about the Northern Patrol and they were astonished at his grasp and knowledge of the most minute details. Characteristically he invited them to suggest any improvements and asked if there was anything the Admiralty could do to improve the lot of the sailors. He had clearly done his homework and pumped Admiral Beynon dry of information before calling aboard *Grey Seal*, for he knew all about the E-boat attack and the novel method used to sink one, and he was fully conversant with the patrol in which *Otter* had been sunk. Then he rose and said gruffly, 'With your approval, Captain, I would like to be shown round your splendid ship.'

Paton grinned and extended his hand in invitation towards the door. A look of grave concern clouded Monsey's face as he rose and said, 'I don't think you'll find it anything like the ships you've been aboard so far, sir.' He forced a thin smile. 'A bit scruffy compared to the *Hood*.'

The First Lord champed hard on his cigar and fixed the speaker with an angry, almost contemptuous stare. 'The mines which produced the coal to fire this ship are also dirty, Captain, but where would we be without them?' And with that he turned to Paton and said, 'Kindly lead the way.'

When Admiral Beynon and Monsey made as if to follow he halted them. 'This is not a formal inspection, gentlemen, more a social call. I'd prefer you to wait here until I return.'

Churchill insisted that Paton should seek formal permission from the men before he descended below decks. 'They are at rest and perfectly entitled to say they are not at home to unexpected callers.' The heavy-jowled face split into an impish grin. 'I do not, for one moment, contemplate a rejection.'

The first lord started in the engine room and chatted cheerfully to Reynolds and the duty stokers who were making final routine checks before moving to the mess deck. It was only with great difficulty that he managed to negotiate the vertical ladder, and when he had set foot in the mess deck he insisted that none of the men should stop what they were doing, and that included those who were resting on their bunks. 'In times of peril when sleep is a precious commodity I always believe that one should never stand when one can sit, and never sit when one can lie down.' The quip brought roars of appreciative laughter. When he observed that a group of men at one table had halted their game of 'uckers' he insisted that they should continue whilst he sat alongside, threw the dice and made a couple of moves. It was all very natural and unaffected. And when Jolson made a tail-wagging appearance and jumped up at the distinguished caller, clearly unimpressed by rank or status, Churchill delighted the men by exchanging a few words with their mascot.

The call was the tonic that the weary men needed. And what delighted them so much was that he seemed genuinely pleased to spend a few minutes with them.

The First Lord nodded to Paton to indicate that the time had come to leave and he began to ascend the ladder leading to the upper deck. Halfway up he paused, looked backwards and said, 'Do not for one moment consider yourselves the Cinderellas of the navy. You are every bit as important to our survival as those mighty ships which have just arrived.'

Someone, Paton could not be sure who, called out, 'Three cheers for Winnie', and the tiny mess deck echoed to their enthusiastic cries. Winston gave a signal with his fingers which was to symbolize the indomitable courage of the British people throughout the years ahead.

Back in the wardroom Churchill turned to the admiral and said, 'They would not have been out of place sailing under the skull and crossbones.'

Captain Monsey again rushed in to apologize. 'It is extremely difficult, First Lord, to maintain appearances in a ship of this nature . . .'

'Appearances be damned. I'd like Herr Hitler to see them. He would immediately realize that he has no possible chance of victory.'

The First Lord solemnly shook hands with the officers and wished them 'God speed and good luck' before turning to Beynon to announce that their visit was over and he wished to depart. On the upper deck the admiral just had time to draw Paton aside and say, 'I'm sitting on the report that Captain Monsey submitted to me. I'm relying on you to see that this is a successful trip. Go along with him as far as you think prudent, but always bear in mind that it is *your* ship. You'll have my wholehearted backing.'

Bugles blared in response to the bosun's pipes as the three trawlers steamed past the long line of moored capital ships and cruisers. Everything aboard the powerful warships looked so spick and span to the men standing on the fo'c'sles and quarterdecks of the cluttered and diminutive trawlers that it was difficult for them to restrain their resentment. The fancy tampians over the muzzles of their enormous guns were a harsh reminder that they had never been fired in anger. Sometimes they sailed so close to the big ships, the decks of which were crowded with smartly dressed ratings who seemed to be doing everything at the double, that their mast tops did not reach the upper decks. Occasionally one of the ratings, bitter at the thought of another patrol, shouted out a taunting remark such as, 'Get some sea time in'. They were immediately silenced by a stern-faced officer who secretly agreed with them. Inwardly the trawlermen felt proud of their role and the ships they sailed in; they had no wish to serve in 'floating barracks'.

Captain Monsey sat on a small let-down seat attached to the bridge bulkhead. He had hardly spoken since the ship slipped its mooring and headed for the open sea, seemingly immersed in his private thoughts, since he had not offered any advice or suggestions – and for that Paton was extremely grateful. Unknown to him, Monsey was fighting his own personal battle: he dreaded the thought of what lay ahead; he hoped for action in order to prove himself, yet was riddled with fear that he would be incapable of measuring up to it. If he had to die he devoutly hoped it would be swift and instantaneous.

He sat there until the group had cleared the boom, then he rose and said quietly, 'I'm going below for a while. If you think I can be of any assistance at any time please do not hesitate to call me.'

Four days passed during which the ship's company were virtually deprived of any real sleep for there were the usual false alarms which meant them being summoned to 'Action Stations' for hours on end, during which nothing happened.

218

And once more the Atlantic lived up to its reputation as the cruellest and most malevolent ocean in the world. They encountered fog and mountainous seas during which whole watches passed without the trawlers ever sighting each other. Paton secretly enjoyed the misery; at least it would show Monsey that none of his complaints had been imaginary. But if the point was driven home Captain Monsey made no comment. He appeared on the bridge for short periods during the day when he asked how things were shaping before retiring to his cabin once more. He seemed to have resigned himself to the fact that there was no possible way of running a trawler like a pusser warship. Paton often detected the faint aroma of cloves when Monsey came close to him, but he just did not care, or even bother to check up on what he was consuming. He had lived on a knife edge ever since they had sailed, waiting for Monsey to fasten on to some slight incident which would enable him to raise the subject which so far had remained taboo. He had not done so, which had made Paton begin to wonder why on earth he had bothered to come aboard. But as the time passed he was quite happy to dismiss it from his mind and just plough on until the patrol was over. It did not occur to him that Monsey was still smarting from the curt rebuke he had suffered at the hands of the First Lord and had resigned himself to the fact that that was one particular battle he was destined to lose. If the men and the ship met with Churchill's approval he had no alternative but to fall into line. If he persisted, more than likely it would result in another black mark and raise further doubts about his own ability.

As dawn broke on the fifth day and the guns crews had closed up for their routine spell of 'Action Stations', the starboard lookout reported a large column of black smoke bearing Green two-oh. Phelp, who was keeping the morning watch, immediately called down for 'Full Ahead' and promptly sent the bridge messenger down to summon the captain.

As Paton arrived on the bridge he asked curtly, 'Make out what it is yet, Number One?',

Phelp shook his head and continued to peer through his glasses. 'Obviously a fire and a big one.'

As he spoke Monsey appeared on the bridge and peered at the smoke through a pair of binoculars. His face was whey-coloured and the glasses shook. 'Can't see a darned thing for smoke. What do you think has happened?' His voice was strained and anxious.

Paton shrugged. 'Won't know until we get closer, sir. Could be anything. A drifting mine, a torpedo, a bomb. Your guess is as good as mine.'

'Damnit, Paton, you've been on this patrol long enough now not to have to indulge in guessing games.'

Paton replied patiently, 'That's all I can do at the moment, sir. We've spotted no planes and had no Asdic contacts. If you have any ideas, sir, I'd be grateful.'

Monsey did not reply but went over to the seat in the corner of the bridge and sat there in morose silence.

An hour later one of the lookouts reported that it was a small merchantman which appeared to have stopped: she was listing slightly to port, and the fire seemed to be confined to aft of the bridge. Paton instructed the signalman to issue a challenge and when there was no reply to the Aldis he was told to keep on trying every few minutes. Meanwhile he was instructed to tell the other ships to keep a careful watch for any signs of the enemy while *Grey Seal* went to investigate.

When they were within three-quarters of a mile's distance, Paton was able to study the merchantman very carefully. There seemed to be no sign of any wake from her stern and the falls dangled lifeless from the boatless davits, giving every indication that the vessel had been abandoned.

Turning to Phelp he said, 'You'd better take over midships. Get a boarding party ready which includes a couple of stokers.'

Paton reduced speed to 'Slow Ahead' and circled the ship warily. He had no idea what she was carrying and he did not want it to explode and take them with it. When he was within two hundred yards he had the loudhailer switched on. 'Ahoy. Is there anybody aboard?'

A figure muffled in a thick overcoat and wearing a soiled and sea-stained cap emerged from the enclosed bridge. 'Are you in need of assistance?' called Paton.

The small figure lifted a megaphone and a broad Yorkshire accent echoed across the dividing space of water. 'Doesn't it look as if I bloody well do? There's a ruddy fire in the aft hold and I've got two men below trying to put it out.'

'Where is your crew?'

'They took to the boats like ruddy rats.'

'What happened?'

'We got shelled, that's what happened. Haven't you got any eyes?'

Paton ran his eyes along the length of the ship and saw a huge, gaping hole in the wheelhouse and another aft, just above the water-line. It was remarkable she was still afloat.

The master continued to shout. 'We had engine trouble and the convoy carried on without us. Typical bloody navy. Then we spotted this ship and asked for assistance. No bigger than my own. But when it got near it hoisted the Jerry flag and structures on the upper deck started collapsing to reveal bloody big cannons. Must have been one of them decoy ships. I was told to abandon ship before they sank by gunfire. The bloody crew – lascars and the dredges of the shipping offices – didn't need any invitation.'

'Why didn't she sink you?'

'Christ knows. She fired a few shots and hit us about three times, then scarpered as suddenly as she arrived. Must have spotted you and mistaken you for destroyers.'

'Who have you got remaining aboard?'

'Me, the engineer, a couple of seamen and an oiler.'

'Enough,' snapped Paton. 'I'll put a party aboard to help fight the fire and get you under way.'

'You bloody well keep clear. I'm not having anyone claiming salvage or prize money.'

'You've no alternative.'

221

'Oh, yes I have. I can wait till the crew comes back. They will if they've got any nonce.'

'What is your cargo?'

The reply came back, 'High explosives. How do you fancy coming aboard now?'

Paton had no idea whether the captain was telling the truth or merely trying to dissuade him from trying to salvage the ship. Not that it mattered, his mind was made up. 'Get some men topsides. I'm sending a boarding party.' He called urgently to the lookouts, 'Keep your eyes peeled. If the Jerry finds out we aren't destroyers he'll be back.'

He had barely passed the message before one of the lookouts screamed, 'Plane approaching. Red five-oh, sir.' The Focke-Wulf Condor long-range reconnaissance bomber clearly had no intention of attacking the trawler force or the crippled merchantman for it remained well out of gunfire range, content to circle round and round keeping observation. It was clearly low on fuel for it departed as suddenly as it had appeared. Paton was in no doubt that it would be in contact with any U-boats in the area and certainly in touch with the armed decoy ship.

He yelled across to the stricken ship, 'For God's sake get some men on deck. Your friend will be back soon to finish off the job otherwise.'

The solitary figure on the bridge disappeared and a few minutes later a handful of men appeared on the upper deck. Paton cupped his hands over his mouth and called down to the first lieutenant, 'Get some lines across as soon as you can. I'm going alongside.'

The sharp crack of the line-throwing Lee Enfield was heard and a thin line went snaking slowly skywards to land on the deck of the merchantman. Eager hands aboard *Grey Seal* secured the inboard end to a heavy steel hawser and Phelp bellowed to the men on the motionless ship, 'Heave away'. The rifle cracked again and another line straddled the deck of the merchantman aft. As soon as the hawsers were secured to bollards the order was given to the men manning *Grey Seal*'s

capstans to take in the slack. Although the sea was comparatively calm, a heavy swell was running and one minute the
lines were taut while the next they were dangling slack as the
ships moved closer together, then were suddenly moved apart
by the force of the swell. From time to time the men working
the capstans had to let slack run out to prevent the wires
snapping like over taut violin strings. Suddenly an agonizing
scream was heard above the shouting voices of the men working the lines, and Paton saw Stoker Cohen fall into the
scuppers, which were slowly turning red. Unaccustomed to
working with wires or ropes, he had stepped into a bight and as
the force of the swell moved the two ships apart it had tightened
and severed his right leg above the knee, as neatly as secateurs
pruning a rose bush. A gout of blood pumped from the leg and
a seaman picked up the sea-boot and gazed in disbelief at the
stump of leg remaining in it. Then he went to the side and
shook it and the stocking-encased piece of flesh plopped overboard. Finally he was violently sick.

Paton turned to Monsey who seemed so silent he could
have been carved out of stone and shouted, 'Can you get
down there, sir, and give a hand?' The request went unheard;
Monsey sat slumped in his seat gazing down at his feet. 'For
God's sake, sir, if you aren't capable of helping get below
where the men can't see you.' But Monsey was transfixed,
incapable of movement or comprehension.

As Cohen screamed and writhed in agony Morris shouted
above the din, 'Flour! Campbell, give me a hand. Quick!' The
huge Canadian needed no further bidding, it was as if he knew
what was in his friend's mind, and the two ex-trawlermen
raced aft ignoring the confused Phelp's order not to desert
their posts. They returned from the galley dragging a heavy
sack of flour across the deck, and savagely pushed aside the
sailors who were muttering encouragement to the badly injured stoker.

'Get out of the bloody way,' roared Rhind as he picked up
the moaning man as if he were a baby and carried him over to
Morris who had ripped open the sack and was busy widening

the neck. He held it steady as the Canadian thrust the raw, bleeding stump into the white powder which for a second began to turn red while the seamen watched in sickened awe as the crimson patch began to spread. Then it suddenly stopped.

Morris looked at Phelp and panted, 'An old trawler dodge, sir. Stops the bleeding by sealing the wound. Like red-hot pitch in the old times. Crude but effective. It's saved the life of many a man who's lost a leg or arm in a warp.'

The first lieutenant held up a rigid thumb in silent tribute. 'I'll see you two later. Now get him below and give him a jab of morphia.' He turned to the men handling the lines, 'Come on lads, let's get alongside.'

As the two ships drew closer together, Chalkie White called out anxiously, 'Signal from *Beaver* sir. Suspected enemy vessel approaching. Am engaging.'

Paton seized the megaphone and yelled down to Phelp, 'Let go everything. Use an axe if necessary.' He did not elaborate and the lines parted with a loud ping as the fire-axe bit through them.

The rescue attempt which had cost Stoker Cohen his leg was abandoned. *Grey Seal* began to churn up a creamy, foaming wake as the engine responded to 'Full Ahead', and she began to head in the direction of the approaching enemy.

'Signal *Vole* to join us,' rapped Paton.

One trawler was no match for the German, but three were. Their combined gunpower – if they could get within range without being blown out of the water – might force the German to withdraw.

Although he had not seen the enemy he was pretty certain from what the master of the merchant ship had said that it was the equivalent to a First World War Q-ship. A vessel which masqueraded as an innocent looking cargo vessel, cynically flying the flags of all nations and often presenting itself as a ship in distress before revealing its concealed armament, to blow some unsuspecting cargo ship which went to its assistance to kingdom come. He had no idea what guns it carried, but they would not be all that powerful: 5.9 inches at the most, and a good, disciplined crew behind a twelve-pounder was a reasonable match.

Paton jammed on his steel helmet, a movement which for some obscure reason made Monsey stir into life. He had seemed totally oblivious to all that had just taken place.

'It's foolhardy, Paton.' He shrugged defeatedly. 'What on earth can you hope to achieve? Far better to cut our losses.'

Paton replied sharply, 'I don't think so, sir. It's three to one, remember. If we can attack from different angles they'll have a problem deciding where to train their guns. They won't be able to engage us all at the same time.' But he might just as well have spoken to himself for Monsey had again lapsed into a total and detached silence; as if having expressed his opinion and been ignored he had washed his hands of everything.

Paton caught sight of *Beaver* and seconds later she opened fire. As the distance between the two ships diminished he could make out the splashes of shells falling around the dogged little trawler which seemed to bear a charmed life. But he knew that her luck could not hold out if he did not get *Grey Seal* within range very quickly and attract some of the German's gunfire. When he called down to the engine room and asked for maximum revolutions, Reynolds replied good humouredly, 'This is getting to be a habit.'

Paton then instructed *Vole* to steam as fast as possible in order to take up station astern of the enemy.

On the twelve-pounder bandstand, Phelp was trying to work out the range. He turned to Jenkins, 'Do you think we're near enough to give her a scare, Guns?'

'I wouldn't have thought so, sir, but there's no harm in loosing off a couple of rounds just to let her know we're not here simply to make up the numbers.'

The ancient gun went off like a clap of thunder and the projectile was clearly visible as it hurtled through the sky. It fell well short, as everyone knew it would, but it achieved its purpose. The German immediately switched one of its guns from *Beaver* and concentrated on the fresh danger. The

German was right on target with his first shell. They were either remarkably good gunners or they had extremely good range-finding equipment. Paton did not know and did not really care; the question was purely academic. A second shell removed two feet from the mainmast and a third scored a direct hit on the bow, but it failed to explode and, apart from removing the anchor, did little or no damage. Paton immediately gave a series of helm orders which made the ship weave like a drunken sailor, and although it made things difficult for his own gunners it made it doubly hard for the enemy.

Grey Seal was now abreast of *Beaver* with about three miles of water separating them. Both ships were well within range of the German and their rate of fire would have brought a nod of approval from any gunnery instructor. Through his glasses Paton saw one shell – he could not be sure whether it came from his own ship or *Beaver* – land close to the bridge of the enemy vessel, and seconds later yellow fingers of flame could be seen flickering on the upper deck. At the same time, *Beaver* received a direct hit amidships which forced her to make a violent alteration to course, but she steadied and once more her twelve-pounder was echoing across the sea. Seconds later *Grey Seal* juddered from stem to stern as an armour-piercing shell struck her a glancing blow on the port side, but failed to penetrate the heavily plated hull. Then the ferocity of the enemy gunfire seemed to relent and Paton realized that *Vole* had begun to attack from astern and forced the German to concentrate one of her guns on the new menace.

Shrapnel shells began exploding overhead and men ducked involuntarily as the screaming chunks of red-hot metal gouged lumps out of the deck, holed boats and rafts and parted stays and rigging. Paton could feel the impact as bits of steel thudded into the padded quilting around the bridge. Miraculously, no one was hit.

As he directed the twelve-pounder, Phelp reflected ruefully: If Lesley could only see me now she'd die of laughing. I'm acting as if this was a ruddy battle-wagon.

The German had now assumed its real identity for he could see the battle ensign fluttering from the mast stay. He could also see quite clearly that they were having trouble training the aft gun. Hopefully, the mounting had been badly damaged.

The much bigger German ship was now like a bear being tormented by tenacious terriers. Individually, the trawlers were no match for her, but combined they presented a formidable opponent and they had the added advantage of presenting much smaller targets. The battle raged unremittingly for five or six minutes, and it was the German who finally adopted the course proposed by Captain Monsey. But a discreet retreat was not all that easy; she was hemmed in by the determined trawlers which had all sustained damage although not to an extent which would force them to disengage. By now they were close enough to open fire with their Oerlikons and the sky was latticed with the glow of lazily looping tracers which were accompanied by unseen, but lethal, high explosive and armour-piercing shells. None of them were capable of inflicting mortal damage but Paton could clearly see they were causing havoc on the upper deck of the enemy ship. The German, however, did not hesitate to retaliate with her own cannons. *Grey Seal*'s decks and superstructure were raked with cannon fire and from the corner of his eye he saw the starboard Oerlikon gunner slump forward over his weapon to be kept in position by the restraining harness. The loader was trying desperately to free him and Paton looked across the bridge to where Monsey was sitting. 'Sir, the starboard Oerlikon gunner has been hit. Can you give his loader a hand?'

Monsey stirred and shook his head as if to dispel some oppressive cloud that prevented clear thinking. Then he rose and moved slowly down to the gun platform like a man sleepwalking. A shell took away the guard-rail which was bolted to the sleepers, then hurtled over the bridge to explode harmlessly in the sea. With the aid of the loader, whose left arm dangled helplessly at his side, Monsey managed to free the gunner from the harness, only to recoil in horror as he

227

gazed into an unrecognizable face that was no more than a bloody pulp. He released his grip of the lifeless man, then turned abruptly and made for the door leading to his cabin. The loader screamed after him, 'You yellow bastard!' But if Monsey heard he ignored him. The one-armed loader uttered a string of oaths, pulled the dead man clear of the gun and with a near superhuman effort clipped on a fresh drum of ammunition and continued to fire the weapon unaided, his lips curled back in a terrifying snarl through which his teeth gleamed white.

Suddenly, the German made a violent alteration to course and began to stream away from the three trawlers. With her superior speed she was soon out of range of their Oerlikons but the twelve-pounders continued to maintain a steady and accurate fire. The enemy was now clearly solely concerned with taking evasive action, although she continued to fire a few desultory and token rounds.

Paton, deeply relieved that the enemy had chosen discretion to valour, signalled the trawlers to break off the action and return to the stricken merchantman.

Vole and *Beaver* had suffered severe damage but they signalled they were capable of making it back to Scapa. Eight of their ship's companies had been killed and several more wounded, and there was no possibility of them continuing the patrol.

While *Grey Seal* headed back to the stricken merchantman, they were ordered to carry out a square search for the men who had taken to the boats.

Grey Seal had been lucky. Apart from the Oerlikon gunner there had been only one other fatality: a seaman on the twelve-pounder had been mortally wounded by a piece of shrapnel. Several, however, had injuries. And although her upper deck looked an awful mess the damage was superficial.

Phelp relieved Paton on the bridge whilst he went on a tour of inspection to find out how the wounded men were faring. The loader who had so heroically operated the Oerlikon literally single-handed was in great pain, but no immediate danger. A lump of his bicep had been blown away and his elbow fractured. The others had suffered minor cuts and bruises. The only man who gave cause for real concern was Cohen whose leg had been severed. If he was to survive it was imperative to get him to hospital and within reach of expert medical attention before gangrene set in. Despite his injury, the stoker was amazingly cheerful. He was lying stretched out on his bunk and even managed to produce a smile from behind the mask of pain. 'Know anyone who wants to buy an odd sea-boot, sir?' he joked.

Paton said, 'We'll try and make you as comfortable as possible till we get back to base. But if there's anything you want, ask.'

Cohen lowered his voice and whispered, 'You would be doing me a favour it you kept an eye on Stoker Danvers, sir. He's likely to take this very badly. If I'm discharged he might not be able to cope.' And with that the stoker went on to explain how he had been writing his oppo's love letters.

Paton said, 'I was aware of that, Cohen. We'll just have to find a way round it.'

'That's not going to be so easy, sir. He proposed in his last letter and she accepted. She doesn't know I wrote his letters.'

Paton patted the injured man gently on the shoulder. 'That's a problem of his own making. It was a reality he would have to face up to sooner or later. The pretence couldn't have been continued indefinitely. Meanwhile, you rest as much as you can.'

It was only after he had completed a thorough tour of the ship and congratulated everyone on the part they had played that he went into his cabin for the unpalatable task of confronting Captain Monsey. He was sitting, a pitiful figure, hunched over the table with a bottle within easy reach, and when Paton walked in he looked up and murmured, 'I didn't measure up to it, did I?'

Paton felt a knife stab of compassion; it afforded him no satisfaction to witness the destruction of another human being, even if he did detest him and deplore the hard veneer beneath which he had hidden his true self. So he remained silent, merely nodded, and poured Monsey another drink. 'I think it would be better for everyone if you remained here for the remainder of the voyage, sir.'

Monsey mumbled, 'I agree. I have no wish to confront any of those men. I can still see the loathing and contempt in the eyes of that loader.' He lifted the glass with a shaking hand, then looked up and said pitifully, 'I suppose you will have to say something when we get back. It's the end for me you realize?'

'I don't want to have to say *anything*, sir. I'd much prefer that you explained the situation. I think you owe me that.'

'You'll find this difficult to understand, Paton. A man who doesn't know the meaning of fear never can. But it's something I just couldn't control. I knew what I wanted to do when I joined you, but I just couldn't force myself to do it. Fear *can* be an illness.'

Paton said harshly, 'There wasn't a man out there – myself included – who wasn't scared to death, but they overcame it. I would have had some sympathy for you if you hadn't tried to break a bloody fine officer for reasons which are beyond my comprehension. You're a tyrannical bastard who cracked the whip to cover up your own shortcomings. Now, if you'll excuse me, sir, I have to get back on the bridge. There are the dead to see to and the merchantman to look after.' He slammed the door without a backward glance.

When he returned to the bridge the stricken cargo ship was less than a mile away and a boarding party was already standing by in the waist of the ship. 'We can't spare a boarding party now, Number One. We'll have to take her in tow. Get the wireless operator to contact base and request an escort to see us home,' he announced curtly.

He took *Grey Seal* within hailing distance and when the truculent master appeared on the bridge Paton wasted no words. 'I'm taking you in tow. If you refuse I'll do what the German failed to do – sink you by gunfire. Wallowing around

230

like that you're a navigational hazard.'

The master accepted the ultimatum without demur and *Grey Seal* was skilfully manoeuvred into a position where her stern was less than twenty yards ahead of the merchantman's bow, which towered above the trawler like a high-rise block beside a bungalow.

The handful of weary and hungry men who had not deserted the ship gathered round the fo'c'sle windlass while the master supervised the unreeling of the insurance wire – the extra heavy five-inch hawser specially carried for such an emergency. The trawler's long-barrelled Lee Enfield sent a thin line snaking skywards to land on the fo'c'sle, where it was eagerly seized and fastened to a manilla, which in turn was made fast to an eye on the insurance wire.

The quarterdeck party on the trawler groaned and grunted as they heaved the manilla across the water. They had to redouble their efforts as the line absorbed more and more water, and Phelp urged them on with words that would not be found in the *Manual of Seamanship*. 'Imagine you're pulling a drunken matelot off your sister.'

Gradually the straining men tugged the manilla closer and when several feet were inboard it was speedily whipped round the drum of the capstan. The rest was easy. The powerful capstan drew it in with the ease of a fisherman retrieving his line. When the eye of the insurance wire was inboard, four hands ran with it to the double bollards amidships and secured it. As an added precaution it was also fastened to the double bollards aft. Only then did Paton begin to steam slowly ahead while the merchantman paid out more line. When ninety fathoms had passed through the fairleads the inboard end was secured to the fo'c'sle bollards on the helpless cargo vessel. On both ships, several feet of wire passing through the fairleads were parcelled with heavy canvas and coated with thick grease to prevent any damage through chafing.

When the operation was completed the towing-wire on the stern of *Grey Seal* and the fo'c'sle of the merchantman plunged into the water at an acute angle. Most of it was below

231

the surface; it was the weight of the wire which would do the actual towing.

Then with *Vole* and *Beaver* keeping a watchful look-out on either quarter, *Grey Seal* began the slow and hazardous journey back to Scapa. Despite a thorough search, the two trawlers had not seen the slightest sign of the men who had abandoned ship. Their fate would remain a mystery.

There was no sleep for anyone aboard *Grey Seal* or her charge that night. The task of towing the engineless merchantman was so precarious that it required everyone to remain on duty. Extra lookouts were mounted on the trawler; the slowness of their progress made both ships sitting ducks for any U-boat that might be in the area, and a working party under Lieutenant Phelp had to be in constant attendance on the quarterdeck.

On the bridge, Paton was kept busy giving a non-stop series of helm and engine orders to ensure that the distance between the two vessels remained constant and the tow did not appear above the surface of the water. If it did, it could part with a vicious twang and a deadly backlash that could kill and maim men in both ships. He was unable to see the tow and had to rely entirely on the messages relayed to him from the quarterdeck.

Several hands were detailed to tend and repair the parcelling and thrust fresh handfuls of grease onto any moving part of the tow. It was a task made doubly difficult because they dared not show a glimmer of light. And so they relied entirely on feel and sound. Within a short time their hands were raw and bleeding and the pain was intensified by the salt water. Ever-present in their minds was Stoker Cohen – a stark reminder of the price one paid for carelessness.

But if conditions were grim for the navy men they were far worse for the handful of men aboard the merchantman. Without any means of propulsion, holding the ship's head steady was a back-breaking task and it needed two men on the wheel to hold the rudder amidships, while the frozen stiff men on the fo'c'sle had to fulfil tasks which would have been a hardship for three times as many. And unlike on the trawler, there was no one available to provide them with a hot drink.

There was only one slight comfort for the men of both ships. They had the consolation of knowing that the fire had been extinguished and there was no longer any real danger of them disappearing in a blinding explosion like the *Otter*. That, of course, did not rule out the danger of Jerry doing it instead.

From time to time Phelp hurried up to the bridge to make a hasty progress report. During one of them Paton turned and said, 'What can you say about a bunch of men such as we've got, Brian? They really did come up trumps.'

Phelp suddenly started laughing out loud. 'You know, sir, when you started steaming towards the Jerry I thought to myself, the daft so and so is going to kill the lot of us. And you know something, sir, I would have been disappointed if you'd done otherwise.' He paused and then enquired, 'How's Captain Monsey? I heard about the incident on the Oerlikon. I suppose he daren't show his face.'

Paton grimaced. 'It's a pity he didn't cop it. It would have been more merciful. He was so preoccupied with saving his own skin that he's committed himself to a living death. The best thing he can do is find a hole and crawl into it. I don't intend saying too much, but the buzz will spread.'

It was shortly after midnight when a concerned Hall arrived on the bridge and asked the captain if he could have a quiet word with him. Paton moved to a corner of the bridge and the steward whispered, 'It's Captain Monsey, sir. I looked in to see if he wanted anything but there was no sign of him. I told the coxswain and he organized a search throughout the ship.' He shrugged. 'Couldn't find hide nor hair of him.'

Paton summoned his number one. 'Nip down and see if you can make sense of it. He's probably skulked off somewhere.'

But the first lieutenant returned to report that Monsey seemed to have vanished into thin air. 'The coxswain says there isn't a part of the ship that hasn't been searched and the quarterdeck party says he didn't show his face there, sir.'

Paton said, 'It's too late now to order one of the other

trawlers to go back and search. Maybe he did the honourable thing.'

Phelp nodded: he had just been going to say that Monsey couldn't possibly have ventured out of his cabin without *some-one* seeing him, but he stopped himself just in time. For it meant that if Monsey had jumped overboard no one had attempted to stop him; and, even worse, it occurred to him that he may have been given a helping hand.

12 Four interminably long days and nights followed during which *Grey Seal*'s ship's company were constantly on duty. They were so tired they moved around the ship like zombies, performing their duties as if by remote control. At times they dozed off while they were standing, and only the terrifying roar of Tiger Read who relentlessly prowled the ship in search of skivers jolted them back to an awareness of the risks they were running by dropping off at their posts. The threats he issued made the ordeal they were enduring seem a picnic. Inwardly they did not resent his non-stop bullying, it was a guarantee of survival. Slow as their progress was with a ship in tow, they were drawn on by the consoling thought that every journey, no matter how long, eventually had to end.

It was the loud, exalted cry of one of the lookouts which made them shake off their tiredness like a snake shedding its skin. 'Ships dead ahead, sir. One cruiser, two destroyers.' Paton snatched up his glasses and quickly identified *Zeus*, one of the cruisers which had arrived at Scapa with the Home Fleet. Dashing round her like frisky dogs were two escorting destroyers. Immediately the powerful searchlight-sized signal-lamp on the bridge of the cruiser began to flash a message and Chalkie White could not conceal his relief and jubilation as he repeated it aloud. 'You interrupted a good tombola school.' The lamp continued to blink and a perplexed White called across the bridge, 'St Luke 15:6, sir. Whatever that means.'

Paton chuckled out loud. 'You should read your Bible more, Bunts. It's one of the navy's favourite passages: "Rejoice with me; for I have found my sheep which was lost". Send back: St John, 7:24, and add, Glad to see you. We heard you were grounded on your own gash.'

White enjoyed sending *that* retort, for it summed up the attitude of small ship men towards the big ships of the pusser navy. When he had finished he turned to his captain and asked, 'What did you say from the Bible, sir?'

'Judge not according to the appearance. It's my way of reminding him we're a wolf in sheep's clothing.' That riposte delighted the bunting tosser even more and he could hardly wait to repeat to the mess deck how the old man had put a bloody great cruiser in its place.

Zeus took up station ahead of the labouring trawlers whilst the destroyers maintained a circling patrol in case any marauding U-boats were foolhardy enough to attempt an attack.

The sense of relief provided a rash of good-humoured signals among the ships in which everyone tried to outvie the other with schoolboyish parodies and witticisms. Eventually the captain of the cruiser intervened with a good-natured rebuke, 'Like Milton, I am blasted with an excess of light.'

A few hours later two sub-hunting Sunderlands and three low-flying Blenheims appeared overhead to be greeted with cheers and waves from the men aboard the small ships. Their arrival confirmed that they were now beyond all danger. Even the *Tirpitz* would think twice about attacking them.

As soon as *Grey Seal* was relieved of her charge by two heavy tugs she turned her head to her own more than welcome berth. As Paton manoeuvred her alongside he was surprised to see Admiral Beynon waiting on the jetty, and as soon as the ship was tied up and the engines silenced the admiral was aboard. He acknowledged the captain's salute with a hand that barely brushed the peak of his cap. He seemed a man who had little or no time to spare. 'I read your coded signals, Paton, and your group are to be congratulated. But you'd better tell me more about Captain Monsey.'

Paton led the way to his cabin and invited the admiral to

join him in a drink before he recounted in detail the events of the patrol. When it came to Monsey's mysterious disappearance, he deliberately omitted mentioning the incident concerning the Oerlikon. It could serve no useful purpose.

The admiral tapped a cigarette against his silver case and appeared to be carefully weighing his words. 'There should by rights be a Court of Inquiry at which any member of the ship's company who could shed some light on this would be interviewed. A bit like an inquest. But if you can assure me that it was a simple accident I see no reason to waste time on an investigation to establish the cause of death.'

'An inquiry into the incident wouldn't disclose any more than I've told you, sir. I made a thorough check myself. No one saw Captain Monsey on the upper deck. But that's not surprising. In the dark you can pass within inches of someone and not be noticed. It's a bit like charcoal on a blackboard.'

Beynon grunted approvingly, 'So he died on active service. I presume you wouldn't quarrel with that?'

'Not at all, sir. It's the truth.'

The admiral relaxed visibly and after a couple of drinks decided to tour the ship and thank the men personally for all they had done and endured. 'Clear Lower Deck' was piped, and as the hands gathered around the fo'c'sle Beynon gazed at the shambles around him. 'If I could find something to stand on and address you I would, in true admiral fashion, but everything seems to have been shot away.' The men laughed at the implied compliment and were extremely glad that the admiral was not going to burden them with a load of flannel about duty, God, King and Country.

'I must say your captain went to incredible lengths to make sure you got your long delayed leave. It'll be at least three weeks before the ship can be made fit and ready for sea again. Therefore I will see that the travel warrants and pay are issued without delay. The sooner you're ashore the quicker the work can start.'

The men broke into a spontaneous cheer that had the admiral beaming happily: it wasn't very often that he had the opportunity of being the harbinger of good news.

When he had finished aboard *Grey Seal*, he repeated his little homily to the other ships in the group.

Back in his office he opened the bottom drawer of his desk and took out the envelope containing the report submitted by Captain Monsey and stood looking at it, deep in thought for several seconds. Then he took out his lighter, flicked the wheel and held the flame under one corner. He watched the flames curling and scorching the envelope, and he twisted and turned it until they were almost touching his fingers. He dropped it in the tin wastepaper basket and watched until there was only a charred pile of ash.

He then sat down and recommended Phelp for a DSC. Paton was an automatic choice for the DSO, while Morris and the badly wounded loader were recommended for the DSM. Midshipman Carnac's name was put up for a Mention in Despatches along with Tiger Read and Chief Reynolds. Beynon thought the whole ship's company should get something, but the allocation of medals was always something of a lottery. Similar lists were drawn up for the other trawlers in the group.

Having completed that most enjoyable task, Beynon sat down to a far less pleasant one: a personal letter to Monsey's widow. The words did not come easily but at least Mrs Monsey would be able to hold her head high and think proudly of her husband.

Aboard *Grey Seal* there was a frenzy of activity as men packed their gear in preparation for their leave. They crammed any spare space in their suitcases with bars of nutty for the kids at home, acutely aware that the chocolate they could obtain so easily was a rare treat in a strictly rationed civvy street. They also wrapped fresh eggs in socks and underwear knowing how much *they* would be appreciated at home.

Old hands like Tiger Read and Reynolds delayed their packing until the very last minute; they had the old seamen's superstition that you were tempting providence to intervene and cancel the whole thing if you got ready well in advance.

Early next morning, *Grey Seal*'s ship's company were standing in a freezing wind on the jetty at Lyness waiting for the ancient steamer to come alongside and take them to Scrabster Harbour on the northern tip of Scotland, the first leg of their journey home.

The quay was a mass of light blue, dark blue and khaki as men from the three Services waited impatiently to go aboard. As soon as planks were put out from the gunwale there was a mad scramble to secure the best berths. Old navy hands who had made the trip before grabbed spaces on the upper deck where they could jam their backs against a bulkhead and their legs against a guard-rail. Experience had taught them it was the only guarantee of arriving safely. Others wedged themselves against davits and even lashed themselves to stanchions or anything else that would support their weight. The Pentland Firth was one of the foulest stretches of water in the world.

Morris and Rhind found a convenient spot above an engine room vent which provided a comforting warmth against the biting wind. Jolson sniffed carefully, turned a couple of circles, then lay down and slept.

In reasonable conditions the trip could take three hours, but in the sea that was running it would take at least five and the men settled down and patiently resigned themselves to a spell in purgatory.

Within an hour the overflowing scuppers were filled with the bodies of men who just wanted to be left alone to die. In what was misguidedly called the saloon, the air was thick with the smell of stale tobacco, vomit, and fuel oil.

When the steamer berthed in Scrabster there was no mad rush to leave, as there had been to board. Many of the servicemen were still lying inert, indifferent to the raucous shouts of the RTO who was urging men wishing to board the London bound train at Thurso to get a move on as the lorries on the quay would not wait for ever.

Eventually everyone managed to get ashore, although there were many who had to be carried bodily to the waiting

239

vehicles; but it was incredible how quickly the effects of seasickness were shaken off as soon as one stepped on dry land, and when the convoy of trucks arrived at the station two miles away, men who a short time previously had been incapable of movement were suddenly galvanized into action. They raced through the entrance to be first in the queues which were forming at the barrier. Space on the double-engined 'Jellicoe' which would carry them almost the entire length of the country was scarce and everyone knew that it was a question of first come, first served.

Morris and Rhind had devised their own plan of action to ensure that Jolson was able to accompany them on the rest of the journey. The penny-pinching navy had not thought it fit to issue a travel warrant for the ship's mascot. And so they stationed themselves well back in the queue, leaving about one hundred servicemen between them and the ticket collectors.

As the barriers were opened and the mad stampede began, Morris commanded Jolson to 'Stay' while he and his oppo raced to the front of the train and grabbed two corner seats. Then Morris went to the door of the carriage and let out a piercing whistle. Jolson shot through the barrier and dodged through the pounding forest of boots and leaped into the carriage. The ticket collector hurled a string of abuse at the dog, but quickly forgot it as the men continued to surge onto the platform.

Twenty bodies piled into a single carriage and suitcases, knapsacks, rifles, gas masks, kit-bags and suitcases were dumped everywhere, as men pushed and shoved for the few available seats. The corridors were just as overcrowded. You could not move an inch without tripping over legs and heavy boots.

It was dark when the train finally set off and the blacked-out carriages and corridors added to the discomfort. Heads lolled against shoulders and the sound of snoring filled the air. But few slept for long. Those stretched out in the corridor were constantly awakened by the non-stop stream of men heading for the toilets where they had to join a queue and wait for as long as half an hour.

It was an incredible journey: through Caithness down to Helmsdale, then Golspie, Tain, Invergordon, on to Inverness, over the Cairngorms down to Perth. Occasionally the train halted and the doors burst open as men piled out to gratefully grab a cup of tea from the waiting WVS. Then the engine would toot a warning and there was another mad race as men hurried to get back aboard.

When it finally pulled into King's Cross the men were bleary-eyed and unshaven. Uppermost in their minds was the thought of a quick hot snack, a couple of pints, and a wash and brush up in the nearest Gents.

Morris and Rhind, with Jolson trotting faithfully beside them, had to employ the same ruse to smuggle the dog aboard a train for Grimsby.

Paton found an empty telephone booth plastered with posters asking users if the call was really necessary and took out the scrap of paper on which Cecily's number was written. He dialled, but there was nothing but silence. He tried another booth, but the response was the same.

He walked dejectedly back to the station and joined a queue waiting for taxis. They were few and far between in wartime London and nearly an hour passed before he was able to clamber into one and give her address to the driver.

The taxi dropped him off at the entrance to the narrow, cobbled mews where she lived, and some indefinable urge made him hasten his footsteps and then, despite the burden of his suitcase, break into a trot. He halted before what had once been her home. The front had been neatly sheered away leaving the ground floor and first floor rooms open to the air. It reminded him of the tiny dolls house that his sister had had when a small girl: the frontage had opened on a hinge to reveal the interior. But the spectacle confronting him brought a

241

feeling of nausea. The walls were blackened and scorched and the floors tilted crazily. A picture hung lopsidedly on one wall, and water dripped noisily from the carpets and hose-sodden furniture. It was a scene that spoke for itself. Of the handful of bombs so far dropped on the city, one had landed on her home.

Paton glanced at the illuminated hands of his watch and realized he had time to reach the theatre before the final curtain came down.

When he reached the theatre he found the audience streaming out onto the pavement. A small notice was spread diagonally across the billboards outside. It simply announced that the part of Miss Grey would be taken over by her understudy. He did not bother to read on but ran round to the stage door where an elderly man sat in a cubicle reading the last edition of the *Star*. Paton rapped on the window partition and the doorkeeper glanced up and opened a small window. 'Can you tell me where I can find Miss Grey?'

The man looked at him, his face full of compassion. 'Haven't you heard, son? She was killed.' Paton nodded dully and turned away. He paused on the way out and retraced his footsteps. 'Will there be a funeral?'

The old man brushed his mouth with the back of a hand dotted with small walnut-coloured patches. 'It's taken place, sir. It was better to get it over and done with quick. It was a direct hit you know.'

Paton walked out into the blackened night. He stopped at several public houses and ordered drinks in a mechanical manner that made one barman suggest, 'Don't you think you've had enough, sir,' but he was cowed by Paton's vicious, 'Don't you think I'm the best judge of that.'

When last orders were called, he walked out into the alien darkness, uncertain and uncaring of where he was, and booked into a hotel without even bothering to look at the name outside. He went straight into his room and telephoned his mother, desperate for someone to share his grief.

'I'm so glad you called, Crispin. I've just had the most

242

dreadful telegram. Your father has been lost at sea. Is there any chance of you coming home?'

'Of course, mother. I'll be there on the very first train.'

13 None of them could recognize *Grey Seal* as they made their way aboard; she looked as if she had arrived fresh from the builders. Her hull and superstructure glistened with a new coat of paint and there was no sign of the damage she had sustained during the battle with the German Q-ship. The quilted padding round the bridge had even been replaced and the tip of the mast which had been shot away restored. But what gave them the greatest pleasure was the discovery that she had been coaled during their absence.

When Tiger Read reported to the captain that all hands with the exception of Stoker Danvers were back aboard, he was surprised to learn that Paton had been back on the ship for several days. He asked in a friendly fashion if he had enjoyed his leave, but Paton brusquely replied that something had cropped up which demanded his early return. He was clearly in no mood to elaborate and the coxswain knew better than to press the matter.

Read reported that replacements for the dead and wounded had also arrived on board.

'I'll see them one by one in my cabin later on, Coxswain, and spell out to them just what I expect of men who join us.' Read detected a new hardness in the captain's tone and devoutly hoped that whatever it was that had brought him back early wasn't going to turn him into a martinet.

'We sail on patrol in twenty-four hours, Coxswain. If Danvers isn't aboard by pipe-down he'll be posted adrift and the naval patrol can pick him up. He'll be for the high jump.'

Read said, 'Don't be too hard on the lad, sir. He's got a lot on his mind. Men do daft things when there's a girl involved. Can't you give him a little longer? Poor little beggar could be eating his heart out somewhere.'

Read thought he noticed a touch of bitterness in Paton's reply, a most uncharacteristic thing. 'We're going to have to learn how to accept disappointments, and become even more determined in our efforts to win this bloody war. I can't afford to have one rotten apple in this ship. But I'll go part of the way with you. If he reports back before we sail I'll deal with him myself.'

'Thank you, sir. He's not a bad lad.'

Lieutenant Phelp knocked gently on the captain's cabin door to report he was back from leave. It was an encounter he was dreading. He had never felt so happy in his life, yet he knew the man he so admired and respected must be experiencing the depths of despair.

When he entered Paton said, 'Nice to see you back, Brian. Hope you had an enjoyable leave. Pull up a chair and join me in a drink.'

The first lieutenant sat down and the words he was loath to speak came tumbling out. He wanted to get it over and done with. 'I'm sorry to hear about your father, sir – and Miss Grey. Lesley told me.'

'I'll learn to live with it. My father's death is something I can accept without too much bitterness. He died as he would have wished. Which is more than can be said for most men. But Cecily's death . . .' He broke off in mid-sentence and his voice assumed a forced gaiety. 'I hear that you and Lesley have decided to take the plunge. Wedding bells in the very near future.'

Phelp sounded embarrassed. 'I said we ought to delay it in view of the sad news, sir. But it was your mother who said we should take our happiness whilst we can, sir.'

'I know, Brian. She told me.'

They sat up drinking until the early hours, and when they finally tumbled into their bunks Paton had managed, at least for the time being, to blot out the memories which had

245

haunted his nights and days by falling into a near drunken stupor.

Coxswain Read knocked on the cabin door and poked his head in before Paton had a chance to answer. 'Thought you'd like to know, sir, Danvers has just reported back from leave. Bit of a pierhead jump, but he made it in time. I've given him a real, ripe rollicking.'

Paton managed to dredge up a smile, his head felt like a jellyfish in a tideway and his mouth was dry and foul-tasting. 'Good for you. Send him up in half an hour.'

Danvers stood nervously fiddling with his cap, his eyes gazing at some invisible spot between his feet, unable to raise them and look into the frozen face of his captain.

'Well, what have you got to say for yourself?' The voice was like an ice-cube down his back.

'Nothing, sir. I'm happy to take my punishment.'

'Did you sort things out?'

'Not really, sir. I laid everything on the line and she said she didn't see how I could expect her to be engaged to a bloke who couldn't even keep in touch. She was quite upset at the thought of Cohen reading her letters. She's going to think it over and let me know the answer next leave.'

'All's not lost then, Danvers?'

The stoker could not hide his misery. 'It ain't exactly rosy, is it, sir? I was so chocker I went on the binge.'

'But you came back.'

'I didn't want to let you down.'

Paton replied, 'It'll be a long time before our next spot of leave, Danvers. Time for you to start learning to read and write.'

'I can do a *little* of both,' he said indignantly. 'I'm not *that* stupid.'

'I'll help you as much as I can. So will the other officers. Whenever you have a spare minute I want you to be studying. That's your punishment. All right?'

The stoker beamed happily. 'That won't be much of a

punishment, sir. You should see her.'

Paton was reasonably confident that Danvers would bust a gut trying to overcome his handicap. He certainly had the incentive.

As the three trawlers steamed past the motionless Fleet, a flurry of ribald remarks was exchanged between the men of the big ships and the small ships. A sailor lolling over a guard rail of HMS *Nelson* shouted, 'See you've had a wash and brush up', and one of *Grey Seal*'s fo'c'sle party retorted, 'Want a tow? Heard you're still aground on the tin cans you've tossed overboard'.

This time the group took a different route. They sailed through the boom at Hoxa Sound, passed between South Ronaldsay and the Pentland Skerries, and headed for the North Sea.

Intelligence reports suggested that Doenitz was contemplating another daring U-boat intrusion into the Flow before the Churchill Barrier was completed. This had been confirmed in part by two trawlers who had recovered a couple of torpedoes caught in the anti-submarine nets. An attempt had clearly been made to blow open a gap and force an entry.

The patrol which stretched from the Pentland Skerries beyond remote North Ronaldsay had none of the hardships of the Northern Patrol, but the boredom it imposed was unimaginable. The only person who was happy with the situation was Danvers, who believed that he was at last catching up on his lost schooldays.

The three ships steamed back and forth on their chosen course without seeing or hearing a thing. Day became night with a monotonous regularity and men who had previously fought to stay awake because they were so tired now found themselves fighting off sleep for an entirely different reason. They couldn't stand the tedium.

The patrol had entered into its second week and the group was well to the east of Copinsay when *Beaver* reported a definite Asdic contact. *Grey Seal* immediately altered course

247

to join her, and within minutes of arriving on the scene her own detector equipment was able to confirm it.

The depth charge crews stood by to launch a joint attack, but the contact disappeared as suddenly as it had been found. The U-boat captain was clearly a wily and experienced hand who had played hide and seek with surface hunters on many occasions. He seemed to be able to anticipate every move the trawlers made, for three times contact was re-established but each time it was lost before a depth charge could be launched.

Paton toyed with the idea of breaking radio silence and asking for assistance, but he rejected the idea: the German would just slip away. It was far better to play a deadly game of cat and mouse. If, as he feared, the U-boat captain was prepared to bide his time and wait for an opportunity to slip into Scapa, possibly beneath the protective hull of an arriving ship, there was every chance of nailing him.

The three ships circled round and round incessantly, their Asdic searching the depths like probing fingers, waiting for the unmistakable sound which would announce they had once more found their quarry. But nothing interrupted the regular ping of the detector. More than likely the U-boat was lying on the bottom in deep water, her crew sitting quietly at their posts and doing as little as possible in order to conserve the air. Her own antennae listening carefully to what was going on above.

'Do you think she's slipped away, sir?' As Phelp addressed his captain he realized he was almost whispering.

Paton laughed out loud. 'You don't have to keep your voice down, Number One. He can't hear you.' In the background the Asdic pinged incessantly. No wonder, he thought, the sick-bays were filled with operators who had been driven half-mad by the constant listening to the same brain-numbing sound. 'I don't think he's skipped. He's been hand-picked for this job and he must know it's a death and glory mission. I think he's just lying doggo hoping we'll give it up. But we'll play him at his own game. His batteries can't last much more than forty-eight hours and he'll have to move and surface somewhere to recharge them.'

Tension mounted in *Grey Seal* as the hours dragged by, but there was still no sign of the German and Paton was forced to admit, 'I think we've lost him, Number One. God knows how, but we have.'

He paced up and down the bridge constantly pausing to enquire if the Asdic had anything to report. But the answer was always the same.

As darkness began to approach he turned to Phelp and said, 'If he's going to make a move I think he'll do it quite soon. If he can break clear and surface he can show us a clean pair of heels.' He summoned Chalkie White to his side: 'Send to *Vole* and *Beaver*. Stop engines and wait for further instructions.'

It was a calculated gamble for there was nothing more vulnerable than a motionless ship, but it was a risk well worth taking. The U-boat captain could be misled into thinking that two of the ships had withdrawn and he now had only one hunter to contend with. If the German fell for it and contact was made, an immediate depth charge attack would be launched.

Kapitanleutnant Kurt Muller sat quietly in the control room on the seat near the periscope, his face an inscrutable mask. He had sailed from Blucher Bridge in Kiel with sealed orders that left him in no doubt that he and his crew would be extremely lucky to make the return journey, displaying additional pennants to those which she proudly displayed whenever she returned to base: red for a warship, white for a freighter, red and white for a tanker. But he was determined to see his mission through to a successful conclusion. He glanced round the confined U-boat at the officers and men who were sitting silently on any piece of equipment that was suitable as a chair. The U-boat had been submerged for a considerable length of time now and her batteries were in desperate need of recharging. And so all non-essential machinery had been switched off, even to the gyro compass, for that emitted a detectable humming noise. No man was even allowed the luxury of a nerve-easing cigarette for the air inside the submarine was already foul. Potassium cartridges had been issued to reduce the amount of carbon dioxide, but that only afforded a short respite. The tired men were even prevented from using the toilet for that could result in a telltale sign on the surface when it was flushed.

But Muller was confident that he would emerge the winner in the deadly duel being played out above and below the surface. The U-boat's detecting equipment was vastly superior to that of the trawlers and he was able to anticipate their moves with uncanny accuracy. By keeping the engines at silent creeping speed he could make slow alterations to course which presented the surface hunters with just a bow or stern on target which was extremely difficult to pinpoint with any real accuracy. Furthermore, the strength of the impulses sent out from the dome on the bottom of the trawlers to bounce off the U-boat's hull to give position, depth and distance, could be affected by variations in temperature and the salinity of the water. Despite the proud boasts of the British, Asdic was still a pretty hit and miss affair.

It was when he detected a marked decrease in the activity above that he decided to make a move. His own 'ears' had reported that only the screws of one ship could be pinpointed above. Everything indicated that two of the hunters had been withdrawn. He gave the order, 'Half ahead together' on the twin electric motors.

Minutes later he realized his error as the *wasserbomben* began to explode around the submarine. Water seaped through seams and pipe joints and the submarine was plunged into total darkness as bulbs shattered, gauges broke and crockery was hurled around the ship. The hull creaked and groaned under the shock waves and men cursed aloud as they were thrown off their feet and hurled into bone-cracking machinery.

Muller joined the cursing; he should have made a slow alteration to his engine speed; abrupt changes made detection so much easier. But he was not too worried; the depth charges

250

were terrifying but they were still too far off to inflict a mortal wound.

He glanced at the manometer and gave orders for the ship to be taken down as deep as possible. The incredibly well disciplined crew worked calmly and methodically amid the maze of valves and levers. As the needle on the gauge flicked round like the second hand of a clock the anxious leitende ingenieur warned that they were perilously close to 'paper depth' when the pressure could crush the hull with a bang like a bursting bag. Muller ignored him. When it was lower than the makers had ever envisaged he resumed cruising speed, and total silence was demanded throughout the vessel.

Muller knew that once he could break clear and surface he was more or less safe, for a surfaced submarine lying low in the water was extremely difficult to spot. And once he was up he could steam at eighteen knots which was too fast for any trawler. In any case, if it did come to a surface battle his ship was more than a match for any trawler. She had a 105mm cannon on her fo'c'sle and one 37mm cannon and two 20mm guns on the deck.

Yet the last thing he wanted was a surface confrontation, for that would spell the end of the mission he was determined to accomplish successfully. He would certainly be awarded the Knight's Cross. It was far better for the hunter to believe he had sunk the U-boat, and so he summoned the engineer and instructed him to release some fuel oil along with odd items of clothing and personal belongings. It was a decoy he had successfully used in the past and he saw no reason why the trawler above should not fall for the old dodge.

The starboard bridge lookout in *Grey Seal* was first to spot the slick of oil that was slowly spreading on the surface of the sea. He pointed to it excitedly and shouted, 'We've got her, sir. Look.'

Paton studied the slick and the caps, shoes, and other jettisoned items that were bobbing slowly up and down. 'I

251

don't think so. There's not enough fuel there. Her tanks must still be pretty full.'

His suspicions were immediately confirmed by the Asdic operator who reported a firm and definite contact. Once more the depth charges were trundled off the stern and hurled into the air by the throwers. The sea erupted in great towering mushrooms as they exploded and Paton signalled to the other two trawlers to join in the attack. The three ships began to plaster the area with patterns of depth charges set at varying depths. The movements of the U-boat had now become desperate as she twisted and turned in a series of violent manoeuvres in an attempt to avoid the explosions which were shaking her to bits.

Grey Seal's Asdic operator reported that he had heard the unmistakable sound of crunching metal which indicated a direct hit or one close enough to have caused structural damage. Soon afterwards a large patch of oil began to spread across the surface of the sea and everyone aboard the trawlers knew that, this time, it wasn't a clever ruse. Nevertheless, the attack was continued with remorseless ferocity.

As the U-boat shook and juddered from the impact of the depth charges, Muller again gave orders for the ship to be taken down to maximum depth, but the engineer and helmsman informed him that the vessel was not responding: the hydroplanes and rudder were obviously damaged. But more serious, there was considerable flooding.

Muller reluctantly gave the order to 'Blow all tanks'. Slowly, like a stricken monster, the 1,100 tons of metal began to rise to the surface and Muller prepared for the engagement he would have given anything to avoid. He looked at the perspiring men busy at the controls and shouted encouragingly, 'Don't worry lads, I'll get you all home.'

The bow of the U-boat appeared like a surfacing whale. Then the rest of the hull began to follow until the whole of the conning tower was clearly visible. She bore no identifying number, but there was a painting of a snarling wolf in the centre of the bridge.

A klaxon sounded and men began tumbling out of the conning tower and racing along the upper deck to take up their positions at the guns. The three trawlers promptly opened fire with their twelve-pounders, Oerlikons and Lewis guns.

The ensign was seen to flutter proudly from the submarine's jackstaff.

Oerlikon and machine gun fire raked the U-boat from stem to stern and men tumbled into the water before they could reach their gun positions. But there were always others rushing to take their place.

A shell from the U-boat's powerful fore'ard gun took a section off *Beaver*'s bow and another passed a few feet above *Grey Seal*'s deck with a deafening scream that made everyone duck. The outcome was, however, predictable. The combined fire power of the three trawlers was too much for the badly damaged U-boat. Several direct hits were made on the hull and superstructure and the 30mm cannon was knocked out. Even so the remaining two cannons continued to fire with commendable accuracy until one was literally blown into the sea. Then a shell exploded directly above the main armament killing the entire gun crew.

Seconds later, men were seen to be diving into the sea and the ensign was hurled down and replaced by the black flag of surrender.

Paton was relieved to see it. The German had fought with incredible courage and tenacity and he did not want to have to continue the pointless slaughter. At the same time he did not underestimate the cunning of Hitler's U-boat commanders and he knew the flag of surrender could be another decoy. Virtually gunless though she was, she was still capable of launching her deadly torpedoes in a death and glory finale.

He called White over and told him to signal the submarine that he was lowering a boat with a boarding party and to warn the captain that fire would resume at the first hint of danger.

As the trawlers turned bows onto the U-boat to minimize the target, *Grey Seal*'s port whaler was lowered with an armed boarding party led by Midshipman Carnac. The men also carried grenades.

Paton watched with mounting anxiety as the whaler pulled towards the submarine, but his fear was nothing to that being experienced by Carnac who was convinced the German would try to pull off some dirty and diabolical trick.

When the whaler was about three hundred yards away Muller, in a white poloneck sweater, his white-topped cap set at the unmistakably rakish angle favoured by U-boat captains, appeared on the bridge with a megaphone in his hand. In impeccable English he requested Carnac not to approach any closer as the scuttling charges had been set and he did not want the whaler or the men in the water to be drawn down by the suction. He would also be extremely grateful if more boats could be lowered to pick up his men.

As he spoke the U-boat began to settle by the stern. A series of explosions echoed across the water and Carnac ordered the men at the oars to cease pulling; Paton would not thank him if he lost a quarter of the ship's company. Glancing astern he saw four or five whalers heading towards the scene, their crews putting everything into the rowing as if they were taking part in a Fleet Regatta. By then some of the U-boat crew were clinging desperately to the side of his boat pleading to be hauled inboard.

As the submarine's bow began to lift out of the water, Carnac yelled out to her captain to leave before it was too late. He wondered whether he was too far away for his voice to carry, for the German simply turned his back. Then to Carnac's astonishment he calmly lowered the black pennant and replaced it with his national flag. As the submarine slid stern first to her doom his last view of her captain was a solitary figure above the snarling wolf's head standing erect and saluting the ensign. Carnac suddenly realized that he too was standing and saluting. To hide his embarrassment at this impromptu gesture he shouted to the boat's crew to get cracking with the survivors; they hadn't got all day. Some of the swimming men began to tread water and someone called for three cheers. There was an immediate response and the sound of their voices drifted across the sea to the waiting trawlers.

When the sodden and shivering men were taken aboard they were handed blankets, cigarettes and mugs of hot cocoa. The more generous members of the trawler crews even gave them 'sippers' of their precious rum.

When the hands fell in for entering harbour there was an aggressive set to their shoulders as they passed through the boom. Several of the survivors were brought up onto the upper deck to be displayed as proud trophies. Each was blindfolded so as not to be able to memorize any of the defence layout of Scapa Flow.

Grey Seal led the three ships into the Flow to be greeted by a lamp from the signal tower ashore blinking a personal message from Admiral Beynon, 'Well done'.

They steamed in line ahead past the huge, grey ships moored at buoys, and loud cheers were heard from the crowded decks of the ships which had been the main target for the incredibly daring U-boat operation. It was most unpusserlike behaviour, but memories of the *Royal Oak* were still fresh in the minds of the men in the big ships.

As *Grey Seal* approached her berth, Phelp stood on the fo'c'sle scanning the quay. He saw a mass of cheering sailors and a group of Wrens jumping up and down with excitement. He soon picked out Lesley and that meant more to him than any praise from an admiral.

That night as Paton, Phelp and Carnac sat yarning over a drink there was a knock on the door. Paton called out, 'Come in,' and an embarrassed looking Rhind stepped into the cabin and presented him with a small wooden plaque. It was beautifully carved and painted and depicted a fouled anchor above a grey seal. Below were the words: 'Our Brethren's Shield'.

Over the Canadian's shoulder Paton could make out the smiling faces of Tiger Read, Reynolds, and several other

255

hands who had jammed into the narrow passageway to witness the presentation.

'We thought it would look nice in front of the bridge,' said Rhind awkwardly. 'The big ships have one, so we didn't see why we shouldn't. After all, we're part of the same outfit.'

Paton said, 'I like the motto, Rhind. Who dreamed it up? It's very apt.'

Rhind said, 'We took it from the hymn "Eternal Father". We've altered it a bit though.'

Paton tried to thank him but the words would not come. 'All right, let's not make a meal of it. Close the door and let's finish our drinks.' His eyes had started to tingle and he realized he was in grave danger of making a fool of himself.

As the door closed he looked at Phelp and Carnac and saw they were grinning from ear to ear.

'It looks like we've come of age,' said the first lieutenant.